Armada's Wake

J. D. Davies is the prolific author of historical naval adventures. He is also one of the foremost authorities on the seventeenth-century navy, which brings a high level of historical detail to his fiction, namely his Matthew Quinton series. He has written widely on the subject, most recently *Kings of the Sea: Charles II, James II and the Royal Navy*, and won the Samuel Pepys Award in 2009 with *Pepys's Navy: Ships, Men and Warfare, 1649-1689.*

Also by J. D. Davies

The Matthew Quinton Journals

Gentleman Captain
The Mountain of Gold
The Blast that Tears the Skies
The Lion of Midnight
The Battle of All The Ages
The Rage of Fortune
Death's Bright Angel
The Devil Upon the Wave
Ensign Royal

Jack Stannard of the Navy Royal

Destiny's Tide
Battle's Flood
Armada's Wake

J. D. DAVIES

Armada's Wake

CANELO

First published in the United Kingdom in 2020 by Canelo

This edition published in the United Kingdom in 2021 by

Canelo
Unit 9, 5th Floor
Cargo Works, 1-2 Hatfields
London, SE1 9PG
United Kingdom

A CIP catalogue record for this book is available from the British Library.

Print ISBN 978 1 78863 936 1
Ebook ISBN 978 1 78863 232 4

Printed and bound in Great Britain by Clays Ltd, Elcograf S.p.A.

1

For the people of Dunwich, past, present and future

Prologue

The ghost stepped forward, stared into the far distance, then remained perfectly still, perfectly silent.

Its expressionless white face seemed not to move at all. But suddenly, without any warning, the mouth opened and began to utter words that reached out into that same distance. The voice was quivering, the intonation eerie, the speech a dreadful message from beyond the tomb.

When this eternal substance of my soul
Did live imprisoned in my wanton flesh
Each in their function serving other's need—

'Too slow,' murmured the dreadful, blood-soaked and rather shorter figure of Revenge, standing at the ghost's side.

'I was a courtier in the Spanish court,' said the ghost, speeding up markedly. 'My name was Don Andrea…'

'Better,' muttered Revenge.

…my descent, though not ignoble, yet inferior far
To gracious fortunes of my tender youth…

The ghost scanned the audience. Most were rapt, in awe of his pale and dreadful visage. A few of the women and children even had hands over their eyes.

Good.

This prologue, which for some perverse reason Thomas Kyd called the Induction, always held the punters' attention, thus proving the old theatrical adage that you never went far wrong with a good ghost. With luck, some of the audience might still be attentive by the second act, after a hefty share of the playwright's unfathomable plotting and tortuous dialogue had ploughed a deep furrow through their goodwill. With even more luck, some of the audience might still be left when the play ended; this had not been the case at Sidcup, nor indeed at Croydon on the previous day.

When I was slain, my soul descended straight
To pass the flowing stream of Acheron;
But churlish Charon, only boatman there,
Said that, my rites of burial not perform'd,
I might not sit amongst his passengers...

Peter Stannard, the ghost of Don Andrea, wrung every emotion he could out of Kyd's words from *The Spanish Tragedy, or, Hieronimo is Mad Again.* As usual, Will Hetherington, the ancient jobbing actor playing Revenge, was gurning at him, murmuring obscenities under his breath, Hetherington being convinced that he should still be playing the much younger Stannard's roles, the Ghost and Balthazar, killer in battle of Don Andrea. But after nearly ten years on the road with one itinerant theatrical company after another, Peter Stannard had the measure of Will and his ilk.

Then was the ferryman of Hell content,
To pass me over to the slimy strand

That leads to— Jesus!

'Kyd didn't write that,' hissed Hetherington.

But Peter Stannard didn't resume his speech. Instead he pointed a trembling finger towards the north-east. The tavern where the company was performing stood at the very northern limit of Bromley, where the lane forked down the hill towards Beckenham. From its yard, where Peter stood upon the makeshift stage, there was an uninterrupted view to the summit of Shooter's Hill, six miles away, which was bathed in the dying sun.

Hetherington moved over to where he too could see what the younger actor was pointing at. There was anxious chatter in the audience, then the screams of four or five women as a brazier flared into life atop the tower of St Peter and St Paul, just south of the inn.

The beacons.

The beacons were ablaze.

In England, even babes still at their mothers' breasts knew what that meant.

Upon the makeshift stage, Peter Stannard knew that no matter how long he lived, and how glorious a career on the stage might await him, he was about to deliver the most important and most dreadful lines his mouth would ever frame.

'The beacons are lit!' he declaimed as if he were performing before the queen herself. 'The mighty Armada is come! Tremble, good people, but then take heart and remember we are Englishmen, and fight for God, St George and Elizabeth!'

One old man in the far corner of the tavern yard stirred himself and cheered drunkenly. Revenge and the rest of the company were already gone, and the sot was all the audience left to hear the words of Peter Stannard, a man who had absolutely no intention of fighting for any of the entities he had just invoked.

-

Two hundred and fifty miles to the west, an unholy cacophony re-echoed across Plymouth Sound. Signal guns fired, trumpets pealed and whistles blew, drums beat, officers bawled commands through speaking trumpets, men bellowed at each other on deck and in the rigging of ninety ships. Anchor cables were hauled up, the capstans groaning, the men on them singing and swearing. Sails were unfurled and sheeted home. Flags and pennants streamed out from topmasts and staffs, the flagship *Ark Royal* hoisting the royal standard itself to the maintop, the red and gold colours bright against the clear blue sky. Small craft carrying last minute supplies and orders bustled between the hulls. Then, almost imperceptibly at first, the great ships of England began to move towards the open sea and the dreadful foe which awaited them. Aboard were stout, valiant men, commanded by the greatest seamen in the kingdom. There, over towards Saint Nicholas island, was the largest ship in the fleet, the carrack *Triumph*, over a thousand tons of English oak, commanded by the famous Sir Martin Frobisher. Just to leeward of her was the *Victory* with Sir John Hawkins, whose fame carried to the far shore of the limitless ocean. Two earls, no less, Cumberland and Sheffield, commanded galleons, going into battle upon the waters just as those of their rank had once charged upon warhorses at Crécy and Agincourt. *Ark Royal* herself began to move, her masts creaking and her shrouds singing, taking to sea the Lord High Admiral of England, Howard of Effingham, sprung from the illustrious line of the dukes of Norfolk. But no commander in the English fleet, nor in the fleet opposed to it, was as renowned as that of the ship from whose deck John Stannard, known to all and sundry as Jack, watched the scene unfold. For this was the vice admiral's flagship, the *Revenge*, and the vice admiral was perhaps the most famous man in the world. For one thing, he was the only living captain who had sailed all the way round it.

Yes, it was truly an astonishing sight, enough to take the breath away, yet Jack, a young man only in his twentieth year, felt unease and disquiet. After all, he had witnessed exactly the same scene only a little more than three weeks earlier, when the same fleet had sailed from the same anchorage. Then they were full of confidence, every man smiling, laughing and singing as the pride of England's Navy Royal put to sea. They were going to the coast of Spain, where they would destroy King Philip's much-vaunted Spanish Armada in harbour at Corunna. After all, had not the living legend who was the *Revenge*'s captain, Sir Francis Drake, done exactly that in the previous year, when the Spaniards lay at Cadiz?

But this time, God was not on England's side. The weather could not have been worse – storms, then a flat calm – and all the while, the fleet's victuals vanished into the gullets of hungry and thirsty men. The ships had to turn back, and then, while they were revictualling and repairing in Plymouth, the Spaniards had put to sea. So the beacons blazed all along the coast of England, inland to London and out again by way of such stations as Shooter's Hill, for King Philip's mighty Armada had come. Now the English were on the defensive, setting out against a vast enemy which had already penetrated their own waters. The cliffs that flanked Plymouth Sound were full of people. Yes, they were watching their own fleet getting under way, but many of them were also pointing far out to sea, towards the array of distant sails just visible on this bright, clear, warm July day. A myriad of sails, so many of them that they seemed to merge into one vast sea monster, intent upon devouring England.

'Well, well,' said a familiar sneering voice behind Jack. 'What have we here? A rat that's scuttled up from the orlop, that's what.'

Jack turned to face Nicholas Fitzranulf, notionally a gentleman volunteer, so thin and pale that he might be taken for a girl, so overdressed in royal-blue silks and satins that he would have been remarked upon even at court, let alone on the deck of a galleon sailing into battle. His three companions, well-born roaring boys like their leader, were only a little less gaudy. They were all laughing and pointing at Jack.

'I have as much right as you to be upon deck,' said Jack.

'Upon deck?' said Fitzranulf. His voice was almost unnaturally high. 'In the waist to use the pissdale, perchance, or in the fo'c'sle buggering a topman, but this is the quarterdeck, Stannard. Reserved for officers – those of rank and honour – and men of the duty watch.'

Nicholas Fitzranulf, a creature of supposedly distinguished but much impoverished Anglo-Irish lineage, had, for reason or reasons unknown, taken an instant dislike to Jack when they both joined the ship at Plymouth at the end of March. While the *Revenge* was provisioning, Jack's duties and Fitzranulf's pretensions kept them in very different parts of the ship. Now, though, with the Spaniard upon the horizon, Jack had no time for such foolery.

'That so, Master Fitzranulf? Then which are you, pray? I hold an office on this ship, unlike you, and I've seen you do no semblance of duty since you've come aboard.'

Fitzranulf turned to his friends, making a mocking face.

'Deputy purser, Stannard? You call that an office? A bean counter, that's all you are, and worse than that, for every sailor in England knows that pursers do naught but cheat good men of their due. A bean counter and a thief, I say!'

Jack had no weapon to hand, but he took a belaying pin from the wale and made to raise it. Fitzranulf's hand went to the hilt of his highly polished and evidently virgin sword.

'*Mister Fitzranulf!*' a familiar voice bellowed from the poop deck, astern of where the young men stood. '*Mister Stannard!*'

With evident bad grace, Fitzranulf and his friends turned and bowed extravagantly to the stocky figure with a small pointed beard, dressed in a simple sailor's shirt open almost to the navel, who stood at the poop deck rail, his hands resting firmly upon it. Jack merely nodded his head.

'I don't know what divides you youngsters,' bawled Sir Francis Drake, 'and I don't care! We have one enemy, one alone, and there he is, my boys. There he is.' The vice admiral pointed out to sea, in the direction of the Spanish Armada. 'You will keep your sword for the Don, Mister Fitzranulf, and when we are done with him, I will be quits with you upon the bowling green. As for you, Mister Stannard, the cook reports to Mister Bodenham here' – Drake gestured towards the lean, priest-like lieutenant of the *Revenge*, who looked far older than his thirty years – 'that some of the bread is already stale. See if this is so!'

Jack nodded again in perfunctory salute and started towards the companionway, exchanging glares with Fitzranulf as he did so. Attending to stale bread when he knew he could wield a sword against the Spaniards to far better effect than a popinjay like Nicholas Fitzranulf. Cooped up in the stench and darkness of the orlop deck when he could work a top yard, serve as lookout, take the helm or man a great gun as well as any foretopman on the ship. Jack Stannard wanted nothing more than to serve England and his queen, to play a real part in the mighty battle that was surely to come.

His oldest brother, Adam, would be far to the east, standing alongside their father Tom aboard the *Eagle of Dunwich*, part of the Narrow Seas fleet watching the Flanders coast in case the Duke of Parma's mighty army should try to come out in boats to meet the oncoming Armada. Adam, so unsuited to the sea, so unsuited to war – so unsuited to this mortal life, if truth were told – yet he would inevitably see more real action than Jack, far below decks on the *Revenge*.

Tom Stannard had used his connections to secure for Jack, by far the best seaman in the family, a place on one of the great ships, but he had not expected it to be Drake's *Revenge*. Jack's father had history with Sir Francis Drake; the exact nature of this was never specified to Tom's sons, but they all assumed it was something to do with their grandfather, after whom Jack was named, who had been lost during the notorious voyage that Drake and their father took to the Indies just before Jack was born. The older Jack Stannard, who would now be in his seventieth year or thereabouts, surely had to be long dead, but he was still held up as an example to the grandson who shared his name. Yet the example oft quoted was that of a fighter, not of a man who assessed the freshness of bread.

The place aboard *Revenge* would serve, though. It paid better than a mere seaman's berth, and in a way, it was Jack's own fault that he found himself fulfilling the tedious duties of a deputy purser, far below decks, rather than being in a place which might see action and honour. He had always been good with numbers, and had been made even better by the teaching of his singular aunt Meg, who had been responsible for all the Stannard accounts for many years. So when the time came for Tom Stannard to seek a place for his youngest son, Jack's fate was decided by the fact that the Navy Royal had plenty of men who could haul on a rope, hold a whipstaff or fire a gun, but precious few who could count to more than ten and keep a half-decent ledger.

As he reached the orlop deck, Jack wondered where his other brother, Peter, might be. Not at sea, that much was certain. He would be somewhere in England, no doubt, probably talking his way into a bed or a fight, the one almost certainly being caused by the other. The Spaniards could land, conquer the kingdom and behead the queen, and it was unlikely that the middle Stannard brother would even notice.

Even if he did, it was very unlikely that he would care, unless King Philip closed the alehouses.

–

It was commonly believed on the lower deck of the great galleass *Girona* – indeed, if rumour were to be believed, even in the officers' quarters at the stern – that the ancient man called Juan could never die.

Even those who publicly scoffed at this, such as Captain Spinola and especially the vessel's unwavering priest, Fra Gordillo, nevertheless colluded in granting the old man certain privileges that would have been unthinkable for any other galley slave, and one of these was an allowance of far more time on the upper deck than was permitted to any other. Indeed, only a need for extreme speed saw Juan being chained to his oar, and even then, it was a purely nominal gesture. He was far too old to contribute much to the rowing. Nevertheless, Captain Spinola regarded him as one of the most valuable members of his crew. While the slaves of the other galleys and galleasses in the navies of the *Rey Católico*, the Catholic King Philip the Second of Spain, worked only to the inexorable beat of a drum, those aboard the *Girona* also kept time to, and joined in with, the still strong and strangely pure singing voice of *el hombre que vivirá para siempre* – the man who will live forever.

It was because of the extraordinary degree of privilege permitted him that Juan was standing at the ship's rail of the *Girona* on that July day in the year of grace 1588, looking out to larboard. All around him, the one hundred and thirty ships of the vast Armada – the Most Fortunate Armada to most, the Invincible Armada to some of the young hotheads among the soldiers – processed in slow, stately and surely unchallengeable fashion. The *Girona*, under sail and not deploying her oars, was accompanied by her immediate consorts, the other three galleasses of Naples, with the *San Lorenzo* as their *capitana* under Don Hugo de Moncada. They were all brilliantly painted in red and gold, pennants streaming from their mastheads beneath the flags of Spain, Naples and the Papacy.

They were sailing just to windward of the squadron of *urcas* led by the *Gran Grifón*. To the south was the squadron of Guipuzcoa, to the north those of Levant and Andalusia, to the west, astern of the rest of the fleet, that of Biscay, commanded by the renowned Recalde. Ahead, to the east, leading the way into the English Channel, were the squadrons of Castile and Portugal, the latter containing the *capitana general*, the *San Martín*, flagship of the entire Armada, flying the royal standard of King Philip at the fore and the sacred banner at the main, displaying a crucifix between images of the Virgin and St Mary Magdalene. Aboard her was the admiral, the Duke of Medina Sidonia, no doubt laying his plans to join forces with the Duke of Parma and the vast army he had assembled on the coast of Flanders. That done, the invincible tide of Spain would wash onto the shores of England.

The tide of Spain, and of God, too. Huge red crosses adorned the sails of every ship, signifying that this was truly a crusade, sanctioned by the Holy Father Sixtus the Fifth—

'Mixed feelings, *anciano*?'

Juan had been so deep in his own thoughts that he had not been aware of Fra Gordillo approaching him.

'We do God's work,' he said, as neutrally as he could. His Castilian was entirely fluent, but even after all these years, it still bore traces of his native accent.

'Very true,' said the thin, pale, black-cassocked chaplain of the *Girona*, crossing himself. Juan always thought the priest resembled an emaciated crow. 'But God's work may involve putting to the sword many thousands of people upon that shore. Your people.' He nodded towards England.

'The realm strayed from the true faith,' said Juan sadly. 'The tyrant Henry was seduced by the heretical Boleyn witch, and now their bastard sits on a usurped throne, the people led astray into false religion, denying the Pope. England has a desperate sickness, Father, and that requires a desperate remedy. The remedy we see all around us.'

Gordillo smiled. 'I so enjoy our talks, Juan. You could have been a distinguished priest, you know. I hear you speak, I watch you during Mass, and you are so sincere, so orthodox in your faith, unlike most of the time-servers in my congregation. But it will avail you nothing, my friend.' His face changed, the smile turning into a grim rictus. 'I still say you should have burned years ago, and you know full well, as do I and as does God, that your soul will burn in hellfire for all eternity as punishment for what you did. Before then, though, you will watch as we carry God's cleansing flame through England. Who knows, Juan Estandar, you may even get to watch as we burn your children and grandchildren.' He made a sketchy benediction, then moved away.

The malevolent priest and his dire predictions of the hereafter no longer scared Juan. In truth, Gordillo was a feeble figure when set alongside the Inquisitors who had questioned him for so long in Mexico; initially so kind when they established that he was of the true faith, then implacable beyond measure when they discovered that, despite this, he had not only sailed alongside the infamous heretical pirates El *Draque* and Juan *Aquines* but had even commanded one of their ships. So he was doubly damned. Spain and the universal Catholic Church condemned him as an apostate, while England condemned him and all his kind as recusants, outcasts from the miserable Protestant uniformity that prevailed under Queen Elizabeth.

Juan strained his eyes. Were those distant sails, emerging from Plymouth Sound? The lookouts' cries began, confirming the old man's suspicion. So the English, his countrymen, were coming out to fight after all; many of his fellow slaves had been of the opinion that the very sight of their mighty fleet would trigger the immediate surrender of the heretical kingdom.

Despite the conflict raging in his heart, Juan realised he was smiling.

Signal flags broke out from the mastheads of the *capitanas* and *almirantas*, and as the old man watched, the vessels of the Armada began to move into their battle positions. Recalde, with some twenty ships, bore away and shortened sail, re-forming to starboard, southward, and fanning out astern of the main body. Don Alonso de Leyva, the noble young genius beloved of his king and of every man in the Armada, did the same to larboard, forming the vanguard directly in the path of the oncoming fleet. The remaining ships remained in the centre, an impregnable floating fortress under Medina Sidonia. If God was looking down from his Heaven, Juan thought, he would have seen a shape that resembled a vast bull's head with two horns.

The old man called Juan had once answered to another name, spoken in another tongue. He had almost forgotten both, yet there was still a part of him that remembered what it had been to be the man called Jack Stannard of Dunwich. With England, his native shore, now in sight, he almost dared to conjure up once again the impossible dream that had sustained him through so much of his captivity: that one day, by some means or other, he would return at last to his home town. His beloved wife Alice lay there, beneath its earth. Perhaps by now his son Tom and daughter Meg did too, maybe even the wife and children of his other, colder marriage. But there would still be living grandchildren, surely. He had known two, if only barely – tiny lads named Adam and Peter – but there must be others, unless the Stannards had been either particularly impotent, infertile, or else unfortunate with pestilence and other sicknesses.

As he looked out towards the distant coastline of the land that had formed him, Juan Estandar – Jack Stannard – had no inkling of the existence of a grandson who bore the very same name, bestowed as a poignant tribute to him. A grandson who, at that very moment, was sailing out of Plymouth Sound aboard Francis Drake's *Revenge*, intent along with every other man in the English fleet on destroying the *Girona* and the entire Spanish Armada.

Part One

This fleet is here and very forcible and must be waited upon with all our force, which is little enough ... this is the greatest and strongest combination to my understanding that was ever gathered in Christendom.

Sir John Hawkins to Queen Elizabeth I, 21 July 1588

One

A single small ship put on sail and outpaced the rest of the English fleet, as if intent on attacking the entire Spanish Armada on its own. Men on the upper decks of both fleets watched in astonishment as the little vessel, no more than eighty tons, steered a determined course directly for the bull's head itself. When it was at the limit of its range, it fired one shot. Juan, still on the deck of the *Girona*, did not see whether it struck a hull or fell harmlessly into the water. All he saw was the distant English vessel wear ship and steer a course back towards the safety of its fleet.

'What was that all about then, old man?' came a voice from behind him.

He turned and made a sketchy salute to Sergio Cala, the grey-bearded bosun of the *Girona*, who was very nearly as ancient as Juan himself.

'A challenge, *señor*. The throwing-down of a gauntlet.'

'A gauntlet? Like the gauntlet *El Cid* took up before Calahorra?'

'Just so. There has been no declaration of war between Spain and England – even we slaves on the oar deck know that, *señor*. Lord Howard, the English *almirante*, is a man of an illustrious and noble lineage, who will act according to ancient honour.'

Cala nodded gravely. 'I had not thought the heretic English possess the same sense of honour as Spaniards do,' he said.

'Perhaps the English will surprise you in other ways too,' said Juan, smiling.

The bosun of the *Girona* took umbrage. 'They won't surprise Medina Sidonia or God,' he said. 'Get you below now, old man, and to your oar. Even your feeble arms may be needed in the coming battle. Not for long, though, eh? One good Spanish broadside and your Howard and your Drake and all the rest of them will shit themselves all the way back to their usurper queen's skirts.'

-

In the hold of the *Revenge*, below the orlop deck, Jack Stannard struggled to keep his lantern steady. He could feel the hull turning into the wind to make another tack, and knew that beyond the timbers confining him, the ship and the entire fleet would be edging ever nearer to the great Armada. He knew he ought to be concentrating on the barrels of beer, salt beef, peas, biscuit, bacon, cheese and stockfish stacked before him, for that was the only way he would be able to keep count. But every creak of the hull, every wave lapping the ship's side only feet from where he stood made him long to be above.

It was a foolish conceit. It would still be a good hour before the fleets closed sufficiently for battle to commence, and in that hour the young deputy purser of the *Revenge* had no more pressing task than counting barrels, then assuming ten fish days and sixteen flesh days per month, with Fridays on half allowance to make up the deficit of two days, additionally allowing a gallon of beer per man per day, then finally recalculating the number of days the ship could remain at sea before being forced into harbour to revictual.

Jack sighed. He owed his place on the *Revenge* to his father, who, the previous autumn, had made a special journey to London to air the matter of his youngest son's prospects with two of his long-standing connections. The first was a certain William Halliday, a very old man who, it seemed, had been a friend of Jack's grandfather. Halliday had once occupied a position of some importance in the Council of Marine Causes, the body that oversaw the queen's Navy Royal, and still had some influence with its members. The second was none other than Sir John Hawkins, the illustrious seaman who held the office of Treasurer of the Navy.

Jack knew that his long-dead mother, whom he could not remember, was distant kin to Hawkins, and there were hints that the old admiral also owed a mighty favour to Jack's father from the time when they had voyaged together to the Carib Sea, some twenty years before. Tom and Jack had both hoped for a volunteer's place on one of the great ships, perhaps even the *Ark Royal* itself, or else on one of the smaller vessels, which were bound to see a share of the action. But Tom had let slip his son's facility with accounts, and Jack's fate was sealed; even more so when the purser of Drake's *Revenge*, Martin Jeffrey, a Devonian kinsman of the vice admiral, proved to be a hopeless sot with brains scrambled by a blow to the head in a tavern brawl. Drake kept his man in the office, drawing pay and allowances, but also petitioned his old friend and kinsman Hawkins for a deputy who could actually do the work.

When Jack had first reported to the famed captain, he had seen Drake's eyes narrow when the new officer spoke his surname.

'Jack Stannard,' he said tentatively. 'A name I have cause to remember. You look like him too, a little. More like your mother, though – I knew her also. Not well, but she was kin to Hawkins, as I am. I sent condolences when she died.'

Jack sensed from the clipped words that his presence, and this history, made Drake uncomfortable, but he could not imagine why.

The thoughts made him lose count yet again. Impatiently he threw yet another crossed-through sheet of paper to the deck and strained to hear the sounds from above his head. Were there more shouts than there had been? Could he just make out the shrill notes of the trumpeters? Were those crashes the sound of the gunports swinging open? Were the two fleets closer to each other than he had supposed? Was battle about to be joined? He took one last look at the barrels, decided that the quantities of salt beef, stockfish and all the rest were most unlikely to diminish significantly before the fight was over, and made his way back up the precarious ladder that led to the hatch in the orlop deck.

In the tiny, stinking space that passed for the purser's store, Martin Jeffrey was sitting on his sea chest raising a jug to his lips. The nominal purser of the *Revenge* slurred something unintelligible, but Jack ignored him, took up his cutlass and made his way up to the main gun deck. Unlike the almost deserted orlop, this was full of men. The ship's great guns, principally culverins on this deck but also with four of the larger cannons-perier, were all in their firing positions, protruding through the gunports. Gun captains were barking their orders and readying their linstocks, boys were running hither and thither with cannonballs and powder, and men, nearly all stripped to the waist, crouched by their guns or made final pernickety adjustments to the running tackle. The twin stenches of sweat and gunpowder pervaded the deck, as did anticipation and determination in equal measure.

The drums started beating as Jack made his way onto the upper deck. From the deep and crowded waist of the *Revenge* he could see only the waves – there was a glimpse of the Devon coast, surprisingly distant – then the splendid galleon went through the rest of her turn and now there was a new sight, much closer than he had expected it to be.

A colossal wall of ships, the towering hulls far higher than those of the vessels sailing to attack them and painted far more gaudily than those of the English men-of-war. There was a preponderance of red and gold, the colours of Spain and King Philip; in the warm July sun, the Spanish fleet appeared like a vast island of fire upon the waves. A forest of masts supporting endless swathes of canvas, all filling with the strong south-westerly breeze, all bearing vast red crosses. The bright summer sun blazed from the highly polished barrels of the enemy's cannon, and from the helmets, pikes and halberds of the countless troops arrayed upon the decks.

Jack was unable to move. His limbs seemed to be locked and he could barely breathe. His eyes hurt. This, he realised, was terror.

There was a strange hush aboard the *Revenge*. Now there was no bravado, no singing, no screaming of obscenities at England's foes. It was as if every man on the ship – every man in the fleet – had been struck dumb and rooted to the place where he stood, staring across the water towards the vast horror before him.

The feeling lasted no more than a few seconds. Jack ran his hand through his curling brown hair, the ship's trumpeters began another fanfare, and a growl of defiance rose from the gun crews. Jack thought of going up to the quarterdeck, but that risked another confrontation with Fitzranulf, so he went forward into the fo'c'sle. Bodenham, the emaciated-looking ship's lieutenant, stood there. He glanced quizzically at Jack, but said nothing. Jack nodded, acknowledging the senior officer's presence, then moved to the ship's side. A familiar face did duty at one of the swivel guns mounted upon the rail.

'Master Stannard,' said Matthew Bradlow, inclining his head slightly in a nominal salute. He was a tall, lean fellow, who according to Jack's father had no more fat on him now than he'd had when he was naught but a callow ship's boy on his first voyage out of Dunwich.

'Matt. All's well with you?'

'Well enough, considering what lies yonder.'

'More than we expected.'

'Aye, double the number we reckoned on. But worse than that, Master Stannard, better ordered, too. You should have seen the way they moved into this formation – flawless seamanship it was. I heard men gasp with awe, that I did. Englishmen awed by the Dons. Who'd have reckoned it?'

The Dons can't sail. Jack had heard the litany countless times in alehouses and on quaysides from Dunwich to Plymouth, and the triumphs of the likes of Drake and Frobisher seemed to prove the point in ample measure. But his father, Tom, knew better, having barely escaped with his life from a Spanish fleet twenty years earlier, and he had impressed the lesson upon the only one of his three sons who showed any inclination at all towards the sea. Matt Bradlow was another who knew better, having sailed with Tom and young Jack's grandfather on that fatal voyage from which the elder Jack Stannard never returned. It was simple chance that placed them both on the *Revenge*.

Jack looked across at the rest of the English fleet and frowned. The ships were formed into a long line, the *Revenge* leading the way, but surely such a formation could not penetrate to the heart of the Armada. Moreover, the fleet's course was set for the rearmost ships, for the northern horn of the Spaniards' huge crescent.

'What are we about, Mister Bodenham?' said Jack to the lieutenant.

Bodenham shrugged. 'Look at them, Stannard,' he growled. 'They outnumber us by so very many. Even though we have the weather gage, what are we to do, eh? Venture between the horns and they'll close in and swallow us. Attack the head and the horns will come up anyway. Get in too close and they can do what the Dons love to do – board and use their soldiers. You know about Spanish soldiers, eh, lad? Invincible. The men who beat the French, and the Dutch, and the Turks. We don't want them anywhere near our decks, by God we don't. So we'll have to fight them a different way. A very different way.'

–

The oar deck of the *Girona* was a low, dark, stinking place, made even more confined by the catwalks bearing swivel guns that were fitted above the oars on each side. The only light came from a handful of lanterns suspended from the beams and from the few oar holes that were not closed by gaskets. The vessel was still proceeding under sail alone, so the three hundred slaves sat upon their benches, leaning on the thirty-two oars but not deploying them. This could change in the blinking of an eye, as Juan knew from long experience, but there seemed no immediate prospect of the rowers being called upon. They were in the middle of the fleet, close to Medina Sidonia's flagship *San Martín*, and the English were far away. Juan was permitted to sit in the rearmost rank so that he could quickly go alongside the drummer and sing when called upon, and he was also allowed the privilege of proximity to an open oar port, giving him a limited view of the outside world. Fra Gordillo blustered at what he called such weak indulgence of a Hell-bound reprobate.

'Well, what can you see?' demanded Spadaro, the little one-eyed Sicilian sitting alongside him.

'Nothing,' he said, 'only our ships.'

'Have the English run away, then?'

'Hoping they have, are you?' laughed Owen Gravell, the lean Welshman on the other side of Spadaro, who then abandoned Castilian for English as he addressed Juan. 'What d'you think, Jack Stannard? Where's Drake?'

'I said I can't see anything,' he said.

Juan's English had been almost forgotten before Gravell appeared aboard the *Girona*. An eternally cheerful fellow who seemed impossibly young but must have been in his late twenties, Gravell had been captured off the Azores in a private man-of-war that the Spanish inevitably condemned as a pirate. English was a second language for him, as it had become for Juan, but it gave them both a connection to the world they had lost.

Juan pressed his face closer against the oar port. Were those flashes in the distance, momentarily visible in gaps between the wall of hulls? And was that gunfire, just audible above the sounds of the creaking timbers and taut sails of the Armada?

Yes, by God. Yes.

He turned towards Gravell and Spadaro and spoke gravely.

'The battle has started,' he said.

Two

'For Drake, Elizabeth and England, give fire!'

Upon Sir Francis Drake's bellowed command, the large bow guns of the *Revenge* opened fire at the nearest ships in the northern horn of the Spanish Armada. Jack Stannard stood by Matt Bradlow, feeling the hull shudder, breathing the choking gun smoke, and praying his ears would recover from the unearthly noise of the cannonade. He had experienced the firing of sakers or falconets on individual ships, but what he saw, heard and felt now was on a scale beyond his comprehension. Truth be told, it was beyond the comprehension of most of the men in the English Navy Royal, which had not fought a battle on anything like this scale for over forty years. Jack could see men gaping, while more than one denizen of Elizabeth's Protestant England surreptitiously crossed himself. His own thoughts turned unaccountably to an argument he had once had with his brother Adam – one of very many – who was berating him for his alleged sinfulness by conjuring up a vivid word picture of Hell as a place of eternal flame, smoke, thunderous noise and unremitting terror. Until now, Jack had never counted his eldest brother as a man of rare prescience.

Astern of the *Revenge*, more and more of the queen's great ships were coming into action. *Ark Royal* herself, following a course further to the east towards the Spanish vanguard, opened fire, the entire flagship invisible for perhaps half a minute as the smoke enveloped her. Hawkins and Frobisher, meanwhile, were close in support of Drake. The English ships passed the rearmost vessels of the Armada in line formation. Each ship in turn fired its bow guns, then wore away, firing the lighter broadside guns as it did so, finally deploying the very large stern guns as it went through a figure-of-eight. It was a terrifying, magnificent spectacle, but as he observed it, Jack felt a mounting sense of disquiet. Men cheered whenever a cannonball struck a hull or ripped a hole in a sail, but he could see clearly that most shots were falling well short and causing telltale spouts of water. Moreover, there was no return of fire. The guns of the Spanish ships were protruding from their ports and men were lining the decks, but there was no answering cannonade. Instead, the vast crescent of the Armada ploughed inexorably onwards, albeit at no more than a walking pace.

'Why do we not close them?' Jack demanded of Bradlow. 'Why aren't we at point blank, or nearer still?'

The older man shook his head. 'Look astern, Master Jack. Half our ships still haven't cleared Plymouth Sound. The admirals won't risk close-quarter action, not yet, at any rate. Perhaps they expected the Dons to break formation once they faced good English gunnery, but look at them, holding their stations as well as any Englishman could. Holding their fire, too. Taunting us. Daring us to close with them. Misjudge such a move by only a few feet and they could do what they long to do, come alongside us and board.'

Distant gunfire suggested that the *Ark Royal* and the ships with her were engaged closer to the centre of the enemy fleet, perhaps with the Duke of Medina Sidonia's flagship itself. After executing one complete figure-of-eight, the *Revenge* and her consorts sailed on, the wind abeam, and made for the other horn of the crescent. As they crossed the open water – the bowstring, had the Armada's formation been a giant longbow – Jack looked off to larboard and saw the vast heart of the Spanish force, a tight mass of large galleons and *urcas* broken only by the lower hulls of four great galleasses, all stern-on to the Englishmen. But the English ships made no attempt to wear around and sail for them. Instead, *Revenge* stayed on course for the southerly horn of the crescent, where the flag of Portugal and an admiral's pennant distinguished a large galleon. A name was being murmured among the gun crews within Jack's earshot: *Recalde.* So then, Francis Drake was seeking a duel with the only seaman in the Armada who came close to rivalling his own fame, Juan de Recalde, Knight of Santiago, second in command of the entire Spanish expedition.

'Give fire!'

On Drake's command, *Revenge* and the ships with her opened fire against the southern wing of the Armada. They were finally in a position, and there were finally enough of them, to execute their favoured tactic, the lead ships of the line approaching upon the wind, firing bow first, then turning through the figure-of-eight to allow them time to reload while the ships behind came up to take their place, thus maintaining a sustained bombardment against the enemy.

The *Revenge* and her consorts carried out this move three times during the course of two hours, and at last it seemed as though the English attack was having an effect. Several Spanish ships broke away from their formation, put on sail, and made for the safety of the centre of the

Armada. But Recalde's huge flagship stood firm against all comers, and Jack fretted when he saw through breaks in the smoke that hardly any shots were hitting her; the English bombardment was impressive, the fleet's complex manoeuvring immaculate, but it was all done at too great a range to have much of an effect. Recalde evidently had no qualms about returning fire, and his ships were giving as good as they got. Worse, Spanish reinforcements in the shape of three large galleons were coming up from the heart of their fleet and beginning to engage with Frobisher's *Triumph*, now at the head of the English formation. Jack could see Drake upon the poop deck, running from side to side, pointing excitedly at this ship or that, all the while shouting orders to Lieutenant Bodenham and the ship's sailing master, Gray. Fitzranulf was there too, part of a gaggle of young men around the admiral; a few of them waved their swords vaguely at the Spanish ships, but otherwise they seemed to fulfil no martial purpose whatsoever.

Now, too, the sea was getting up. Jack could feel the hull of *Revenge* rising, falling and rolling more markedly beneath his feet, could see and hear the sails filling and groaning in the strengthening wind. Drake was barking orders, sending men aloft and out onto the yards, but it was all to little avail. The state of the sea would make it harder for the English to keep their sailing formation, so much more intricate than that of the Armada, and equally difficult for them to maintain accurate fire. If a mere stripling like Jack Stannard knew this, he thought, then Sir Francis Drake most certainly did too. So it was no surprise when Jack saw a white flag being hoisted from the foretop, the signal for the fleet to break off the attack and fall away.

It was at that precise moment that Lieutenant Bodenham finally seemed to awaken to the implications of Jack's continued presence on the fo'c'sle.

'Pusser Stannard, there!'

'Sir.'

'The men are uncommon thirsty, Mister Stannard, but the distribution of beer is uncommon slow. I'd be obliged if you and the cook would attend to the matter expeditiously!'

Jack bowed his head. 'As you say, Lieutenant.'

As he turned away from Bodenham and Matt Bradlow, one of the Spanish vessels nearest to Recalde's flagship blew up.

–

'The *Salvador*,' said Juan, squinting his eyes as he stared through the oar hole of the *Girona*. '*Madre de dios*, the *Salvador* has gone.'

The galleass was towards the rear of the Armada's main force and had turned to larboard to make way for a galleon tacking back to join the reinforcement of Recalde's rearguard, so for a few minutes Juan had enjoyed a view of the battle astern. Although the smoke was blowing northeasterly, towards the heart of the Armada, the firing was sufficiently intermittent to allow him to identify individual ships, even the flags of St George flying from the mastheads of the English vessels.

'The English?' said Owen Gravell. 'If their gunfire is that good…'

'I doubt it,' said Juan. 'The range looks too great for it to have been even a lucky shot. *Jesu Maria* help those poor souls.'

The colossal pall of smoke surrounding the *Salvador* cleared sufficiently for Juan to be able to make out some of the carnage. Most of the galleon's upper works and all of her sterncastle were gone, and Juan, whose eyesight had not deteriorated much with age, could just make out the tiny shapes of men jumping from the sides of the burning hull.

'Damnation, old man, tell us what you can see!' cried Spadaro, echoed by the fellow slaves near him.

'The powder magazines can't have blown up,' said Juan. 'They'd have torn the hull apart. And the English… aye, the English are falling astern. They're breaking off the fight.'

There were some feeble cheers on the oar deck. None of the men there should have had cause to love King Philip, yet most, including Juan, had been incarcerated for so long in galleys or galleasses that Spain, which at least fed them and kept them alive, was now their country.

Juan's view of the *Salvador* vanished as the *Girona* swung round slightly to starboard. As he continued to look through the oar hole, he was also aware of the headway coming off the galleass. The ships now within view, including the flagship *San Martín*, were backing their sails, while the flagship of the galleasses, the *San Lorenzo*, already had her oars deployed and was beginning to swing around through the points of the compass. So it was no surprise when Bosun Cala appeared on the platform at the rear of the oar deck and bellowed his orders.

'All hands, man your oars! Prepare to deploy outboard!'

The three hundred rowers shuffled into position, their manacles rattling as they did so. Juan, who was unchained, stood and saluted Cala.

'A song, bosun?'

'Aye, Juan, a song. The drummer will be at his fastest beat, so you'll need something to keep up with him.'

'The fastest beat? Then we're turning to fight the English?'

'Fight the English? Why? Your countrymen are standing off, Juan Estandar. They're running away. They can't hurt us, and they know it. No, we're going to save the *Salvador*. Saving the saviour, eh? It's the paymaster's ship, Englishman – my money's aboard it, so is Captain Spinola's and the admiral's, and we'll all be damned before we see it go to the bottom of the ocean!'

Upon Cala's orders, the gaskets were removed from the oar ports, and the oars themselves swung outboard. Then, as the drummer began his fast and steady rhythm, Juan Estandar sang a song that, as Jack Stannard, he had first heard sung in the Pelican in its Piety in Dunwich, only a matter of days before he left home to become a choirboy in the short-lived Cardinal College at Ipswich.

There were three brothers in merry Scotland
In merry Scotland there were three
And they did cast lots which of them should go, should go,
should go
And turn robber all on the salt sea…

The men heaved upon their oars, and the *Girona* gained speed as she closed the *Salvador*.

-

Jack spent the next few hours below decks. Not only was his nominal superior, Purser Jeffrey, a hopeless sot, but so too was the ship's cook, a one-legged fellow named

Damerell who had been on Drake's world voyage, where his limb had fallen victim to gangrene. This meant that the task of ensuring that the ship's crew were victualled at the correct times, and with the correct portions, devolved to a considerable extent upon Jack's young shoulders. Yes, he would rather have been on deck, manning a gun; but if this was how God had determined that he should serve his queen and country, then so be it.

The advantage of having good cause to move frequently and easily along each deck and between each mess was that Jack was known to many in the crew, and he knew them in return. It also meant that he was privy to more of the whispers, rumours and downright libels that pervaded the lower deck than many of the other officers. Such chatter was rife during the long afternoon and evening after the first fight with the Spanish Armada. The ship that blew up had been saved, it seemed, Medina Sidonia having stopped the entire fleet and dispatched his manoeuvrable galleasses to secure it. But men said that another large Spanish ship had run into difficulties, colliding with some of her consorts and ultimately losing her foremast. She was somewhere out there still, but the Armada was under way again and England's Navy Royal, with *Ark Royal* and her consorts now back in company, was bound to follow it.

Some of the grizzled old foretopmen talked of how they had been up on deck when a pinnace came across from the flagship bearing orders for Drake to set the night watch for the fleet – in other words, to be the lead ship, lighting her large lanterns for the rest of the ships to follow in the dark. But other men, who had just come below after the end of the first watch, swore that the lanterns had not been lit. That could not be right, Jack thought.

If the Lord Admiral of England had ordered the watch to be set by *Revenge*, then set it surely would have been. So there must have been no such order, and some other ship had to be leading the fleet: the *Triumph*, perhaps.

Such were his thoughts when one of the ship's boys caught up with him in the galley, where he had gone to remonstrate with the cook about the burned fish provided for supper.

'Sir Francis's compliments, Master Stannard,' said the lad, who looked impossibly young, 'an' he orders you to attend upon him in his cabin.'

Perplexed, Jack made his way to the upper deck. The first faint streaks of dawn were apparent in the east, and there was already enough light for Jack to make out the utter strangeness of the scene. The sea was all but empty. There was no sign of the two huge fleets; it was as if they had never existed. There was only one other ship in sight, a vast, darkened hull a few cables away to starboard, but that was all.

Jack's thoughts did not dwell upon this strange state of affairs. Instead, they raced with more immediate concerns. Why in God's name would Drake himself wish to speak with him? Had complaints about the fish reached the admiral? Had Fitzranulf been making trouble for him? Such imaginings, and even stranger ones too, were racing through his mind as he was admitted into the great cabin.

The renowned mariner was seated upon an incongruously elaborate oak chair, drinking wine from what appeared to be a fine silver goblet. He was barefoot and dressed only in a rough shirt and breeches; but for his bejewelled earrings, he might have been taken for an ordinary foretopman.

'Sir Francis,' said Jack, making his salute.

'Stannard. So what have you made of battle, eh? I saw you on the fo'c'sle earlier. Not a place for a mere clerk.'

Jack's hackles rose. 'Clerk in name, perhaps, but as able a seaman as any on this ship—'

Drake raised his hand. 'Spare me,' he said. 'I know you Stannards of old – argumentative fellows and keen for a fight. Your father for one, but your grandfather most of all. You know I remember him in my prayers every day?'

Jack knew his eyes were as plates, but he could not help himself.

'You do, Sir Francis?'

'Just as I remember San Juan de Ulúa each and every day. I hate Spain and the wicked falsity of the Church of Rome with a passion, Jack Stannard, and everything I do aims to atone for what happened that day in the Indies. To be avenged for those we lost – those like your grandfather, whose name you share. So I know why you want to argue with me. I know you want nothing more than to prove yourself a fighting man who'll stand alongside me as we do battle for England, the true Protestant religion and our glorious queen against the dark forces of the Antichrist. I was only a little older than you when I was at San Juan, Jack, and I remember how it feels to be young. And for what it's worth, I'd rather have a lad like you, who's handy with a blade and keen to fight for his queen, out there on deck in case we come to close quarters with the Don, rather than making up an inventory somewhere in the hold.' Drake took a little more of his wine. 'But there are times when inventories are needed, and when adding and subtracting are just as useful to England – to the queen, and to me – as the sword. At sunrise, you will experience one of those times.'

'I don't follow, Sir Francis.'

'You've seen the Spanish galleon yonder, Master Stannard? *Our Lady of Rosario*, so some of the oldsters who've been in the Don's galleys tell me. She lost her foremast in the fight, and Medina Sidonia didn't see fit to send aid to her. Thus God, the just God we Englishmen worship, has delivered her into our hands. She's drifting, and when the sun rises, I intend to take her as prize in the name of the queen.'

Jack frowned, thinking of the categorical report that Drake had been ordered to set the night watch. If that was true, then the admiral's protestations of fervour towards God and Elizabeth sat uneasily with his apparent disobedience of orders and pursuit of this prize. But Jack knew better than to speak his mind and risk the wrath of Francis Drake.

'And I have a part to play in this, sir?' he said, tentatively.

'That you do, Master Stannard, and a critical part at that. As I say, I need a man who knows how to handle both a weapon and an abacus. Once, Purser Jeffrey would have been that man, but now…' They both knew why Drake had no need to complete the sentence. 'Jeffrey was a man I could trust, Jack Stannard. A man loyal to me, who would guard my secrets with his life. Can you be that man for me in his stead?'

'What is it you would have me do, Sir Francis?'

'Do I have your loyalty?'

Jack's father, who had told him much about Drake's reputation, would have counselled caution. But Tom Stannard was not there, in the great cabin of the *Revenge*, standing a few feet from England's finest seaman, the most famous man in the world. And Jack had one thought above all at the forefront of his mind. If he did Drake's bidding, and if the Armada was defeated, then who knew what advantage might accrue to him? So when all was said and done, there was only one answer he could give.

'You have my loyalty, Sir Francis.'

Three

The surrender of the *Rosario* was accomplished swiftly and bloodlessly. Just after first light, the Spanish galleon was hailed and ordered to capitulate. Her captain prevaricated, but must have seen that his position was hopeless; his foremast had fallen back against the main, the sails and rigging were inextricably entangled, and it was impossible for the ship to manoeuvre. If he resisted, Drake would simply circle the *Rosario* at will, blasting her into matchwood. The *Revenge* would need no seconds, which was as well because no other ship from either fleet was in sight. All around, the sea was entirely empty.

At length the Spanish captain came aboard. Word quickly spread among those watching on the upper deck of *Revenge* that this was one Don Pedro de Valdes, a tall, haughty fellow in black and gold half-armour. He exchanged a few sentences with Drake, who had donned a pristine white doublet and matching coat for the occasion; Jack knew that the admiral had picked up enough Spanish over the years to be able to dispense with an interpreter. Valdes then walked away and leaned heavily on the *Revenge*'s rail, looking across to the *Rosario*. When he turned back, his face was red with emotion. He walked across the deck, slowly drew his sword and, with evident bad grace, presented it to England's admiral. Drake accepted it, bowed, and grinned broadly before inviting Valdes to take wine with him in his cabin.

Lieutenant Bodenham took a large boarding party across to secure the prize, and Jack went with him. He had orders directly from Drake to seize or kill any man who dared plunder cargo from the galleon, but at first the Englishmen's self-restraint and discipline seemed remarkable. Jack worked methodically through the officers' cabins at the stern, his sword drawn and with a half-dozen men at his back. Bodenham had selected these for their dependability, but Jack insisted that the party should include Matt Bradlow, the one man aboard *Revenge* upon whom he knew he could count. Even so, there seemed at first to be no need to provide the deputy purser with such a formidable escort.

As he scoured the ship, Jack found sea chests unopened, bejewelled crucifixes and rosaries untouched, even loose bags of coin lying undisturbed. He knew of Drake's reputation – what man, woman or child in England did not? – but still struggled to comprehend its potency. Yet even English seamen, perhaps some of the most avaricious creatures on God's earth, seemed to at least half believe in the same ferocious legend that terrified their Spanish foes: the legend of *El Draque*, the dragon, the man who was, perhaps, the Devil incarnate and whose wrath would consign them to eternal hellfire. So the riches of the *Rosario* were gathered up, noted in proper form by Jack, then taken to the boats for ferrying across to the *Revenge*.

There was still no sign of either fleet.

Jack made his way methodically through the gun deck of the prize, although he knew that the seamen's humble mess tables were unlikely to produce anything worthy of dispatch to Queen Elizabeth's treasury. Finally he descended to the orlop and the various storerooms located there, where he expected to find the richest pickings of all.

'Smells different to an English ship,' said Bradlow. 'Sweeter.'

'Mayhap the Spanish don't shit in their bilges so much,' said Jack.

Bradlow barely smiled. 'Their galley more like,' he said. 'Made a voyage to Bilbao once, tried some of the local food. The wine, too. 'Tis little wonder the Dons are mad enough to fight bulls—'

Jack raised a hand to silence him, and gestured to him to extinguish his lantern. There were voices somewhere ahead of them, speaking in low tones. Low English tones; the voices of men who did not wish to be discovered.

Jack crept forward, trying not to trip on the piles of tackle the Spaniards had left scattered across the deck. If a Spanish man-of-war had a similar layout to an English one, then he was probably approaching the equivalent of his own space aboard the *Revenge*, namely the purser's office and store. The bulk of the gold and silver held aboard the ship would almost certainly be located there, and these men, whoever they were, knew that.

He pressed himself hard against a huge knee timber, whispered to Bradlow at his back, then carefully leaned forward. He could see one man holding a lantern, and two others who were tearing open canvas bags and scooping the contents into smaller bags fastened to their belts. The light from the lantern was weak, but sufficient to glint from the gold and silver coins. Jack's eyes were now accustomed to the light, so he was able to identify the men. Two of them were gentlemen volunteers, Carver and Mabbs, younger even than Jack, prideful fellows who bragged endlessly of all the important people they knew at court. Although his back was turned, Jack had no difficulty in identifying the third man, their leader, Nicholas Fitzranulf.

As Matt Bradlow crept away, as silently as he could, Jack Stannard drew his sword and stepped forward.

–

Far to the east of the battle off Plymouth and the drifting prize *Rosario*, the second of Queen Elizabeth's fleets lay at anchor in the Downs, the broad anchorage off the coast of Kent. This force had three roles, although in truth, it fulfilled only one of them at a time. As things stood, it watched the coast of Flanders, ready to sally forth if Parma's army used the approach of the Armada as cover to make a sudden dash for England. In reality, though, most of the work of watching and harrying was being done by England's allies, the Dutch, who had a squadron of some twenty small men-of-war in the shallow coastal waters, which they knew much better in any case. The Narrow Seas fleet's second role would come into play if Howard and Drake were still fighting it out with the Armada when both fleets reached the Straits of Dover; then, the eastern fleet would join the western, and God willing, the combined force would finally defeat the dreadful threat from Spain. The third role was the one Tom Stannard and every other man aboard the ships in the Downs hoped and prayed they would never need to play. For if the Armada had already defeated Hawkins and Drake, or defeated them here in the Straits, then the Narrow Seas fleet, England's last hope at sea, would throw itself into a last, desperate suicidal attack.

For suicide it would certainly be. As the sun rose and he looked around the anchorage from the deck of his *Eagle of Dunwich*, Tom Stannard could see but thirteen ships of the Navy Royal proper, only five of them fit to trade gunfire with the mighty Spanish galleons. True, there were also eight London ships of a good size, but the rest, the *Eagle* included, were a motley assortment of thirty or so coasting ships from the likes of Harwich, Ipswich, Aldeburgh, Yarmouth and, of course, Dunwich.

The previous evening, their admiral had assembled all his captains aboard his flagship, the mighty race-built galleon *Rainbow*, and given them a fine speech about how they were the pride of England, how they would humble the Don, and how no single soldier of Parma's army would ever set foot in Queen Elizabeth's realm. It was Tom Stannard's first encounter with Lord Henry Seymour, admiral of the Narrow Seas fleet, and he was suitably impressed. Nephew of a queen, cousin to a king, Seymour shared the red hair of both, and of his long-dead father, the Duke of Somerset, once protector of the kingdom, whose head had been cut off for the heinous sin of being too generous to the poor folk of the realm. Yet to Tom's surprise and approbation, Seymour dressed plainly, almost indistinguishable from a common seaman but for the whistle of command hanging from a golden chain around his neck. He had an easy, good-humoured manner, seeming to take every man, no matter how humble, into his confidence. So Tom went back to the *Eagle* in good spirits, a happy condition that lasted only until he discovered that his son had returned to the ship earlier that morning.

Tom sighed. He had hoped Adam was still ashore, berating drunks in the street or elsewise annoying the early risers of Deal by assuring them they were all damned for their manifold sins. But he greeted his son amiably enough, and related the gist of the admiral's speech.

'He did not speak of the certainty of God's divine intervention to succour His chosen people?' said Adam Stannard, frowning.

Adam was a broad, dark fellow, in marked contrast to his brothers, who were lighter and fairer. Over the years Adam had also become markedly ugly, a consequence, his father reckoned, of never doing anything but frown, as he was doing now, and taking even less care over his appearance than seemingly every other man in England. His lank hair and beard both stank and seemed alive with insects, while his stained shirt could not have been washed for months. One of the few consolations Tom Stannard took from the death of his wife was that she had not seen what her eldest son, once her pride and joy, had grown to be.

'Not in so many words, no.'

Adam's face, which had rarely smiled since he was two years old and terrified out of his wits by a hellfire sermon in Plymouth, was a stern mask of disapproval.

'As I have told you before, Father,' he said solemnly, 'the only reason why we might fail is that we are not godly enough. That our leaders are not godly enough. Seymour and all the rest of them, Drake excepted, cannot see that we are upon a crusade here. We are holy warriors fighting to bring down the Whore of Babylon, but there is too much ignorance in this fleet. Aye, in the whole kingdom. Scoffing, whoring, drunkenness, neglect of the word of God.'

Tom wondered whether Adam was thinking of his brother Peter, but humour was lost on the eldest of his three sons. He could just as easily have been sniping at Tom himself, for the father suspected that this son found him a sore back-sliding disappointment.

Even leaving his appearance aside, Adam Stannard was an utter mystery to his father. Jack, the youngest of his three sons, was a dreamer, cast from the same mould as his namesake, Tom's own father. Peter, the middle boy, was a cheerful soul, wild and free since the day of his birth, but also a practical, ingenious creature, just as his mother had been. But Adam… God alone knew what perverse strain far back in the Stannard bloodline had hatched that one. By the age of six he could recite whole passages of the Bible by heart, usually the bloodier parts of the Old Testament or the Book of Revelation. By ten, he knew Foxe's Book of Martyrs intimately, and could hold forth for an hour or more on the evils of transubstantiation, sodomy and a thousand other sins. By twenty, he risked arrest and execution with almost every public word he spoke. Now he was a hedge-preacher and a Brownist, one of the strange new sects that seemed to be proliferating among the wilder fringes of those named 'Puritans'.

One wild night, though, as Tom Stannard walked upon Dunwich cliff in a storm to clear his head after too many tankards at the Queen's Arms, a strange thought came to him. Perhaps Adam was not such a mystery after all. Perhaps, in truth, the son was the exact mirror image of the father.

It was not a reassuring revelation, and he had swiftly put it out of his mind.

For the time being, though, father and son were joined in a single cause, a cause that united them with Lord Henry Seymour and even the queen herself. Defeating the Armada and preserving Protestant England: nothing else mattered. To further that end, Adam Stannard had browbeaten his father into allowing him to sail on the *Eagle* as a kind of unofficial chaplain. Adam was no seaman, he could not wield a sword, and the one interminable sermon his father had allowed him to preach had offended those few crewmen who either understood it or who had not started to chatter among themselves about half an hour into the diatribe. So yes, Tom regretted his weakness in agreeing to his son's request. Jack would have been useful, Peter would have been fun, and both would have fought like demons if fate required it; but perhaps if Adam's endless prayers played some small part in bringing victory over the Spanish Armada, it would all have been worthwhile.

–

'Fitzranulf.'

'Stannard!' cried Mabbs, who nearly dropped the lantern he was holding.

Fitzranulf and Carver turned abruptly, both of them spilling coins to the deck as they did so.

'Well, gentlemen,' said Jack lightly, 'it seems that even Sir Francis's orders are not powerful enough to restrain the greed of some. For shame on you, who should be showing an example to the lower orders.'

Even in the dim light, it was possible to see that Fitzranulf was blushing.

'Sir Francis's orders?' he said, recovering some of his bluster and glancing at his friends for support. 'Why, Stannard, we're here by those very orders.'

'Is that so?' asked Jack, deploying a measure of sarcasm of which his brother Peter might have been proud. 'Shall we get him to confirm that when we return to the *Revenge*? Because his orders to me – and me alone – were to ensure that every coin on this ship was properly accounted for so that it should all reach the queen's treasury. Strange that he should then give a completely contradictory set of orders to you, Fitzranulf.'

Jack saw the panic in the faces of Mabbs and Carver, but their leader remained ostensibly defiant.

'Ah, but you're a sharp fellow, Jack Stannard.' Fitzranulf smiled, but it was a rictus of hostility. 'The queen's treasury, you say? And Drake said that, did he? Well now. You see, I think I know the great Sir Francis better than you. So let me inform you of a great truth. Aye, he'll send a goodly share to the treasury, enough to keep himself in the good graces of Her Majesty, but d'you believe for a moment that every coin here on this deck will make that journey? Don't you think, my friend, that an equally goodly portion of this treasure will take the other journey, just a short way up the river from Plymouth? To Buckland Abbey, no less?'

'The admiral has no such intent,' said Jack, although he had no confidence in his words, for he knew that Buckland Abbey, Drake's grand home – far grander than any Devon mariner could expect to possess – was certainly not built with the pay he had officially drawn from the queen over the years.

Fitzranulf stepped forward, seemingly unafraid of the naked blade that Jack held out before him.

'We're reasonable men,' he said, his brazen arrogance now restored in full measure, 'and there's more than enough bullion in this one cabin alone to keep everyone happy – the queen and Drake, Mabbs and Carver here, you and I. Look at all these unopened bags, Stannard.

Each of us could buy an estate, a hundred horses and the services of every whore between Plymouth and London, and the queen and our beloved admiral would be none the wiser. Come, Jack, you know I speak true. Where's the harm in it, man? Who's hurt by it? The queen and Drake won't think they've lost a farthing if you don't write anything down on that list of yours – what's never owned can never be lost.'

'The queen owns it, Fitzranulf. Aye, every last farthing of it.'

Fitzranulf's face hardened. 'Well then, if I can't persuade you with words, perhaps I can do so by other means. Persuade or dispatch. Look at the odds, Stannard. Three of us, one of you.' He drew out his knife, Mabbs and Carver following his lead. 'Such a tragedy, that the deputy purser of *Revenge* should be slaughtered by a desperate renegade Don while doing his duty.'

The three thieves stepped forward, but Jack remained resolute.

'I've sent for Bodenham,' he said. 'He'll be on his way this very moment. Think on it, Fitzranulf. Aye, there may well be renegades hiding out somewhere in the ship, so do you truly think Drake would send just one man to take possession of all the bullion on the orlop? Empty your bags, man. Make it seem as though you're helping me collect spilled coins, and you may live.'

There was a distant shout. It was Bodenham's voice, calling out for Jack, and the sound of running footsteps on both the orlop and the gun deck above suggested he had many men with him, one of whom was sure to be Jack's loyal messenger, Matt Bradlow.

Mabbs and Carver looked desperately at Fitzranulf.

The Irishman raised his knife, pointed it between Jack's eyes, then swept it downwards and swiftly cut the bags from his belt. Scores, then hundreds of coins bearing the head of King Philip of Spain fell to the deck of the *Rosario*.

Four

Peter Stannard sat at the edge of the glum, contemplative body of actors who formed Lord Carnforth's Men. They were in the courtyard of the Bell at Bromley, where the performance of *The Spanish Tragedy* had ended so abruptly and to which they had all drifted back shamefacedly after their precipitate flight from the stage. By rights, they should have been staging Marlowe's *Tamburlaine* at that very moment, but the entire nation was now upon a greater stage of its own, acting in a drama that might yet prove a tragedy, and lesser actors had no audiences.

'They say King Philip is quite favourable towards the theatre,' said Will Hetherington, who was very far gone in his cups. 'His daughter, who they say he'll make queen here, even more so.'

As one, the men of the company turned and studied every door, every corner. No one seemed to be within earshot.

'God's blood, Hetherington,' hissed Rob Wasdale, the vast, hirsute actor-manager of the troupe. 'For once in your life, act the part of a mute!'

'All well and good for you to say that,' slurred Hetherington. 'You can go back to the mercer's trade, or wring coin out of your brother the archdeacon. But what of the rest of us? No performances, no audiences, no money. What are we to do, eh?'

Peter Stannard and every other man in the company stared intently at Wasdale, but now it was the huge man who was mute. The truth was that Wasdale, like the rest of them, had no idea of what might happen, and thus of what they should do. Perhaps Peter's father and brothers, and the rest of their kind who manned England's ships at sea, would defeat the Spanish Armada in short order, the theatres would swiftly reopen and the inns that hosted the touring companies would be filled with relieved citizens, celebrating the triumph. Or else, of course, the Armada might win, in which case the Duke of Parma could be in London in a week, bringing the Inquisition in his wake.

The bell of St Peter and St Paul tolled the hour, and Peter realised his doxy was late. He made his excuses, receiving a torrent of knowing ribaldry in return, and made his way out into the bustle of late afternoon on the streets of Bromley. He took the road towards the palace, hoping to meet her upon the way.

Arabella Dowling.

At first it had seemed to be the usual business that Peter had already experienced a hundred times. There was a kind of woman – of any age – who was seduced by the stage. This one, a well-built maiden with dark, curling brown hair, had been in the front row of their performance of *Master Arden of Feversham* some ten days earlier, and her unwavering gaze upon him had been truly unsettling. Later that night, lying alongside each other with their bodies finally and utterly spent, he asked her why she had given herself to him so quickly and willingly. Oh, she said, it was the words, and the beauty with which he had uttered them. Not my own beauty, then? he had asked. No, for you are a plain brute, she said, perplexing him, but you are an actor, and you have a sturdy body, and you can make me dream that Sir Philip Sidney himself lies in my arms as he takes me.

A very strange creature.

His brother Adam would have castigated him for his weakness against the wiles of an heiress to Eve, she who had brought sin into the world. Adam would also have upbraided him for fornication. But then for as long as he could remember, Adam had been upbraiding him for one thing or another: everything from picking his nose to doubting the very existence of God. Their younger brother Jack, loyal until death to the queen and thus to her Church, always laughed at the pair of them, bickering like old fishwives.

Inevitably, therefore, Peter Stannard was immediately besotted with Arabella Dowling as he had been with no woman before.

She was witty, she could read and write, but she was naught but a scullery maid at the palace. This edifice, the residence of the Lord Bishop of Rochester, dominated the town even though it stood somewhat apart from it. Many of the local folk worked there, or were married to someone who did, or else supplied it with victuals or labour. But Arabella, whose parents were long dead, had ambitions to better herself, and seemed to see Peter as the means by which she could do so. She was already talking of going with him when Lord Carnforth's Men returned to London, as they had planned to do when the usual plague season was over. But the arrival of the Armada had thrown all such schemes into confusion, and Peter was meant to be meeting with her that day to discuss what they might do. It was unlike her to be late; indeed, she had always been early to their previous encounters. Peter

Stannard never imagined that the part of the ardent lover could be so tiring.

He turned a corner into a narrow alley, which he knew provided a shortcut to the palace, and was nearly knocked off his feet by a woman running into him.

'Hell's flames, woman, watch your— *Arabella!*'

She looked up, her eyes not registering him for a moment. She was weeping already, but now burst into a torrent of tears and violent, heaving sobs. He took her in his arms, noting as he did so that her shift was torn at the shoulder.

'Peter,' she said, struggling to speak, 'Peter, he…'

There was a commotion behind her, and a large, sweating fellow, well dressed in a green doublet and wearing a chain of office, came running down the alley from the other end.

'Unhand that little bitch!' he cried. 'She's mine, by Christ, and needs to be taught some manners!'

Peter pushed Arabella behind him and stepped forward, raising his arm to stop the oncoming creature. The man looked at him in astonishment, then his face grew redder and redder until it was a portrait of utter fury.

'*Do you know who I am?*' he blustered.

'No,' said Peter, 'nor do I wish to. All I know is that you're an oaf and a bully who's frightened this poor maiden.'

'*Maiden?* You're a Bedlam-fellow!' The large man raised his own arm to knock Peter's aside. 'She's a whore, and she's *my* whore! Out of my way, churl!'

Peter sagged, as though acknowledging defeat. Then, as his adversary stepped forward towards Arabella, he unleashed his right fist directly into the fellow's jaw. The man staggered backward and wiped blood from his lip. He stared angrily at Peter.

'I know you,' he said. 'You're one of the actors who's been at the Bell. Well, you'll not act again, sirrah!'

He drew a long, wicked blade from a pouch at his hose and thrust directly at Peter. Although Arabella screamed, the younger man sidestepped neatly. He knew all the moves of stage fighting, of course, but he was also well versed in the real business, having been taught by a father who had fought to the death countless times, and having learned other forms of fighting in countless tavern brawls in London and several score of provincial towns. Almost casually, he drew out his own bollock knife. Such a weapon was indispensable for an actor; for some reason, there were always loud, jostling fellows who reckoned those who trod the boards, oft dressed as girls, were both fair game and easy targets.

The assailant was evidently one of these. He laughed at the sight of Peter's weapon and thrust again with his own. Peter countered and drew blood, scratching the back of the large man's right hand.

'You're a dead man,' hissed his attacker.

Arabella screamed again as Peter stepped backwards to evade the onslaught, but the noise brought no throng rushing to see what the issue was. This, after all, was England, and if a young woman screamed it was most likely because she was giving birth or receiving a righteous beating from her husband. No one else's business, that was for certain.

The screams seemed to pour fuel on the fire of the large man's rage. He roared like an animal and struck hard three times in quick succession. Peter, pressed back against the wattle-and-daub wall on one side of the alley, defended himself ably, then thrust his knife arm swiftly upwards, seeming almost to lift it from his toes. The blade struck home into his assailant's chest. The man dropped his own knife and clasped at Peter's, perhaps hoping to pull it from his body. Then his eyes rolled and he fell backwards, quite obviously dead before he hit the hard ground.

Arabella ran to Peter, clinging to him and sobbing mightily.

'No tears for me,' he said as bravely as he could, although in truth he was shaking from what he had just done. 'Nor for him neither. He'll not harm you again, Bella.'

She looked up at him, her face a lake of tears.

'He will, and he'll harm you too, Peter Stannard. He was right. You're a dead man.'

'How so?'

Arabella gulped down her tears and her fear.

'He is – he was – Henry Ballard, the Bishop of Rochester's steward. The bishop's right hand here in Bromley, if not through half of Kent.'

Peter looked at her in horror, then glanced up and down to see if there were any witnesses. God be thanked, there were none. But his doublet and shirt were stained with Ballard's fresh blood, and there must have been plenty of people who had seen him enter the alley from one side or a young woman pursued by one of the most recognisable men in the town from the other. Even the most bovine of parish constables, not to mention the clever university-trained flunkeys who were bound to surround a senior prelate of the Church, wouldn't need to be a Thomas More or an Erasmus to draw the correct conclusion from such evidence.

Peter Stannard had seen hangings in both Dunwich and Plymouth, and suddenly felt a mighty tenderness for his own neck.

–

The large black rat, Meg's only company in the Dunwich lockup, moved unhurriedly about its business, pausing from time to time to give her a contemptuous stare across the muddy floor. She had chased after it at first, trying to shoo it away, but that was before the manacles on her ankles scraped off so much skin that she could barely walk, let alone pursue an elusive rodent. Instead, it amused her to name the rat Nevill. It bore no resemblance to her principal persecutor, Sir Nevill Bourchier, Justice of the Peace, but she found gallows humour in imitating his nasal whine and projecting the words as though the rat was speaking them:

'*Witchcraft or treason, Goodwife. For which of those to prosecute you, that is my dilemma. For certain, though, you are heinously guilty of both.*'

Those were the words the self-satisfied Bourchier had spoken to her on the night when she was dragged from her cottage upon Dunwich Heath by the borough constable, old Fanning, and taken before the magistrate in his elegant, recently acquired house over towards Darsham. Her arrest did not come entirely as a surprise to Meg. When she reflected upon it in her cell – and she had much time to reflect – the only real surprise was that it had not come sooner, perhaps years before.

Her recent persecution had begun about the time of the second false alarm from the beacons, when the sight of the flames all along Suffolk's shore saw children running screaming through the streets of Dunwich. In truth, though, people's tempers had been altering slowly for many years, since that fateful day so very long ago when word came of a papal bull excommunicating Elizabeth, she whom ignorant folk called the Queen of England, and making it incumbent on all good Catholics to seek to kill her. In truth, Meg had no great love for Elizabeth, bastard child of the Boleyn whore who had seduced King Harry from the true path, but she had even less love of murder. But as tempers frayed during that hot summer of 1588, as fears of the Spanish grew ever more fevered, she found herself ostracised in ways she had never once known during the more than fifty years of her life. Families who had always come to her to heal their sick children now turned their backs on her in the street. Women spat upon their thresholds as she passed. Boys jeered her, calling her 'witch' or 'popish witch' or 'Spaniard's whore'. Men in the alehouses murmured that the storms of the previous winter, which had taken away more land from the town than any of the previous forty years, could only be due to witchcraft, or God's judgement against Dunwich and England, or both.

Meg could brush off such flea bites; she still had friends in Dunwich, and her name, her maiden name, meant something in the town. But the case was altered when a grandly dressed fellow with a generous beard, mounted upon a splendid grey, rode one day along Duck Street accompanied by Francis Birkes and Robert Spatchell, the two bailiffs of Dunwich, and pointed at her as though he already knew her.

'Who is that crone yonder?' the proud fellow demanded.

'Yonder?' said Birkes, in his early thirties and thus young to be bailiff. 'Oh, that is the Widow de Andrade. A healer, much respected in the town.'

'De Andrade? Hardly a Suffolk name?'

'Spanish. She was married briefly, many years ago, to—'

'*Spanish?* You have a Spaniard among you, and you tolerate it?'

Francis Birkes, who had a fondness for Meg from his childhood, stiffened at that, and looked in alarm at his fellow bailiff.

'She is as English as you or I, Sir Nevill,' said Spatchell, a much older man who had his own fondness for Meg, 'and from a family with a considerable name in Dunwich.'

'Families who claim to be as English as you or I pray for the victory of King Philip, Master Spatchell,' said Bourchier gravely. 'Who is to say that this crone's sympathies do not still reside with her husband's countrymen? If she has been swived by a Spanish pintle, then she has become Spanish, I'd say. And her faith? What of her faith?'

'The Widow de Andrade attends sometimes at St Peter's,' said Francis Birkes uncertainly, unable to think of any more truthful words he could utter.

'Sometimes? Just a sufficient "sometimes" to disqualify her from recusancy fines?'

Birkes and Spatchell could find no response. Of course, they did not know then the real reason why Sir Nevill Bourchier, newly ensconced in the area and newly minted a justice of the peace, should be taking such a precise interest in the affairs of Meg de Andrade, maiden-named Stannard.

The *Girona* was under easy sail, and Juan Estandar had been allowed to go on deck again. There was no prospect of action. After the brief fight off Plymouth, the English fleet had simply disappeared. Some murmured that the heretics had turned and run, returning in shame to their harbours, but Juan knew better. Even so, it was unaccountable. It should have been impossible for a following fleet with the advantage of the wind to lose both its formation and all contact with the fleet ahead of it, yet somehow the English had managed this, and in their own waters, too. Juan recognised the distant coast just visible to northward, for he had sailed along it often enough when he bore the name Jack Stannard. It was Dorset, and the waters would usually have been full of fishing craft and coasters out of Lyme or Bridport. Now, though, the sea was empty.

There was a shout from the lookout, echoing calls from the other ships. Juan looked astern, and after a few minutes he managed to make out specks on the horizon to the south-west. Sails, there was no doubt of it, and they could only belong to the English fleet. His countrymen had not given up after all, but their cause was increasingly desperate. Every mile the Armada sailed brought it closer to Flanders and to Parma's invincible army, and God alone knew how the English would attempt to stop it.

The ship's bell sounded, summoning those who were not on watch to assemble in the waist and celebrate Mass. Juan shuffled over to join them, receiving roughly equal numbers of respectful nods, *signa cruces* and terrified stares as he passed. He saw Fra Gordillo, splendidly attired in full canonicals, elevate the Host, and managed with the assistance of the younger men around him to fall to his knees in veneration. Gordillo enjoined them all to pray for the success of the fleet, and Juan smiled.

After all, the priest had not specified which fleet he was meant to pray for.

Five

Even in the moments before he was fully awake, Jack was aware that something had changed and that something was wrong. He picked himself up from the blanket on the deck that served as his makeshift sea-bed, stepped out of his tiny cabin below the quarterdeck and steadied himself. The motion of the ship was different: more pronounced, with a marked roll. He made his way out onto the deck and looked up at the sails, then out to sea. The wind had changed in the night. Now it was blowing from the east, and that spelled profound danger for the only recently reunited English fleet. The Spanish now had the weather gage, and the rearmost ships of the Armada, some of its largest and most powerful vessels, were turning north and west. Turning to attack, and now they held the advantage of the wind.

Jack spotted Drake pacing the poop deck, Fitzranulf and another half-dozen of the gentlemen volunteers standing close by him, as were several of the ship's officers. They were all looking intently towards *Ark Royal*, leading the fleet, which was slowly turning north-east towards the distant but unmistakable bulk of Portland Bill, the vast headland that protruded from the coast of Dorset.

'Mister Bodenham! Mister Gray!' cried Drake to the lieutenant and sailing master of the *Revenge*. 'Close-haul, gentlemen! Fall into *Ark*'s wake!'

The rest of the English fleet was doing the same. Jack could see the reason at once, for it had been an unspoken fear on every mess deck even before the fleet sailed from Plymouth. The Armada was known to be carrying many thousands of troops; that, after all, was why the Dons wished to close and board, rather than fight an artillery duel. If it had the right wind, though, there was always a risk that Medina Sidonia would find irresistible the prospect of coming inshore and landing his men. Why share the glory with Parma when perhaps he could conquer England on his own? At the very least, the Armada's troops could establish an invincible bridgehead and await reinforcements. Now the Dons had the perfect wind, just as the English had found one off Plymouth, and for all Drake, Lord Howard and the rest of them knew, they might be sailing to invade and overrun Portland Bill, if not the whole of Dorset.

Jack turned towards the poop deck again, catching the eye of Fitzranulf, who scowled at him. God knew why; he had probably saved the rogue from manacles in the hold at the very least, if not a summary hanging at the yardarm. Bodenham was clearly suspicious of the reason why Fitzranulf and his friends might have been below decks on the *Rosario*, but was assuaged by Jack's assurances and had not reported his doubts to Drake. That Fitzranulf was ungrateful was an understatement.

'And where's the gold now, d'you think?' he had hissed to Jack during the afternoon of the previous day, when they were both on deck as the *Revenge* rejoined the fleet. 'Under Drake's bed, and in his sea chest, and in his privy, and up his arse. Anywhere, Stannard, but bound for the queen's coffers. You had your chance, man, we could all have been rich, but you're naught but a fool. Where's your precious inventory of the prize goods now, eh? Have you asked yourself that? Being edited by Drake, that's where it is. I wonder how similar the paper that'll end up in the Lord Treasurer's hands will be to the one you actually wrote. There's a thought for you, eh, bean counter?'

Jack did not want to admit the truth of Fitzranulf's words, but he had heard Frobisher bawling at Drake from the poop deck of the *Triumph* as the two great ships sailed side by side.

'Where was our light, Drake? Where was your lantern for the fleet to follow? Aye, you and I know the answer full well, Frank Drake! You wanted the prize for yourself, so you kept close by her all night. You thought to cheat us out of our shares of fifteen thousand ducats, but we'll have our shares or I'll make you spend the best blood in your belly!'

Jack knew he could speak to no man on the *Revenge* of his suspicions, but he had a terrible sense that perhaps Nicholas Fitzranulf was right. He was a fool. He was complicit in enriching Francis Drake at the expense of the queen, and perhaps in preventing an English victory over the Spanish Armada too. As he watched his own fleet and the Dons' huge galleons sail towards each other on converging courses, each trying to get between the other and the coast of England, he prayed that he would have a chance to redeem himself.

-

'Give fire!' cried Drake. 'Henceforth, gun captains, fire as they bear!'

The great guns of the *Revenge* opened fire on her assailants.

'Steady, men!' Jack shouted. 'Make every shot count!'

He was striding up and down the ship's waist, waving his sword at the oncoming Spanish ships, their huge hulls looming through the gun smoke like demonic monsters sailing straight out of Hell. It was not his duty to do so, but he was an officer of the *Revenge*, and as far as he could see not one of the gentlemen volunteers had any intention of leaving the quarterdeck or poop.

The Dons had won the race for the weather gage, cutting off the English fleet from their own coast. To avoid being trapped against a lee shore in the strengthening easterly breeze, Lord Howard had ordered his ships to come about and bear away south-westward, making for the open sea. But that gave the other Spanish ships, coming up to support their outliers, an easy sail to close with their enemies, and a ferocious battle had begun. A huge galleon was bearing down on the *Revenge*, clearly intent on grappling to her rigging; Jack could see the men in her beakhead, standing ready to throw the hooks, and behind them the morion helmets and pikes of the Spanish troops waiting impatiently to carve through English sailors like butchers through sides of beef. The trumpeters and drummers of both ships kept up their own duels, adding to the cacophony caused by the cannon.

The range for the great guns was now at point blank, and even muskets were joining the fray, albeit at the limit of their range. One, though, was accurate enough or lucky enough to hit the gun captain of the demi-culverin nearest Jack. The fellow spun round, his mouth open as though he was about to commence a song. But he would never sing another note, nor speak another word, for where his right eye should have been was a terrible bloody hole.

The man's gun crew made towards his body, but Jack stepped into their way.

'Stay at your posts, men, he's beyond mortal help now! Await orders, in the name of the queen!' He waved his sword threateningly, then stooped down to look along the barrel of the gun. 'Two more points of elevation!' he cried.

'You know the business of gunnery, pusser?' demanded a broad-chested, black-bearded fellow. The expression on his face suggested that he already knew the answer to his question, and did not like it.

Jack smiled. 'This one's a bit bigger than any I've fired against Scottish or Breton pirates,' he said, 'but aye, I know it.' He pointed at the gun. 'Demi-culverin, shot of nine and one third pounds with eight pounds of powder per shot. Point blank by the quadrant, twenty paces.'

Blackbeard frowned, then broke into a broad grin, and the other men in the gun crew looked at each other and nodded. 'Aye aye, sir!' he said, knuckling his forehead as he did so, and he and his fellows adjusted the gun according to Jack's order.

Jack looked along the barrel again, and reckoned it was aimed directly at one party of fellows with grappling hooks in the bows of the oncoming Spanish galleon. He took up the fallen captain's linstock and readied it over the hole in the barrel.

'Give fire!' he shouted, applying the linstock to the powder, then stepped back from the recoil as the demi-culverin fired its ball and its dragon's tongue of flame.

The easterly breeze blew the smoke back into his eyes, and he tasted the bitterness of the powder. It took perhaps a minute for the stinging sensation and the involuntary tears to clear enough for him to be able to see the carnage he had wreaked. A couple of figures, terribly maimed, were still moving among the shattered timbers and torn rigging of the Spaniard's beakhead. But no man there would be throwing a grappling hook against the *Revenge* on that day, or, if God willed it, on any other.

Jack wished his father could have been there to see the moment his youngest son came of age. He had fired one of the great guns of one of the queen's finest men-of-war. He was a warrior of the Navy Royal now, whatever any man said.

He glanced up towards the stern of the *Revenge* and saw Francis Drake looking down at him. He awaited the inevitable order to return to his station below decks, but it did not come.

Instead, the queen's world-renowned admiral smiled.

-

From the deck of *Girona*, Juan Estandar watched as the two battling squadrons of England and Spain fought their way slowly south-westward, further out into the open sea. Medina Sidonia himself was leading the attack, and the Spanish ships seemed to have the upper hand. Even so, Juan had lived long enough and seen more than enough to know that not all was as it seemed. The Spanish ships kept trying to close their English opponents in order to get near enough to grapple and board, but the English always edged away to maintain their distance. Moreover, their rate of fire was far faster than those of the Spanish batteries. Those manning the English guns knew their business, Juan thought.

He felt the bow of *Girona* begin to come round more towards the north-west, and saw that the other three galleasses were doing the same. The reason why was immediately apparent: downwind of the Spanish ships lay a small squadron of English men-of-war, just west of the towering cliffs of Portland Bill and hove-to off the lee shore of Dorset in calm water. Five of them seemed to be merchantmen, but the sixth was a very different case, a carrack that could stand comparison with the largest and most powerful ships in the Armada. Juan guessed what Captain Spinola and his immediate superior, Don Hugo de Moncada, would be thinking. The heretic vessels must have misjudged their course north-easterly earlier that morning, then found they were too close inshore to turn and beat back into the open sea. The huge English carrack would be a splendid prize to offset the loss of the *Rosario* and the *Salvador*, and the galleasses could easily manoeuvre in such confined waters regardless of the wind.

But they were wrong.

He stared long and hard at the statue of the Madonna standing above the ship's bell of the *Girona*. The black-robed Gordillo knelt before it, his hands raised in supplication to the heavens. The trumpets were sounding and Bosun Cala was shouting orders, but Juan was only dimly aware of the noise as he struggled with his thoughts. He could speak up and betray England, or remain silent and betray Spain. There should have been no choice to make, but it was not as simple as that. He prayed to the Madonna for guidance.

Whether or not the intercession of the Virgin was responsible, he had a moment of epiphany. He made his way towards Cala, who was berating two men for their slackness in securing a cable.

'Bosun,' he said, 'I must speak with Captain Spinola. Urgently, as God is my witness.'

'You wish to speak to the captain *now*, when we are about to go into battle? He has more urgent matters to attend to than conversing with an ancient slave.'

'It's a trap, bosun! The English ships—'

'You are the trap, apostate,' said Fra Gordillo, stepping towards him. 'You dare to call upon God as your witness? I call upon Him to witness the folly of permitting you ever to stray from your chains.'

Juan looked imploringly at Cala, but the bosun shook his head. He was a devout man, and Gordillo's ferocity in the confessional was a byword.

'All hands are needed at the oars,' he said hesitantly. 'Even yours, *anciano*.'

Juan bowed his head and went below, sensing Gordillo's hostile eyes following him as he went. It seemed the Madonna really had interceded and demonstrated God's will after all. Let the Dons suffer the consequences, then.

-

The wind had changed.

Jack Stannard was still captaining his gun crew, for no man had ordered him not to, so he was still on the upper deck of the *Revenge* as the strong breeze shifted more southerly. There was a blessed respite, for *Revenge* and a dozen or so of the other great ships were coming round and bearing up on a northerly course. This manoeuvre took them out of range of the Spanish men-of-war, which were changing course in their turn to cut off the English.

One of the ship's boys ran up with a tankard of beer, which Jack seized greedily, quaffing a long draught. The lad often ran errands for the *Revenge*'s purser, and looked in frank astonishment at the sweating, half-naked creature before him, who by rights should have been the least warlike of the ship's officers.

'What, Tom Rayment?' said Jack, a mock-serious expression on his face. 'You didn't know that a man could both count and fight? Let this be your lesson for the day, then.'

The lad looked confused, and went off to draw more beer from the open barrel by the mainmast.

As the *Revenge* completed its turn, Jack could see what Lord Howard's intention was. Frobisher's *Triumph* and five of the London merchantmen lay between Portland Bill and the westerly coast, and four huge galleasses were steering a course to attack them. Howard was leading his ships to reinforce Frobisher, but Jack knew these waters better than the Lord Admiral. Not better than either Frobisher or Drake, it was true, but better than the Dons, for certain. At any rate, the Spanish galleasses would never reach Frobisher.

-

The *Girona* pitched and yawed more crazily than she had ever done in the waters of Biscay, that wild sea that had forced the Armada's Portuguese galleys to turn back. On the oar deck, slaves were spewing copiously over their oars and each other. The drummer was still maintaining his steady beat, but no more than a handful of oars were cutting the water. A sea which had seemed almost perfectly calm minutes earlier was now a raging torrent, slamming against the hulls of the galleasses and flinging the men within in several directions at once.

'*Jesu Maria!*' cried Spadaro, whose chest was caked with his own vomit. 'This is Hell! No, worse than Hell!'

'Believe it,' said Owen Gravell. 'Drake's summoned his friends, the dragons and devils. This is King Philip's payment for dreaming he could snatch the queen's crown from her head.'

Another strange wave, unaccountably forceful in such a relatively light wind, struck the side of the *Girona*, causing the entire hull to shudder.

'Is he right, Juan?' said Spadaro fearfully. 'Is the Devil fighting for England?'

'No devils here,' said the old man, 'nor dragons neither. Portland, the headland yonder, breaks up the sea and creates a tide race. I first sailed through it forty or so years past. My ship was nearly overset, and it took me near a whole day to escape it – aye, and then I had to waste a fortnight in Bridport being repaired.'

Gravell, who seemed utterly immune to the violent motion of the sea, turned to Juan and smiled.

'Perhaps you should have told them that, *hen ffrind*.'

'I meant to,' said Juan, 'but Gordillo thought it would offend against God's will for me to speak to the captain. Perhaps it's now God's will that the reverend father is spewing his guts up, eh?'

Gradually, though, the *Girona*'s movement became less violent. Juan could see through the oar hole that the sea was calmer, but also that their three consorts were all well astern, still trapped within the tide race. Astern of them, and further to the west, was a vast wall of smoke, through which glimpses of sails, hulls and flashes from gun barrels could be seen. Ships of both fleets were fighting their way towards the galleasses and the English ships ahead of them.

Juan turned and craned his neck to look forward. There was the mighty English galleon, her flags and pennants streaming in the breeze and her guns run out, the armed merchantmen manoeuvring to second her. It was as Juan had suspected. The English ships were not here because they had made a terrible error in navigation; they were here entirely by design. The captain of the English galleon, whoever he was, had set an irresistible trap for the Spanish, and the Dons had blundered straight into it.

Aye, blundered into it because one arrogant priest had not deigned to listen to the one man in the Armada who could have warned its commanders of the Portland Race.

The thought was still in Juan's mind as the starboard battery of the English galleon erupted in a billowing sheet of flame and smoke. He felt the oar he was gripping jerk violently away from him – a shot must have snapped it in two – then the hull of the *Girona* shattered, slaves screaming and fouling themselves as great splinters of wood flew across the dark confined space of the oar deck, spearing or decapitating any man in their path.

'*Madre de dios!*' screamed Spadaro, while Gravell cried out something unintelligible in Welsh.

Strangely, Juan Estandar was very calm. He had a sudden thought of his old mentor, Thomas Ryman, who had perished on the long-lost *Mary Rose*. He had almost forgotten what Ryman looked like, but it seemed as though the sometime friar's face was suddenly before his very eyes, clear in every detail.

Another shot struck the hull of the *Girona*, Juan felt a blow to his head, and Ryman's face was the last image he registered before the darkness came.

Six

Once again, men and women alike were running screaming through the streets of Dover as the church bells rang out in alarm. Someone in the town must have convinced themselves that the sails just sighted to southward were the vanward of the Spanish Armada, rather than, say, some French ships bringing wine from Rouen. If there was any imminent threat, Tom Stannard thought, the admiral would surely have fired the guns and beaten the drums to recall all men to their ships, and the Narrow Seas fleet would have put to sea at once. As it was, every hour brought some wild new rumour that terrified the good but credulous people of Dover. The Spanish had landed upon the Isle of Wight. The Spanish had come ashore in Torbay and burned Exeter. Parma was slipping out of the creeks of Flanders at that very moment, not even deigning to await the arrival of his escorting fleet. Why, said others, he had in fact already landed – some said at Yarmouth, some Canvey – and was marching on London. The queen had been shot dead by a Jesuit, or else, according to one account, butchered by seven Irishmen with broadswords. The Pope himself was at Antwerp, waiting his moment to take ship for England.

Such, at least, had been the rumour in the alehouse where Tom had betaken himself for a little relief from the hectoring of his son. Like every other man in the fleet, he had nothing to set against the fears and hysteria of the people. Only very limited intelligence from the main fleet had reached the Narrow Seas squadron in the Downs, and all of it was second-hand, trickling down from London. Even less information was filtering out from the flagship to the lesser ships. It seemed there had been a fight off Plymouth and that Lord Howard, Drake and the rest were following the Armada up the Channel, but it was in the nature of such things that this had been the state of affairs some days past. Perhaps for all Tom knew – for all Lord Harry Seymour knew, come to that – one or more of the fearful rumours sweeping through Dover might be truer than the intelligence they possessed.

So there was a madness in the town, and a madness in himself.

Several of the terrified running folk crashed into Tom Stannard, but he was nearly oblivious to them. Any who took notice of him at all might have mistaken him for yet another drunken mariner staggering unsteadily back down to the quays. It was true that Tom was in drink, but his swaying gait and blank expression was not due solely to Dover ale. He had deliberately chosen an alehouse well away from the harbour, and as he had hoped, he knew no man's face within it. None of the voices belonged to men of Suffolk, and any Plymouth men from the flagships were evidently elsewhere. No faces he knew, a quiet stool in a corner, and a flagon refilled at regular intervals. But the ale brought maudlin thoughts. Perhaps tomorrow they would sail out against the Armada and be destroyed. Mayhap this was his last day on earth. Perhaps Adam was right, and Tom and all of England were damned for their manifest sins. Tom knew there was one sin above all of which he was guilty; a sin he had tried his utmost to conceal and suppress for as long as he could remember. But there, in that low-roofed alehouse in a back lane of Dover, his thoughts about that sin became more ambiguous.

It might indeed be his last day on earth, and the bosun of a Norwegian timber ship, drinking just across the room with some of his crew, seemed to be glancing in his direction from time to time. Tom Stannard lowered his tankard and smiled at the foreigner.

It was fast and it was confusing. Even though it had happened within the last hour, Tom could not remember exactly what was said, or what signals had been exchanged, or who had led the way to the small lean-to in the alehouse yard. All he could remember was that he and the Norwegian had been frantic in their desire; that he had been lost in pleasure.

Then he had seen Adam's face, no more than ten feet away across the yard. A face frozen in horror and revulsion. His son stared at him, then turned without a word and ran from the scene.

As Tom staggered back towards the quay and the boat that would take him out to his *Eagle of Dunwich*, all the secret fears of his life seemed to crowd upon him. He had tried for so long to forsake the mortal sin to which he was prone. He had nearly convinced himself that he was now too old and was safe from temptation. But God and the Devil had found him out and sent Adam as their messenger to punish him.

The Spanish Armada held no fears for Tom Stannard now. The only thing he feared in this world was the contempt of his eldest son, and the only thing he feared in the next was the possibility that Adam was right and that eternal damnation awaited him.

Meg de Andrade attempted to chew upon a piece of mouldy cheese, but it was hard as oak timber and she spat it out.

That it had come to this pass, she reflected as she looked around the confines of her cell. Once, hard men, big men, the sort of men who went out on the Iceland ships in earlier days, had knuckled their foreheads in deference to any and every member of the Stannard family.

In those times, the Stannards had wealth and highly placed friends, whereas now they had neither; the war with Spain had ruined their usually lucrative trades with Flanders, and the balance sheets she managed had been precarious for some time. Beyond that, though, the family had always been united in both the cause they pursued and the love they bore each other.

Meg shook her head bitterly. The love they bore each other now, some of them? Oh, what a fine jest that would be, were it not so tragic. The love of Cain and Abel was akin to that of Abelard and Héloïse when set against that of—

The key turned in the door of her cell, and the gaoler bowed as he admitted a spectacle of femininity attired in a gaudy outfit that might have been remarked upon even at court. A red kirtle emphasised her ample breasts, and a black overgown trumpeted her wealth – or at least, the wealth of her lover. A concealed farthingale thrust the skirt outward. The wearer of this confection, as unlikely in Suffolk as an Arctic bear, was a woman in her middle thirties; the sort of woman whom the more cock-led of men called beautiful. She fixed Meg with a broad smile, revealing a set of nearly perfect white teeth. Just like her mother, in that as in so many other ways.

'You look like the whore you are,' said Meg levelly.

The smile remained fixed, but the flash of anger from the visitor's eyes told a different story.

'And you, dear sister, look like the filthy hag you are,' said Mary Stannard.

'I have little opportunity to attend to my appearance.'

Meg's half-sister nodded. 'Soon, I assure you, you won't need to worry about your appearance at all.'

'Your bedswerving gandermooner's bought enough witnesses, then? Pressed enough silver into enough palms?'

It seemed that Mary would rise to the bait, as she invariably did, but perhaps her grand clothes and airs made her more approximately the sort of lady she had always aspired to be. She merely sniffed.

'It might avail you better not to speak ill of Sir Nevill, especially as you will shortly face examination before him. Besides, the Don is upon the coast. The militia are marching for the camp at Tilbury, and the people are sore distracted. Nobody will care what happens to an ancient wretch like you, sister. None will even know.'

'There is still law in England, sister. And beyond that, there is the law of God.'

Mary laughed coldly. 'Oh, call on any law you like, dear Margaret. Your brother is at sea, and who knows if he'll come back alive. He's the only one who'd have lifted even a finger to save you.'

Meg made no reply, for it was true. Tom, the only other child of their father's first marriage, had always been close to her, but he was far away, as were his sons, two of whom, dear blessed boys, had shown nothing but love towards their aunt. Mary's brothers, spewed forth from the womb of the older Jack Stannard's second wife, had always banded together, as did their children in turn. So Meg was alone in the world, with those who should have been among her nearest kin seeking her destruction.

'Well then, sister, you have had sufficient time to gloat,' she said. 'Behold my reduced condition. This is what you've always wanted, so relish your moment. But mark me in this, dear Mary. Sir Nevill Bourchier will never marry you. Oh, he will enjoy your cunny for as long as it retains a semblance of youth—'

Mary Stannard's restraint vanished. She flew at Meg, screaming and scratching, but Meg had grown large with age and had always been strong. Her fists struck Mary's chest, then her face, bloodying her mouth. Mary wiped her lips and stared upon her own blood, disbelieving. Her eyes widened.

'I will see you hang,' she hissed in a low voice. 'Or burn. I shall ask Nevill if you may burn.'

She turned on her heel and left the cell.

Meg sank to her knees and nodded a greeting to Nevill the rat, who had appeared out of the fouled straw in the corner.

'So shall I burn, Nevill?' she asked, grinning. The rat stared back impudently, but made no reply. 'Or shall deliverance come from the east, from the returning sons of Jerusalem, as John's gospel says? What do you think, eh?'

The rat shuffled off into the other corner, to the tiny hole that allowed it, but not Meg, egress to the outside world. She could not be certain whether or not the rodent agreed with her sentiments, but for her own part, Meg's faith was unshakeable. The Armada would come, bringing Parma's army from the east, and the returning sons – the faithful Catholics who had been driven into exile by thirty years of persecution – would include her long-lost father, Jack Stannard.

–

'Must it be?' asked Arabella.

'I have no choice,' said Peter. 'London isn't the answer. The bishop holds plenty of sway there, many people know my name and face, and there are informers in every doorway. No, my fair love, this is the only way I can throw them off my scent.'

They lay in a barn by a meadow in the valley between Bromley and Beckenham. There was no sign of a hue and cry as yet, no *posse comitatus* scouring copses and outbuildings. But there would be, that was certain. The only reason why there was no hunt as yet for the killer of Henry Ballard was that the justices of the peace and the sheriff were all consumed entirely by the preparations against the Spanish Armada, while the Lord Lieutenant, Lord Cobham, was on a mission abroad to talk peace with, of all people, the Duke of Parma, the man who was expected to lead the invasion of England. Meanwhile, the Bishop of Rochester was in London, and might only just have heard of the slaughter of his loyal servant at remote Bromley.

'I will go with you,' said Arabella, albeit without much conviction.

'You know as well as I what sort of women go where I'm going,' said Peter.

'You've known me ten whole days or near enough, Peter Stannard,' she said, smiling at him. 'A lifetime. You think I concern myself with my reputation?'

'You are the most singular woman I have ever met,' he said, settling back onto a bale of old hay.

'Then you haven't met the right women.'

'Mayhap that's true.'

He certainly had not met her sort of woman before, Peter thought. He had always scoffed at the notion of one man and one woman spending their lives in domestic harmony, unlike his brother Jack, who refused even to tumble more than a handful of the more willing Dunwich girls because he was waiting to meet the one enduring true love of his life. Yet this strange, irresistible creature, whom he had known for such a short time…

He pricked up his ears. That new sound – surely it could only be a distant drum? Sure enough, a few minutes later they could just make out a voice, and soon after that it became clear that this was a man bellowing as loudly as he could.

'All good men and true! Don't cower by your hearths, men of England! The Don is coming to rape your wives and your mothers and your daughters! Only you can stop him, men of England! The army masses to defend the realm, and needs every able-bodied man! Matters not if you've ne'er held a pikestaff or even a billhook, we'll train you in ample time to put it to good use and stick it in a Don's guts! Come with me, my brave boys, and fight for your queen, for St George and England!'

Peter Stannard grimaced. All his life he had hoped to avoid fighting for any cause at all, other than perhaps the favour of a woman. He certainly had no interest in fighting for England, nor for Dunwich, that lost cause that meant so much to so many of his near kin.

But then he certainly had no interest in dangling from a rope in Bromley, either.

He stood, brushed himself down, and helped Arabella to her feet. As they left the barn, they saw the recruiting party at once: a sergeant, a corporal, two troopers, all in grubby cuirasses, followed by a gaggle of two-score men who seemed to include three boys, two ancient creatures with limps, a fellow who appeared to be blind, a man leaning upon a crutch, and several who bore the telltale signs of having been beggars until hours or even minutes before. They marched to the beat of a tiny child striking a drum, while one of the troopers carried a tattered flag of St George before them. They were on the road north, down the valley and towards the Thames.

Peter turned to Arabella, who was weeping. He took her in his arms, hugged her and kissed her, murmuring his undying love for her. Then he let her go, waved farewell and turned towards the small party of would-be warriors.

The sergeant watched him approach, looking him up and down.

'Your name, fellow?' he demanded.

'Dowling,' said Peter, glancing back towards Arabella. 'Peter Dowling.'

'You look like a sturdy lad, Peter Dowling. You've fought? You've been a soldier?'

'Oh yes, Sergeant. I've fought.'

That, at least, was true, although not in the way the sergeant probably thought. Peter Stannard had never been a soldier. But as he fell into the midst of the company shuffling behind the colours, he smiled to himself.

He might not have been a soldier, but he knew exactly how to play one.

Seven

'*El hombre que vivirá para siempre.*'

The first voice Juan Estandar heard in Hell was that of Fra Gordillo. Good, thought the soul who had once answered to the name of Jack Stannard. Not even holy orders were sufficient to save a foul shit like Gordillo from the eternal fires.

'Once again Satan does not claim you,' said Gordillo, who, Juan realised, was evidently and disappointingly very much alive. 'What demon watches over you and protects you, Juan Estandar? It's certainly no saint or no angel, of that I'm certain.'

Juan was aware of the pain in his head and could feel his limbs. So it was not death, that longed-for condition. He was upon a pallet on the low, dark orlop deck of the *Girona*, one of the patients under the galleass's surgeon.

Gordillo was right, damn him. Somehow, the man who will live forever had survived once again.

'What's the state of the battle?' he asked.

'Oh, fear not, *anciano*, your heretic friends haven't triumphed. How could they when the Armada has God so manifestly on its side?'

'Thanks be to God,' said Juan, knowing it would be what Gordillo wanted to hear.

'There was a great fight,' said Gordillo. 'The admiral himself came up to support us, and the English attacked in a line. They fired much shot at us, but there is little damage.'

'The English ships are nimbler,' said Juan, 'but they dare not come close.'

'Of course not,' said Gordillo, 'for they are cowards, as all heretics are. Creatures who are not brave enough to accept the manifest truth that the only true faith, the only sure way to salvation, is the Church of Rome under the Holy Father. So they broke off the battle, and we sail onward to glory, Juan Estandar. I have seen the charts. There is a large island ahead of us.'

'Wight,' said Juan in English, 'the Isle of Wight.'

'As you say. But beyond it, there are no more obstacles. Nothing between our fleet and Parma's army and victory. The utter extirpation of heresy throughout England. God's will be done.'

Gordillo crossed himself and moved away to attend to more of the sick and injured men of the *Girona*, laid out on trestles upon the orlop deck.

The man who had once sailed these waters under the name of Jack Stannard could remember each and every cliff and every seamark of the coast they were traversing, and which the Dons were yet to encounter. Gordillo, a man utterly ignorant of the ways of the sea, was right, albeit inadvertently so: once the *Armada* was beyond the Isle of Wight, its path would be irrevocable. There could be no turning back, and once the Solent was passed, there were no more anchorages it could occupy. Juan thought of the time over forty years before when another huge enemy fleet had approached Wight, and he had sailed to do battle with it. The threat had been repelled that time, albeit at terrible cost – most notably the loss of the great *Mary Rose*, taking with it his friend and mentor Thomas

Ryman. Now Juan was counted among the enemies of England. He prayed that wherever Ryman's soul resided, the erstwhile friar would understand and forgive him.

-

For the first time, some men on the lower deck of the *Revenge* were whispering about defeat. As he went from mess to mess, Jack Stannard heard the talk and tried to ignore it, but could not. He knew, for the gunner's store was adjacent to the purser's, that the *Revenge*, like most of the other great ships in the fleet, had almost exhausted her stock of ammunition during the fight off Portland. The battle had been ferocious, the roar of the guns incessant, but it was apparent to Jack and every other man with a view of the fight that the Spanish ships were virtually untouched. When the English fleet broke off the engagement off Portland, having almost no more shot left to fire, the vast enemy hulls simply turned away in stately contempt, resumed their close formation with immaculate precision and continued unhindered up the Channel. Now men murmured that the English had given everything and achieved nothing. The Dons would go into the Solent, they said, and occupy Wight. From there, they would be able to dictate terms for the surrender of England.

Drake himself, pacing the poop deck relentlessly, seemed quieter than usual. If even the legendary dragon of England was distracted, some men said, then perhaps the prospect was dire indeed.

Jack would not join with the fainthearts. God was on England's side. The queen was glorious and noble and virtuous, and she would triumph.

She had to.

–

Juan prayed that the blow to the head had not affected his singing voice. He hummed four or five notes, steadied himself and looked out over the expectant ranks of his fellow slaves, then began to sing.

Wake, wake, you young and valiant men,
Wake to serve him our noble King of France!
And heed the call, each loyal son,
To right the wrongs that we've been done!

Janequin's '*The Battle of Marignano*' – always a firm favourite even of the Spanish, despite it recounting a crushing French victory many years before; a battle in which, as it happened, Juan's old friend Thomas Ryman had fought as a mercenary. Soon, almost every man on the oar deck was joining in, the French slaves captured in the Azores campaign singing most lustily of all.

Ta ri ra ri ra ri ra reyne,
Pon, pon, pon, pon,
La la la…
Courage, France, courage!
Hit them hard!
Blast, strike, torch, gouge,
Rape and plunder, rend asunder!

All the while the *Girona*, like the other three galleasses, was slowly coming about, their oars cutting the water as their helms were put hard over. Juan, who had just come down from the upper deck, knew why; indeed, he had seen why. The *Gran Grifón*, a cumbersome leviathan hired from Rostock, had fallen behind the main body of the Armada. Juan had overheard Captain Spinola opining that she must have sustained some damage, and an order had come from the flagship for the galleasses to turn directly into the wind – which, of course, only they could do – and rescue the stricken ship. But it was likely to be a desperate business. Juan saw a single English galleon put on sail, detach itself from the main body of its fleet and make directly for the *Gran Grifón*. Just before he was sent below decks, Juan heard the word spread from mouth to mouth, and saw Fra Gordillo cross himself.

'*El Draque*,' men said, pointing fearfully at the distant English ship. '*La Venganza*.'

Francis Drake, then, aboard a ship called the *Revenge*. Built since Juan's days in England to the fine lines the English had come to favour, she cut the water elegantly, her bow rising and falling with the waves. Flags and pennants streamed from her mastheads.

Yes, a fine sight, but Juan Estandar had other thoughts on his mind. Thoughts of the harbour of San Juan de Ulúa in the Carib Sea twenty years earlier, and of a ferocious battle between John Hawkins' English squadron and a much larger Spanish fleet. Memories of how Francis Drake had fled from the fight, leaving the others to fend for themselves. Remembrance of how his son Tom had got away, albeit barely, but also how he, Jack Stannard, had surrendered to the Spanish. Memories of the long forced march to Mexico City, of the endless interrogations by the Inquisition, of the eventual condemnation to the galleys. Thoughts, too, of the other Englishmen who had been taken prisoner, never to see their homeland again; of

Paul Hawkins above all, nephew of the admiral, who had stood trembling alongside him on the deck of the captured flagship *Jesus of Lubeck*. Poor Paul, whose prospects should have been so fair.

And now, all these years later, here was Francis Drake once again. Juan reprised '*The Battle of Marignano*', this time with even more vigour, adding embellishments to every line.

He did not want Englishmen to die. The Armada was a crusade, its righteous purpose being for the ultimate good of every soul in England. But there was one Englishman for whom he was prepared to make an exception, one Englishman he wanted dead. And if the *Girona*, turning to engage the *Revenge*, was to be the instrument of Francis Drake's death, then so much the better.

-

Jack Stannard stood in the fo'c'sle as the *Revenge* closed the lone Spanish ship struggling in the wake of the Armada. After his performance in the Portland fight, there was tacit acknowledgement by everyone from Drake downward – everyone, at any rate, except Fitzranulf and his friends – that Jack should be considered a *reformado* officer, entitled to an undefined yet real fighting role. So it was as a fully fledged fighting man that he looked around him. A few miles north-east lay the coast of the Isle of Wight, with the western entrance into the Solent. But no fleet would consider attempting to enter the anchorage that way; the currents were ferocious, the rocks murderous and the channel more than halved in breadth by a huge sand spit that protruded from the coast of Hampshire. No, if the Dons had ambitions to anchor in the Solent, they would seek out the broad, easy eastern entrance, but England's fleet would do everything in its power to prevent that. The first proof of this was the advance of the *Revenge*, her sails cracking in the strong south-westerly breeze. Ships out of Weymouth and Poole had brought fresh ammunition to the fleet, and even some of those who had been most dire in their opinions a day or two earlier were cheered once again as the *Revenge* closed the larboard beam of the wallowing Spaniard.

'Once more for old England and the true reformed faith, my lads!' cried Drake, who had come down to the quarterdeck rail to address his men. 'A noble prize or an ignoble wreck, it matters not to me! Starboard gun captains make ready! Damnation to Spain and the Pope! God for Elizabeth and the Devil for Francis Drake!'

The men laughed and cheered, Jack joining in with the throng. Then, though, it was all business, with gun tackle being readied and shot rammed home. Jack sought out Matt Bradlow at his usual station with his swivel gun upon the larboard rail.

'All well, Matt?'

'Aye, Master Jack – sir, I should say.'

'We're both men of Dunwich, Matt, so no need for distinction.'

'Aye, well then. A mighty tall hull with this one – and look at the number of troops on her deck! One mistake that takes us so close they'll be able to board... not a prospect I want to consider, Master Jack.'

'Come now, Matt Bradlow! D'you reckon Sir Francis is so callow as to mistake our course? And he has Mister Bodenham and Master Gray at his side. No, Matt. Let the Dons yonder learn what Englishmen can do!'

Matt Bradlow nodded, but Jack sensed he was not convinced. In truth, his words did not even convince himself. The Spaniards looked utterly formidable, and the English had everything to lose. The very kingdom itself, in all truth.

The *Revenge* closed to point blank, the gun captains poised with their linstocks, awaiting the command.

'Give fire!' cried Drake, and the large bow guns of *Revenge* bellowed, followed in short order by those on the broadside, flinging hundreds of pounds of roundshot into the hull of the Spanish ship.

The return of fire was desultory, the immobility of the Dons telling against them. Besides, they too might have exhausted their ammunition in the previous fight, Jack thought.

'Lesser men would have surrendered already,' he said.

'They have courage, 'tis true,' said Bradlow.

The *Revenge* sailed ahead, then tacked back before completing the full figure-of-eight, coming as close to the wind as she dared so that the larboard battery too could fire against the same side of the Spaniard. Jack was impressed. Drake instilled high standards into his men, and for certain not every ship in the English fleet could have carried out such a manoeuvre so briskly.

Matt Bradlow readied himself at his gun, a small fowler firing a shot of one pound. Such a relatively light weapon could be crewed by only one man if necessity demanded it, and Jack watched as Matt, who knew his business, prepared the charge and the shot, then looked down the length of the barrel.

'No shortage of targets,' said Bradlow, nodding towards the massed ranks of armoured Spanish troops thronging the upper deck of the great ship.

A handful of great guns on the enemy vessel opened a ragged fire, but the range was too long to harm the *Revenge*; a sure sign that the Spanish gun captains and their superiors were panicking. One ball struck the ship's side, but the rest fell well short, sending up spouts of water as they plunged into the Channel. Drake's men, perhaps foremost among their colleagues throughout the English fleet, had better discipline – or maybe greater confidence in their own abilities, born of pride in the enigmatic creature who ruled over their little floating world. So they waited, eyes turned towards the uncharacteristically still figure of Sir Francis Drake, awaiting his command.

'*Give fire!*'

Matt Bradlow fired nearly in the same moment, the recoil almost striking Jack, whose eagerness had made him incautious.

At point blank, the effect of the *Revenge*'s broadside was more profound than that of the Spanish artillery. Holes were apparent all along the side of the enemy vessel, although few of them seemed to penetrate right through the hull. On the upper deck, the swivel guns like Bradlow's brought screams of agony, with stricken men staggering blindly into their neighbours, and momentary confusion. But it was only momentary. Silently, other Spanish troops advanced into the positions of those who had fallen in the front ranks. Dressings were taken up and platoons re-formed, all in less than a minute. The Dons remained unbroken and defiant.

The *Revenge* now turned smartly to come abeam of the wind and astern of the Spaniard, firing her mighty stern guns as she did so. Once again Drake gave the order to fire, this time a raking broadside into the elegantly carved and splendidly adorned stern of the enemy ship. There was a loud cheer as the smoke rolled away and it became apparent that one lucky shot had taken the head off the centrepiece of the transom, a large and gaudy carving of the Virgin Mary. But the cheer died away as the *Revenge* emerged from behind the Spaniard. Jack and the men of the fo'c'sle were the first to see the awesome spectacle now before them.

It seemed as though the entire Spanish Armada was turning to beat a few points into the wind, four magnificent galleasses leading the way – undoubtedly the instruments by which the enemy would extract their straggler.

There was no doubt what Medina Sidonia intended to do. The wind was southerly, and would favour both fleets equally once the Dons were on their new course. They sought finally to close the range, force a general battle, grapple and board the English ships and win a decisive victory that very day.

There was silence aboard the *Revenge*. Jack looked back towards the poop deck and saw Drake leaning heavily upon the rail. Even *he* seemed uncertain. Mayhap in his heart of hearts he wanted nothing more than to put on sail and lead the attack against the Armada there and then. But if the English fleet, so much smaller than the Spanish, lost that day, in a fight of Medina Sidonia's choosing – if it lost to the west of Wight, giving the Dons free rein to enter the Solent and establish contact with Parma at their leisure – then England was doomed. If even Jack Stannard, naught but a youthful deputy purser, knew this, then Sir Francis Drake most certainly knew it in spades, and so did Lord Howard and all the other high commanders.

So it was no great surprise to Jack to see men's arms pointing westward, towards *Ark Royal*, coming up at the head of the fleet. A flag was breaking out at her mizzen top; the signal for the fleet to break off. The flagship's bow was already beginning to turn. There would be no more fighting that day.

Eight

Dawn, and no wind.

Juan was below decks, chewing tentatively on a piece of solid green bread.

'God bless the victuallers,' said Owen Gravell, looking suspiciously at his.

'The free seamen and soldiers get little better,' said Juan, shrugging. 'Even the officers.'

'I heard Gordillo complaining about the offal,' said Spadaro.

'He has the least cause to complain of any man aboard,' said Gravell. 'If he feels hungry, he can just gorge himself on Mass wafers.'

The three men, and the half-dozen or so closest to them, laughed, but it was gallows humour. They were all old enough hands, Juan above all, to know the prospect before them. The hull of the *Girona* was not moving at all, and the sea, glimpsed through the open oar ports, was utterly still. Like glass, Juan thought. A vast, limitless mirror in which the ambitions of both kingdoms were reflected. More immediately, though, a flat calm meant that only four vessels could move independently, and the *Girona* was one of them.

Sure enough, Cala soon appeared on the platform at the stern, giving the command for all men to ready their oars. Juan stood and made his way to the bosun's side.

'The tempo, bosun?'

'Slow, *anciano*. Slow and stately. We're going to be towing *Rata Encoronada*.'

Juan frowned. The *Rata Encoronada* was de Leyva's flagship, one of the strongest, proudest vessels in the entire Armada. She was also one of the largest.

'She's disabled?'

'No. But two more ships have fallen behind, and we're ordered to rescue them, as we did for the *Gran Grifón* yesterday. One of the English flagships is trying to come up with them, being towed by her boats.'

'*Revenge* again? *El Draque?*'

'Not Drake this time. There's no sign of Drake.' Cala turned to address the entire deck. 'All hands! Stand by to ship oars!'

Within half a glass or so, the *Girona* was moving across the placid waters of the English Channel, towing behind her the towering hull of the *Rata Encoronada*. Two of the other galleasses flanked her as they inched westward towards the two stragglers from the Armada. It was so still that across the water, aboard Sir John Hawkins' mighty carrack *Victory*, under tow towards exactly the same target, some men with particularly good hearing swore that they could make out a distant English voice singing '*Greensleeves*'.

-

The wind was getting up at last, and the English fleet was dividing. From the fo'c'sle of the *Revenge*, at the very southern extremity of the fleet, Jack Stannard could see Frobisher moving away northward, leading a squadron towards the eastern end of the Isle of Wight. Much closer, no more than a mile or two north-east, Hawkins' *Victory* was finally casting off her tow boats and moving under her own sail to engage the three galleasses and the single great galleon moving towards the two Spanish ships that lay between the two fleets. Behind *Victory* came the main body of the fleet, *Ark Royal* leading the bulk of the ships. That was where *Revenge* should surely be – where Drake should be. Yet as the wind got up, and their sails filled, *Revenge* and her consorts were moving away from the developing battle.

Jack could see men murmuring among themselves, and could hear some of the whispers. Drake had orders to sail ahead, flanking the Armada and joining up with Seymour's fleet in the Narrow Seas. Perhaps this was because intelligence had come that Parma's invasion barges had emerged from their estuaries and were even now making for the coast of England. Perhaps Lord Howard expected to lose this day, and Drake and Seymour would unite to make one last desperate stand off Dover. But the most damning rumour of all came from an unlikely source.

'He's running,' said Nicholas Fitzranulf, seemingly far gone in his cups despite it still being well before the middle of the morning. The gentleman volunteer had come up to the fo'c'sle to use the heads, and one of his boon companions – Jack could not make out which – was sitting alongside him.

'He'll run for France, offer his services to the French king,' said Fitzranulf, slurring his words.

His friend tried to quieten him, but Fitzranulf persisted.

'He'll not make me a traitor, damn him,' he said.

Jack went below and waited for Fitzranulf to come inboard.

'Mister Fitzranulf,' he said, 'your voice carries more than you think. It bears inadvisable words, too.'

'Eavesdropping now, bean counter?'

The men at the guns and mess benches were rapt.

'Advice for your benefit – think of it that way.'

'My benefit? *My benefit?* You denied me the greatest opportunity for my benefit, Stannard. Denied it because you can't see where your loyalty should lie. Not with *him*' – Fitzranulf pointed angrily towards the stern – 'that's for certain.'

Several men were rising from their places, evidently unsettled by the spectacle of two of their officers and betters warring between themselves.

Jack raised a hand. 'I'd advise you to lie down in your cabin, Mister Fitzranulf. You are not well, and I don't wish to have to summon Lieutenant Bodenham.'

Fitzranulf swayed upon his feet. He seemed about to deliver an angry riposte, or even to draw the vicious knife in his belt, but Matt Bradlow appeared at Jack's shoulder, a belaying pin gripped tightly in his hand. In that moment, the Irishman's companion – it was Carver – came in from the heads. Soberer than his friend, he immediately assessed the situation, took hold of Fitzranulf's elbow and led him away, glaring at Jack as he did so.

Jack and Bradlow went back up on deck.

'He'll end badly,' said Bradlow calmly.

'Maybe this very day, if any man reports his words to Drake.'

'He's a favourite with Drake, though Christ in Heaven knows why.'

'My father once told me of a man called Thomas Doughty, who was a gentleman volunteer too, on Drake's world voyage. He was another great favourite of our admiral, my father said – a great favourite until the day Drake accused him of treason and witchcraft, then had his head cut off.'

Bradlow smiled. 'Aye, I heard that tale off your father too. He fares well?'

'He did, the last I heard before we sailed from Plymouth.'

'He delivered me a great mercy once, when we were in the Spanish Main. A very great mercy – which is why I will always be true to any man who bears the name of Stannard.'

Jack could not read the curious expression on Bradlow's face. Instead, he looked about and saw that the two main fleets were now far to the north, the prospect of them receding all the time. The gunfire from the ships already engaged was like distant thunder upon the shore of Wight, yet still Drake's squadron put more and more distance between itself and the battle.

Jack had one thought, and that was an uncomfortable suspicion that Fitzranulf might be right.

What the devil was Drake doing?

-

The *Girona* was no longer under oars, and was fighting under sail. The other two galleasses had towed the stragglers to safety before the wind got up, and *Girona* and *Rata Encoronada* had engaged the English flagship. With no immediate prospect of the oars being deployed again, Juan was allowed up on deck, receiving a glare from Fra

Gordillo as he emerged into sunlight. The priest was blessing the gun crews, sprinkling holy water upon the barrels and chanting the rosary as he did so. The English flagship was still close, a few hundred yards across the water, but was primarily occupied with *Rata Encoronada* off her starboard bow.

Juan took in the spectacle. There seemed to be English ships to northward – they would be off St Helen's Bay, for the great mass of Wight stretched across the sea to the north. Medina Sidonia's flagship and some of the other large galleons from the left wing of the Armada were sailing that way to intercept them. Most of the Spanish ships, though, lay undisturbed and serene, waiting to deploy in support of either de Leyva or Medina Sidonia as occasion dictated.

Juan furrowed his brow. The English fleet seemed much smaller; had the Armada really caused so much damage to it in the Portland fight?

He looked northward again. The eastern end of the Solent, that was where the decisive business would be done. If Medina Sidonia could overcome the English ships that had gone that way, clearly to obstruct his course, then the Armada would enter the Solent, drop anchor and await the most propitious moment to meet with Parma.

'Steady as she goes, my boys!' cried Captain Spinola, resplendent in blue Milanese armour at the quarterdeck rail, Fra Gordillo making extravagant signs of the cross before him. The galleass was closing with the English galleon.

Spinola drew his sword and pointed it at the enemy. 'For God, Philip and Spain!' he cried.

The men on the upper deck echoed his call, and the first shots thundered from the great guns.

The *Girona* advanced to support *Rata Encoronada*, firing the six forward-facing heavy cannon in the bows as she did so, a tactic that forced the Englishman to divide his fire. As the first clouds of smoke cleared, Juan looked hard at the quarterdeck of the English galleon. There was an old fellow – well, perhaps ten or so years younger than himself – in a breastplate, waving his sword vigorously. The men around him were deferring to him.

Juan felt a prickling sensation down his spine. Although it was a warm day, he suddenly felt colder than he had done for many a long year.

Oh, the hair was grey now, but there was still plenty of red in the beard, and even at this distance, the nose was unmistakable. Juan Estandar, Jack Stannard, had last seen those features in a Carib harbour twenty years before, amid scenes of utter carnage, as his last hope of escape and freedom steered away from the doomed flagship *Jesus of Lubeck*. He had watched that same face recede, then lost sight of it as he surrendered his sword to the Spanish officer taking command of his prize.

Although he knew the Englishman would never see him, and would never recognise him if he did, Juan raised a hand to wave at Sir John Hawkins.

The lookout shouted something rapid and indecipherable from the masthead. Juan saw Spinola swing around, saw the men around him pointing away to the south. There were sails upon the horizon, perhaps two dozen of them, closing rapidly. Suddenly, trumpets were sounding and drums being beaten aboard the previously unengaged ships of the Armada, which were hastily hoisting more sail.

Juan smiled to himself. After all, he was probably the only man on the *Girona*, and one of very few in the entire

Armada, who now knew exactly what the English were doing, and why.

-

There was no more murmuring aboard the *Revenge*. Now her upper deck was a spectacle: ranks of grinning, determined men at their action stations, their thoughts accompanied by a cacophony from the drums and trumpets. Upon the quarterdeck stood Francis Drake, who had donned his best cuirass and burgonet, the latter sporting an extravagant plume that blew wildly in the wind. He had his eyes raised to Heaven, and declaimed the words of Deuteronomy in a loud and fervent voice.

'Vengeance is mine, and recompense; their foot shall slip in due time; for the day of their calamity *is* at hand, and the things to come hasten upon them.'

He lowered his eyes, and spoke even more loudly so that all could hear.

'Glory be to God! Glory be to his handmaiden, our sovereign lady Elizabeth! Glory to his chosen people, the good men of England! Onward, aye onward, *Revenge*!'

One of those in the throng around the admiral was Nicholas Fitzranulf, who was studiously avoiding Jack Stannard's gaze.

The *Revenge* and the squadron astern of her had all sail set, and were bearing down on the complacent, slow-moving southern flank of the Spanish Armada. The flashes and smoke of gunfire indicated the positions of the battles around Howard, Hawkins and Frobisher, the last of whom had taken his squadron into the mouth of the Solent to close it to the Spaniards. Word had at last filtered down to the under-officers, and thence to the lower deck, of the fleet's strategy. While Frobisher went northward, Howard and Hawkins would hold in the centre. Meanwhile Drake would sail far to the south, feinting as if to run up the Channel and away from the fight. But that would not have been Francis Drake at all.

Instead, the *Revenge* plunged through the waves, the banners of England streaming from her mastheads. Ahead of her, the surprised Spanish ships swiftly hoisted more sail, and those nearest their admiral attempted tentatively to move north-west, back towards the mouth of the Solent. But they were too many, too tightly packed, and too slow. Jack had heard his father speak of the 'race-built' galleon, supposedly the invention of John Hawkins, and of how much better it cut the water than the cumbersome Spanish hulls. The *Revenge* was one such, and she seemed veritably to be flying towards the confused Armada.

'Well, Master Stannard,' said Lieutenant Bodenham, 'Sir Francis and I reckon you've earned your spurs these last days, so you have the watch upon this deck. We're going to be fighting both sides of the ship, so I'll go below to assist the master gunner.'

Jack was dumbfounded, but still managed to say, 'Aye, aye, sir.'

He turned and saw Matt Bradlow grinning at him.

'You'll be an admiral yet, Master Stannard,' he said, and knuckled his forehead in salute.

'Steady all hands!' cried Jack, although he knew his words were superfluous. Even if they had never seen a shot fired in anger before, the battles of the last few days had turned the men of the *Revenge* into veterans.

The *Revenge* came up with the Dons, aiming for a gap between two towering *urcas*. As Drake and Gray, the sailing master, navigated her through it, the starboard and larboard batteries fired almost as one. Jack felt the ship shudder mightily, the planks moving beneath his feet, and it seemed as though the hull would break apart. But the *Revenge* held and her men cheered, for it was clear they had made several hits on both their targets. Now the English vessel turned slightly eastward and more weatherly, running along the larboard beam of one of the *urcas*.

'Fire at will, lads!'

The swivel gunners fired, but once again the range was too great and the Spanish hull too high for their shot to have much effect.

But the impact of the attack as a whole was very different indeed. As Drake and Gray manoeuvred *Revenge* back out into the open sea, their consorts were engaging in a similarly furious manner. The southern ships of the Armada were all turning north, away from the ferocious English onslaught.

'Got 'em on the run, Master Jack!' cried Matt Bradlow triumphantly.

Jack drew breath. 'Aye, seems so. Although...'

'Master Jack?'

'Surely all we're doing is herding them towards where they want to go anyway? Into the Solent?'

Bradlow smiled. 'Ah, well now, Master Jack, you've not sailed these waters much, I can tell. But I have, and long before that, your father taught me about 'em, as his father, the one you're named for, taught *him*, or so he said. The Dons ain't going where they want to go, mark my words. They ain't going anywhere near it.'

-

'Like Scylla and Charybdis, then?' said Spadaro.

'Who?' said Gravell.

'Yes, like Scylla and Charybdis,' said Juan.

He had learned the legend from old Thomas Ryman back in King Harry's time, before the present occupant of the English throne was even born. His masters at Cardinal College in Ipswich were impressed that he came to them already possessed of such knowledge when most of the pupils were dolts. Little good his learning had done him since, particularly in the last twenty years of captivity at the pleasure of the *Rey Católico*.

'What?' said Gravell.

'A monster and a whirlpool on either side of a narrow strait,' said Juan. 'The old Greeks had it that between them they destroyed countless ships – avoiding one threw you into the way of the other, and so on.'

'And that's where we are?'

'Precisely where we are.'

'But there are no monsters, my friend,' said Spadaro, 'and England isn't known for its whirlpools.'

'Not a whirlpool,' said Juan, 'but a great shelf of rocks called the Owers. It protrudes from the east end of the island we Englishmen call Wight.'

The *Girona*'s hull groaned; the helm was being put over. Through the oar port, Juan could see their consorts making the same change of course. The entire Armada was turning eastward, away from the Solent and the last anchorage available to it before the Straits of Dover. There was no choice in the matter. To westward and northward, the flags and cannon fire of the lead English ships were clearly visible. The mighty fleet had been hemmed in, the last straw being the sudden attack from the south. Changing course back to the east was its only chance of avoiding utter destruction upon the Owers.

'Rocks, then,' said Owen Gravell. '*Chwarae teg* – fair enough. But where's your monster, Jack Stannard?'

Before Juan could answer, Spadaro said, 'Francis Drake. The Dragon. What other monster could there be?'

Owen Gravell grinned. 'Ah, a dragon. *Duw dad*, now that's the monster indeed.'

Nine

'So, then, Widow de Andrade,' said a smiling Sir Nevill Bourchier, 'when did you become a witch?'

Meg was standing in chains before the magistrate, who sat in an elegant carved oak chair behind a large table within the principal room of his own house. Fanning, the parish constable of All Saints Dunwich, stood to one side, while a young clerk sat at the end of the table, making notes of the examination. There was no sign of her sister Mary, but Meg did not doubt that she was somewhere within earshot, perhaps even looking upon the proceedings from a place of concealment. Mayhap she was even pissing herself with excitement.

Meg was very tired. They had deprived her of sleep for three days before the examination began, but she knew what they were about and was determined not to oblige them. Silently she prayed to God and the Blessed Virgin to give her strength.

The first questions had been merely for the record – her name, her quality – but the interrogation swiftly took a more serious turn.

'Your parents?' said Sir Nevill.

'John Stannard of Dunwich, sir, and Alice his wife, born Easey.'

'Both inveterate papists?'

Meg had expected some sort of a question to that effect.

'They were of an age when every man and woman in England was a papist, as you call it,' she said, 'your own parents among them.'

Bourchier bridled at that. 'I'd advise you against insolence, woman,' he said petulantly. 'But note for the record, Master Clerk, that John Stannard of Dunwich was reputed to be a notorious papist until he disappeared, presumed killed, in the Indies.' The young clerk nodded, and made a note. 'So. Your mother was a witch, then?'

'No, sir,' said Meg, moderating her tone, 'she was never that.'

'But her good-sister was a different case, was she not? Your father's sister – Agatha, I believe her name was. I have it upon good authority, Widow.'

Mary, thought Meg. She would barely have known their aunt Agatha, who had died when she was a child, but she must have taken as gospel the opinion of her mother Jennet, who always despised and plainly feared Agatha Stannard.

Meg made no reply. After all, even she knew that Agatha had often gone far beyond the bounds of mere healing, and she would gain nothing by trying to defend a woman who had been dead for the best part of thirty years.

'Accused does not deny that her aunt was known to be a witch,' said Bourchier. 'So let us continue to explore your family a little, Widow de Andrade. Let us consider, say, your grandfather. He was a leper, was he not? The last leper of Dunwich?'

Meg was cautious, trying to focus her fuddled thoughts. Her grandfather had once possessed a certain fearsome reputation in the town of Dunwich, and her sister Mary knew that as well as she did.

'He was, sir.'

'Ah, then,' said Bourchier, smiling, 'is not leprosy a punishment from God? What is so evil in your family that such a dire punishment was sent down from Heaven, Margaret de Andrade?'

'Sir, does not the Bible say that the sins of the fathers shall not be visited on their offspring?'

This evidently confused the magistrate, though whether his perplexity was caused by the quotation from scripture or the fact that it was being quoted by a mean, unwashed suspected witch was a moot point.

'I thought it said the opposite,' he said hesitantly. 'But no matter. Master Clerk, merely note the fact of the accused's grandfather having been leprous. It shall be for the grand jury and then the assize court thereafter to judge what weight to give to it.'

The clerk nodded and scribbled on the sheet before him.

After a silence during which he seemed lost in thought, Sir Nevill Bourchier leaned forward with his elbows on the table, steepled his fingers and smiled. 'Well then, Widow de Andrade, let us come to the crux of the matter. When exactly did you become a witch?'

–

'Make more haste!' cried Tom Stannard.

Venn and Harrison, the oarsmen rowing him ashore from the *Eagle*, grunted and bent their backs. Tom knew he was being unduly harsh on them, for the harbour at Dover was crowded and a direct passage to the quay impossible. Every ship was getting under way, so small craft thronged the anchorage, carrying men back to their vessels or else bringing out fresh victuals or ammunition. The galleons, led by the flagship *Rainbow*, were already at sea, but the tide was turning and it was unlikely that *Eagle* and most of the other merchant ships would be able to leave harbour until it ebbed again. The sense of urgency was palpable, for the lookouts on the ramparts of Dover Castle and in the crow's nests of the queen's great ships reported that two vast forests of sails were in sight far to the south-west, off the French coast. They could only be the Spanish Armada and Lord Howard's fleet.

England's moment of destiny was imminent, but Tom had quite another concern. He trusted his men to ready the ship for sea without him, but if the mission upon which he was now embarked brought him to trial before the admiral for deserting his station, then so be it.

The boat drew alongside the quay, and he leapt to shore with the vigour of a much younger man. Not waiting for his two crewmen, he ran through the crowd thronging the quayside, then through the gateway in the ruinous town wall. Progress was difficult. The curious multitude making for the harbour to watch the fleet put to sea collided with the tide of the fearful, their possessions piled high in sacks over shoulders or in handcarts, seeking to flee to the greater safety they expected to find further inland. There were angry shouts and not a few raised fists, but slowly Tom neared his destination, the open space in front of the town's principal church. This contained a third crowd, and unlike the others, this one showed no desire to move in either direction, but was rather content to remain where it was, surrounding a pillory that contained a half-naked, groaning, bleeding bearded wretch. The fellow was barely recognisable as Adam Stannard.

Tom struggled to get closer to his son, but the crowd was tightly packed. Men, women and children seemed to be competing with each other to fling the coarsest insults imaginable, while others threw dung or even stones at the defenceless Adam. As he pushed his way through, Tom heard snatches of conversations.

'Called himself the new Christ, that he did! I heard him, I tell you!'

'Said we're all sinners and all damned! Looks like he's damned now, for certain!'

'Preached on naught but sodomy for six hours, barely drawing a breath. He reckoned it's why the Dons are coming against us – God's instrument to punish us for sodomy, he said.'

Tom pressed on, finally reaching the front, and made for the constable, a fat, sweating fellow standing a few feet back from the pillory to avoid the barrage being directed at it.

'You've the key?' he said angrily.

'What's it to you?' replied the constable, bristling.

'I am Thomas Stannard, captain of the ship *Eagle of Dunwich* in the queen's fleet. The fellow yonder is my chaplain. It'll gratify me if you'll release him forthwith.'

'Your chaplain? Damned unorthodox chaplain, I'd say, proclaiming himself the Messiah and other such heresies. Mayor Tench ordered him placed in there, but the vicar's demanding he be sent before the justices.'

'With the Armada in sight?' said Tom. 'Haven't we all more important matters to occupy us? He's needed on the ship. Look at him, man. Whatever spouts from his mouth, he's a good strong fellow. England needs every such man to defend it!'

The constable shook his head.

'Mayor Tench's order,' he said, albeit less confidently than before.

A few at the front of the crowd, who had overheard what had passed between Tom and the constable, were restive and starting to jeer and hiss. Tom looked around and saw that Venn and Harrison had finally caught up. Both men were large and ugly, both were disfigured by hideous scars, and both had cudgels in their hands; these, of course, were precisely the reasons why Tom had chosen them to accompany him. A passage cleared in front of them as it had for Moses in the Red Sea.

Tom wore a battered old sword, and now, to gasps from the crowd, he drew it from its shabby leather scabbard. The constable took a couple of paces backwards.

In ordinary times, what Tom was doing might well get him hanged. But the times were anything but ordinary, and regardless of whether England's fleet won or lost against the mighty Spanish Armada, he reckoned that the mayor of Dover and his constable would have more important things to occupy themselves with. And if he did not survive the dreadful fight that was sure to come, then the criminal act he was about to commit – mayhap an act of rebellion, or treason, or whatever other charge a devious lawyer like Tom's half-brother George might conjure up – would be of no import to anyone left on God's earth.

'I'd trouble you for your keys, Constable,' he said.

The fellow handed them over, his eyes never moving from the point of Tom's blade.

Tom went to the pillory and unlocked it. Adam groaned loudly, sagged and fell. Tom caught him, and as Venn and Harrison came to his side, glaring defiantly at all around, he turned his son's face towards him.

'You're safe now,' he said gently. 'We'll get you back to the ship.'

Adam seemed not to recognise him at first, but then his eyes narrowed.

'Leviticus,' he whispered, his words little more than gasps. 'One Corinthians. God's word damns you. It damns all sodomites. My own father is an abomination unto me. An abomination unto God's law.'

With that, Adam Stannard fainted.

-

'So, Widow de Andrade,' said Sir Nevill Bourchier smoothly, 'when was the first time you lay with the Devil?'

Even at the sixth or seventh time of asking, the question sounded so comical that, despite herself, Meg laughed, swaying upon her feet as she did so. She was very tired, but was still alert enough not to be wrong-footed by her adversary's sudden switch of tack.

'I have never seen the Devil, Sir Nevill,' she said, 'so how can I have lain with him?'

Aye, a switch of tack, but an interesting one. Meg knew full well, for her aunt Agatha had told her this long ago, that there were two kinds of charge laid against suspected witches: *maleficium*, the harming of kinsfolk and neighbours by one means or another; or else alleging that the suspect was in league with the Devil. Obtaining a conviction depended above all on the suspect confessing.

With this foreknowledge, Meg was confident of denying all charges.

Certainly the questioning about suspected *maleficium* seemed feeble in the extreme: one neighbour (unnamed, but Meg suspected the drunken Goody Fawcett who lived close by Hen Hill) alleged that Meg had caused the sickness and death of her baby son, father unknown, when it was well known throughout Dunwich that the mother had dropped the child head first onto a hard floor when in drink; another, almost certainly old Jephson down by Minsmere, alleged that Meg had cursed his cow by making her milk dry up. But Jephson was known to be a simpleton who had previously testified against three other alleged witches; all three cases had been thrown out by the grand jury and never reached the assizes. No matter how tired she was, Meg could deny such charges until the day of judgement. But alleging a pact with the Devil was a very different matter.

'Constable Fanning,' said Bourchier, 'by your statement, you say that you searched the cottage of the accused during the forenoon of the twenty-first of July.'

The feeble constable nodded several times, shuffling upon his feet as he did so. 'That I did, m'lord,' he said.

Meg scowled at him. Fanning was a dirty, fawning creature, forced into the post of constable because no better man would take it, but he was related somehow to the Cuddons, long-time rivals of the Stannards in Dunwich.

'And these are the items you discovered?' Bourchier waved his hand over the strange assortment of objects on the table. There were small jars of unguents and herbs, pins, needles, candles, a few animal bones and Meg's paternoster.

'They are, m'lord,' said Fanning.

'Very good,' said Bourchier. 'Well then, Margaret de Andrade. What explanation have you for these?'

Meg struggled to keep her eyes open, but still weighed her words carefully. 'The jars contain substances for healing, sir. Any physician will testify to their efficacy.' She thought she heard a noise behind one of the doors into the room, and wondered if it was her malevolent sister.

'You set yourself on a level with a physician, woman?'

'No, sir, of course I do not. But these things have been known since time immemorial, and known to be good.'

Bourchier removed the lid from one of the jars, sniffed, recoiled, and replaced the lid. It was obvious to Meg that he was uncertain; for sure, his knowledge of medicines was negligible, and no match for hers. Instead, he lifted the paternoster and waved it before her.

'And this?'

'You know as well as any man in England what that is, Sir Nevill. Possession of it is not a crime.'

'I have warned you about your insolence, woman! You deny, then, that this abomination is your means of praying to your master, Satan?'

'It is a means of praying, Sir Nevill, but not to Satan. You know that. Every judge and jury in England will know that. I do not deny that I cleave to the old faith – have never denied it. But that is not witchcraft.'

He stared hard at her, then finally settled back into his chair with a heavy sigh, flinging the string of beads back onto the table.

'And the bones?' he demanded.

'They are foolish keepsakes of a favourite cat, long dead,' said Meg, too swiftly, realising her mistake at once.

Bourchier sat bolt upright. 'A cat, you say?' He smiled. 'A familiar, then? A Satanic imp, no less!'

'No, Sir Nevill. Just a cat.'

'I had cats as a child, Widow. As a man, I have dogs. When each of them died in their turn, I felt no compulsion to keep their bones. What purpose can the remains of a cat serve, other than to conjure up curses against goodly innocent folk? Confess now, woman! Confess to both *maleficium* and carnal knowledge of the Devil!'

There was another noise from outside the room. Sister Mary must be stamping her little foot in ecstasy, Meg thought.

'I am innocent, as God is my judge,' she said firmly.

'Oh yes, God will indeed be your judge, Margaret de Andrade. I shall summon a jury of matrons, and they will search your body for the Devil's marks!'

For the first time, Meg de Andrade felt real fear.

Ten

From his now familiar station in the fo'c'sle of the *Revenge*, Jack Stannard joined in the thunderous cheering from every quarter and every man of the English fleet. Truly the sight before them was one to lighten heavy and weary hearts. Under full sail on a south-easterly course directly towards them came the great galleons of Lord Harry Seymour's Narrow Seas Fleet, led by the flagship *Rainbow* with the equally formidable *Vanguard* and *Antelope* astern. Fresh ships with crews eager to see action, bringing full magazines and powder stores. Behind them came the rest of Seymour's ships, a collection of well-armed and nimble merchantmen, the true representatives of England's maritime power. Jack strained his eyes to see if he could make out the *Eagle of Dunwich*, carrying his father and brother Adam, but the throng of ships and sails was too dense, and the *Eagle* was not a big vessel.

Like every man on the upper deck of every ship, Jack counted hulls, adding the number that had sailed from Plymouth to the reinforcements coming out from Dover and the Downs.

'A hundred and forty, give or take,' he said to Matt Bradlow, who was close by. 'We now outnumber the Dons, by God.'

'All well and good, Master Stannard,' said Bradlow, remembering the proprieties of their respective stations, 'but we outnumber them only barely, and we still have to beat them. And somewhere over yonder' – he pointed northward – 'lies Parma with ships of his own, and the barges to bring over his army.'

'Aye, but God is on our side, Matt Bradlow. On our noble queen's side.'

Bradlow made no reply. Instead the two men looked out again at the welcome sight of the English reinforcements, the flagships of the Narrow Seas fleet taking up station on either side of *Ark Royal*. The intent was clear, and was confirmed a few minutes later when whistles blew aboard the *Revenge* and the ship's longboat was hauled round from the stern and laid alongside. Shortly afterwards, Sir Francis Drake emerged into the ship's waist, elegantly attired in shining half-armour bearing his heraldic emblem, the wyvern – which to any untrained eye looked remarkably like a dragon. He climbed down into the longboat, and as hurrahs echoed from the deck of *Revenge*, his oarsmen began to row him towards Lord Howard's flagship. The same scene was evidently being played out on all the ships that bore those entitled to places in the council of war: longboats were setting out from *Triumph* with Martin Frobisher, from *Victory* with John Hawkins, from *Elizabeth Bonaventure* with the Earl of Cumberland and from *White Bear* with the Earl of Sheffield. The boats bearing Lord Harry Seymour and Sir William Wynter from *Rainbow* and *Vanguard* respectively were already alongside the fleet flagship. The greatest seamen in England were going into conference, and Jack, along with every man in the fleet, had no doubt what they would be discussing. They were planning exactly how and when they would destroy the Spanish Armada.

–

Peter Stannard knew Gravesend of old. He had played there the previous summer, when Lord Carnforth's Men staged *The Three Ladies of London* before a baying, drunken audience. The town itself was a low, marshy place, full of stinking alehouses that made fortunes from the scores of ships that always lay in its anchorage, awaiting favourable winds and tides to move up- or downstream. Now, though, Gravesend had suddenly become the centre of the world. Countless regiments of regular troops and militiamen thronged its streets, or else formed up on its shore. Splendidly attired cavalrymen and officers in gleaming cuirasses and morion helmets rode up and down, calling out for the unwary to get out of their way. Oxen pulled huge field guns down towards the Thames. All of this military activity was directed towards one point in the town, low down on the shore beneath the church, and to one structure. Floating upon the Thames was a bridge of boats that connected Gravesend to the far bank, namely the shore of Essex. The bridge was secured by anchors, cables and ropes, covered by guns in hastily erected bastions at either end, and had crane-like devices in the middle that allowed it to be opened to let vessels through.

'Jesu and Judas,' said Bennet Barnes, the old grey-bearded trooper resting heavily on his pike alongside Peter, 'I wouldn't take a mouse across that, let alone an army.'

The bridge was indeed swaying and dipping crazily as a single small cannon was pulled across it by a recalcitrant horse.

'I'm sure the engineer who built it knows his business,' said Peter cheerily, adopting his time-honoured character of hail-fellow-well-met.

'Engineers? Fuckwits, every man of them,' said Bennet, spitting onto the dusty ground.

Bennet Barnes claimed that his first campaign had been the fall of Calais thirty years before, which might or might not have been true, but it was plain that the oldster had more than enough experience to speak with authority upon the subject of engineers. Also upon the subjects of generals, cavalry, artillery, victuallers, whores, transubstantiation, the French, the Spanish, ale, Yorkshiremen, the Irish, and very nearly everything else under the sun too, it seemed.

From his own observation, though, Peter had to admit that his ancient companion had a point about the bridge. The fragile structure was all well and good now, when the weather was relatively calm and there was no urgent hurry to get men and equipment across to the other side. But if word came that the Dons had landed in Kent, contrary to expectation, and the entire army had to be got back across the river again with the greatest of haste – aye, especially in inclement weather – then God alone knew how they would fare.

For now, though, the bridge of boats served Peter Stannard's purpose admirably. It would get him swiftly out of Kent, away from pursuit by any hue and cry that the sheriff or the Bishop of Rochester might have proclaimed by now. Once over in Essex and thus on the other side of the Thames, he could easily vanish into very nearly any part of the entire kingdom. Or else, of course, he could seek to reunite with Lord Carnforth's Men in London, once the alarms from both Bromley and the Spanish

Armada were over. Better, he could reunite with Arabella, whose irresistible body, sly smile and earthy common sense held sway over his thoughts and dreams. Peter was not much given to prayer, unlike his brother Adam, but he prayed every waking hour that she was safe and that somehow he would soon see her again.

But until that day came, he would continue to play at being a soldier, and that meant crossing the bridge to the vast armed camp stretching as far as the eye could see upon the flat, marshy land of Essex, behind the small blockhouse lying at the river's edge. Banners flew from voluminous officers' tents, the clank of arms and armour vied with the shouted orders of sergeants, while the stench of a thousand dung pits wafted across the river, where it came together with the foul odours of the tidal mud to create a rare and hellish confection.

This, then, was Tilbury.

-

One by one, the ships of the Spanish Armada dropped anchor. Aboard the four galleasses the slaves were allowed upon deck for some air and exercise, always under the watchful eyes of heavily armed soldiers.

'Is that England?' said Spadaro, pointing to the nearby shore and the large town surrounded by strong walls in whose anchorage the Armada now rode.

'That is England,' said Juan Estandar, pointing off to the west towards a distant line of white cliffs. 'This is France. Calais.'

The fleur-de-lis of King Henri were just visible on the flags flying from the nearest towers.

'France is Spain's ally now?' said Spadaro incredulously.

'Her king needs all the friends he can get while he fights his Protestants,' said Juan. 'But it'll suit him to assist the Armada. If King Philip's eyes are on London, they won't be on Paris.'

'I sailed here once,' said Owen Gravell, who was looking out towards Calais. 'Back in eighty, I think, or eighty-one. A poor harbour. Too exposed in westerlies.'

'I sailed here countless times,' said Juan, 'even in the days when it was still English. But you're right, this is no roadstead for a great fleet.'

He inclined his head to Fra Gordillo, who was moving astern prior to celebrating Mass once again. The priest glowered at him.

'So we'll not be here long?' said Spadaro.

'Not long in either case,' said Juan. 'Either Parma is ready to bring his army out, or the English will attack before that can happen. This is where it'll be decided, my friends – the entire fate of this enterprise of England.'

He looked south-west towards the towering cape that protruded into the Channel, mirroring Dungeness on the English shore. Off it stood the English fleet, unmoving and menacing, the bows of his countrymen's galleons pointing directly at the anchored Armada.

The time of decision had come.

Part Two

I know I have the body of a weak and feeble woman; but I have the heart and stomach of a king, and of a king of England too, and think foul scorn that Parma or Spain, or any prince of Europe, should dare to invade the borders of my realm; to which rather than any dishonour shall grow by me, I myself will take up arms, I myself will be your general, judge, and rewarder of every one of your virtues in the field.

Commonly accepted version of the speech delivered by Queen Elizabeth I to her army at Tilbury, 9 August 1588

Come on now, my companions at arms, and fellow soldiers, in the field, now for the Lord, for your Queen, and for the Kingdom … the enemy perhaps may challenge my sex for that I am a woman, so may I likewise charge their mould for that they are but men…

From one of two completely different versions of the queen's speech

Eleven

The summons to the *Rainbow*, flagship of the Narrow Seas fleet, came as an utter shock to Tom Stannard. As the *Eagle*'s longboat took him across the calm water of the Channel, between the hulls of the queen's ships and the hired merchantmen, he attempted to assemble his thoughts into some sort of order. But it was an impossible task. He could think only of Adam, gagged and tied to a sea-bed within the locked master's cabin, guarded by two of the trustiest men in the *Eagle*'s crew. Whenever the gag was removed, Adam poured forth the bitterest invective against his father, citing biblical texts he never completed, often becoming so angry and red in the face that his words were utterly unintelligible. Tom feared that news had somehow reached Lord Harry that the captain of the *Eagle of Dunwich* had a madman aboard his ship, or else that complaint had come from the mayor and burgesses of Dover against the pirate who had stolen a violator of the public peace from righteous justice.

Tom had been aboard the flagship before, but never in such circumstances. As he emerged onto the upper deck, he could see the ships of the Spanish Armada lying as plain as day off Calais' shore. Like the other vessels around her, the *Rainbow* had taken in all but the smallest vestige of sail. She was not at anchor, but it was as though she and her consorts were idling upon the spot. There was nothing idle about the flagship's crew, though. Gunners were checking their tackle and swabbing their barrels, while soldiers in gleaming breastplates were sharpening their blades or cleaning their muskets. Men grinned at each other, but there was a determination to the grins. Every man knew, as did Tom Stannard, that the final battle for England was about to be fought.

A scowling guard admitted Tom to the great cabin at the stern, and the half-dozen or so men within fell silent. Tom recognised the admiral, Lord Harry Seymour, clad in the simplest seaman's garb, with no badge of office to distinguish him. He could easily have been taken for the meanest foretopman. Alongside him was the far more splendidly attired vice admiral of the Narrow Seas fleet, Sir William Wynter, an ancient greybeard who, it was said, had first gone to sea in the Scottish expedition of the year forty-four, when Tom's long-lost and lamented father had first distinguished himself in battle. He knew none of the others, but they had the look and the clothing of lawyers rather than men of action.

'Thomas Stannard of the *Eagle*,' said Lord Harry. 'Welcome, my friend.'

His friend? The two words threw Tom into utter confusion, and this was compounded when Wynter smiled, stepped forward and clapped him on the back. Plainly, whatever this summons was concerned with, it could not be about Adam. Perhaps it was about his other son, Jack – had he been killed aboard the *Revenge*? But surely the admiral himself would not deign to summon him to tell him that.

'My… my lord,' said Tom, recollecting his duty. 'Sir William. Gentlemen.'

'Of course you're wondering why we summoned you,' said Lord Harry. 'Tell me, Goodman Stannard – you're of Suffolk, yes? Of Dunwich, that place of past glory and renown?'

'You know of it, my lord?'

'Oh, every man of parts – of knowledge – in England knows the legend of Dunwich. The mighty city lost beneath the waves. Isn't that the case, Sir William?' Wynter nodded. 'So, Tom Stannard, I'd wager that any man of Dunwich would want to do all in his power to save his hearth and home from the Dons, wouldn't that be so? Because if they land, my friend, there's a decent chance they'll land somewhere near those parts. True, the army is assembled at Tilbury, and I'm informed the queen herself has a mind to go there, but the Dons yonder know that as well as you and I. So they may seek to land a little further north and outflank our army, and you'll know better than I that Suffolk has many fine beaches, ideal for an invading army to storm ashore. My point is this, Tom Stannard. Your Dunwich may be one of the first places in England that sees Parma's men in its streets. You've loved ones there, yes? Pray for them, my friend.'

Tom could say nothing. He swayed upon his feet and was entirely mute. Lord Henry Seymour, one of the queen's most trusted admirals, was confiding in him. *In him*. Yet there had to be a purpose to all this...

'The truth is,' said Sir William, seemingly a little irritated by Lord Harry's rhetoric, 'we need your ship. The queen needs your ship.'

'She already has my ship, Sir William.'

'You misunderstand me, Captain Stannard. What we need, what the queen needs, what England demands, is the sacrifice of your ship.'

The *Girona* lay at anchor towards the southern flank of the Armada. Aboard her, as on every ship in the mighty fleet, Mass was said that evening with even greater urgency than usual, Fra Gordillo's imprecations being carried heavenward with the prayers of an anxious crew. Those of the galley slaves who were not heretics or Mahometans shuffled forward in their turn to take communion, and Juan saw the young priest's hands trembling. Captain Spinola stood at Gordillo's side, as though to provide reassurance, but even his face looked drawn and anxious. On the *Girona*, as on every ship close to her, the watch on deck had been strengthened, soldiers reinforcing the seamen who would normally be on duty. Pinnaces ringed the fleet, constantly moving between and around the anchored hulls, ready to respond to any eventuality.

Even as their thoughts should have been only upon beseeching God for succour, many men's eyes turned surreptitiously to the south-west, to the brooding mass of shipping lying there.

Earlier, as they ate a weak, tasteless broth below decks, Juan and his companions had joined in the single topic of conversation, or rather the two whispered questions that were being repeated in a score of different forms: *What will the English do?* and *Is Parma ready?*

'There's a council of war on *San Martín*,' said Adil, a strapping young Mahometan who had been captured in a Tunisian galley off Majorca. 'Moncada's gone over for it.'

'When I was last on deck,' said Owen Gravell, 'I heard cheering from a few of the big Biscayan ships, and saw Recalde being rowed over in his pinnace. They say de Leyva's over there, too. All the great flagmen. Maybe word has come from Parma.'

'And what if the word says that Parma's not ready?' said Juan. 'I know this roadstead; we can't stay here for long, least of all if the weather gets up. And the English – they'll make sure we can't lie here for any time at all.'

'There's talk they've got hellburners,' said Adil.

Spadaro crossed himself, while Juan exchanged a glance with Gravell. Every man in the Armada feared hellburners more than anything else. Nearly three years before, these infernal devices, packed with thousands of pounds of gunpowder, had killed hundreds of men and even wounded Parma himself when they were used against the Spanish besiegers of Antwerp. In awed whispers, men said that the world had never heard explosions so vast, nor witnessed carnage so terrible. The hellburners had been designed by an Italian engineer named Giambelli, and he was known to be in England now, in the employ of Queen Elizabeth.

'They'll not use hellburners,' said Juan. 'They'd take more powder than the queen has in her entire kingdom.'

'You haven't been in England for twenty years,' said Spadaro, 'so how the hell can you know that, old man?'

'Just so,' said Adil. 'Why employ this Giambelli at all, if not to re-create this terrible weapon of his?'

Juan Estandar shook his head. In truth, the questions were unanswerable. He had no way of knowing if his countrymen had hellburners or not; he only had his instinct, and that told him the English would not waste such colossal quantities of gunpowder on creating only a massive explosion or two. For one thing, they did not need to. As he looked around the deck and saw his fellow slaves murmuring among themselves, the Catholics among them crossing themselves frequently, Juan knew that Francis Drake, John Hawkins and the rest of them needed to do only one thing to trigger the mounting panic that was creeping insidiously through the mess decks of the Spanish Armada.

–

Tom wished for nothing more than to return to the *Eagle*, but Seymour and Wynter insisted on entertaining him, and the other captains in the same position as him, to a lavish dinner in the great cabin of the *Rainbow*. He should not concern himself, said Seymour. The new crew being assigned to the *Eagle* would send back all his possessions, and as much of the stores, armaments and weapons as they could, and then dispatch boats with the Dunwich crew, including his son, Adam. In turn, the new crew – all long-serving veterans of the Navy Royal proper – would take across the materials they needed and prepare the *Eagle* for the great business in hand.

Tom was uneasy, but Seymour was all reassurance. Were not the terms being offered on the queen's behalf markedly generous? Indeed they were; more than four hundred pounds for the ship itself, the same again for the gear and stores in her. Tom would be able to afford a new ship better than the *Eagle*. And he need not worry about his son, Lord Harry said. The *Rainbow* had a most excellent surgeon aboard, and if the case warranted it, Adam could be sent ashore to the hospital in Dover. If Tom wished it, his other son Jack, of whom he had spoken to the admiral, could be released from his duties aboard *Revenge* to support his father and brother in their time of trouble.

All the while that Tom and his fellows were being treated as equals by Lord Harry Seymour and Sir William

Wynter, boats ferried goods and men back and forth between the flagships and the *Eagle* and the other seven chosen ships.

The afternoon sun was fading into evening when Tom emerged once again onto the upper deck of the *Rainbow*. He saw men milling around in the waist of the ship, and longboats and pinnaces moored alongside her hull, but there were no familiar faces from *Eagle*.

'Ho, Bosun Laine!' he called.

The boatswain of *Rainbow*, distinguishable by the whistle of office around his neck, recognised Tom from his arrival on the ship.

'Master Stannard?'

'Where are the men from *Eagle*, I beg you? *Eagle of Dunwich?*'

Laine shrugged. 'Gone to *Vanguard* or *Antelope*, most like, or else to one of the ships from the western fleet. We've spread 'em round the galleons.'

'They were meant to come here! My son is sickly – Lord Henry assured me your ship's surgeon could treat him, or arrange for him to go ashore.'

'Don't concern yourself, man, he'll be perfectly safe on any of the other ships.'

'I must find him!'

Laine looked uncertain. He was of an age to be a father, and perhaps had a sense of Tom's anxiety.

'Tell you what, Stannard, we've got a boat about to go to *Vanguard* and *Antelope* to deliver orders for the night. Mister Carey's going as messenger – he's one of the gentleman volunteers. We'll get him to see if he can find out which ship the men from *Eagle* are on and bring back word. What think you?'

Tom thought only that he wished to go in the boat himself, to find Adam, to see if his rage had subsided, to offer more words – any words – that might placate his son and assuage the unbearable guilt he felt. But he could not challenge Laine, for in a matter of this kind, it was certain that Seymour would support his officer. So Tom watched anxiously as the boat pulled away from *Rainbow*, bound for the other great ships. He went from one end of the deck to the other, seeing if he could catch a glimpse of its return or else of the *Eagle itself*, but the combined English fleets were in such close formation that it was impossible to see through the colossal wall of wood before him.

It was well after dark before the boat returned. As it secured to the side of the *Rainbow*, Tom could see at once that it did not contain Adam. There was a familiar face among the boat's crew, though: Luke Fletcher, master's mate of the *Eagle*, a quiet, competent man.

'Where's Adam?' Tom demanded as soon as Fletcher came aboard the flagship. 'Where's my son?'

'Begging pardon, Master Stannard, he told us to leave the ship before the navy crew came aboard. Said he'd make a final check that all was in order before he handed it over to them, then he'd come off when they did, in their boat.'

By the dim light of the lanterns illuminating the deck of the *Rainbow*, Tom could see the doubt in Fletcher's face. He knew almost as well as Tom did that Adam Stannard knew little more of ships than the difference between one end and the other, so the idea of him checking the *Eagle* for anything at all was simply inconceivable.

'And you believed him?' said Tom.

Fletcher looked downcast. 'He's a Stannard of Dunwich. He's your son.'

'How did he seem when you left him? In his right senses?'

'Aye, Master Stannard, happier than I've seen him for many a long day, too. He kept repeating "Matthew nine, verse one", over and over to himself,' said Fletcher, a godly, self-taught fellow.

Tom felt a clamp close around his heart, and a terrible coldness consume his flesh. He did not know scripture as well as his father had done, nor as well as his sister Meg did, although her use of it was invariably either mischievous or incendiary, principally to prove the supposed truth of the Church of Rome. Even so, there were certain chapters, certain passages and certain verses he knew well enough; and like many men who used the sea, these included all the references to ships and the boundless waves.

Matthew nine, verse one: *Then he – Jesus – entered into a ship, and passed over, and came into his own city.*

And Adam Stannard, in his lunatic delusions, imagined himself to be the new Jesus.

There was a sudden loud cheer from the direction of *Ark Royal*, closer to the French shore, then from the ships around her. Up on the fo'c'sle of *Rainbow*, men were pointing excitedly to the north-east, towards where the Spanish Armada lay at anchor. Tom took hold of a shroud and hauled himself up to get a clearer view. In the distance, he could see eight small fires, exactly like the beacons that warned England of the Armada's approach. As he watched, they seemed to get smaller, then grew larger. Within what seemed a matter of moments it was even possible to make out the ghostly shapes of blazing hulls, masts and yardarms moving slowly across the sea towards the distant Armada.

One of the fiery ships was the *Eagle of Dunwich*, and Tom knew in his heart that Adam would have found some way of concealing himself aboard when her naval crew left, shortly after firing the fuses they had laid.

Tom Stannard was the only man in the fleet who did not exult as England's blazing harbingers of doom sailed onward, surely destined for glory and immortal fame.

-

There was a frenzied hacking, then a colossal jolt as the anchor cable of the *Girona* was finally cut through and the galleass suddenly rode free. From his limited viewpoint, looking through the oar hole, Juan could see and hear the same scene being repeated all around. The Armada was freeing itself from its moorings with all possible haste, and the reason why was suddenly visible as two galleons lying to larboard of the *Girona* began to gain momentum as the wind filled their sails. Now Juan could see blazing hulls approaching the Spanish formation, doubtless unmanned but still carried inexorably forward upon wind and tide. Their cannon fired, surely manned by invisible, infernal gun crews drawn from the ranks of the satanic army.

Up above, the free sailors and soldiers who were witnessing the spectacle in its entirety were screaming in terror, their cries reaching the slaves down below. Strangely, perhaps, the galley slaves themselves were almost entirely silent; even if one of the burning ships struck the *Girona* and destroyed it, some, such as the fatalistic Spadaro and the Moor Adil, would look upon such a fate as deliverance from an unrelenting captivity. Juan Estandar had no such thoughts. Very old though he was, he still wished to live, and if God willed it, he would see Dunwich again.

'Hellburners! More sail, in the name of God! Absolution from any sin, I promise it!'

Juan could hear Fra Gordillo's shrieks from the deck above, carrying above even the shouts of the men setting the sails, the shrill calls on Bosun Cala's whistle, and the heavy rumbling of the great guns being rolled into position.

'Have you gone mad, old man?' said Owen Gravell. 'You're smiling, *mawredd mawr*. How can you smile when everything might be blown to the heavens in a moment?'

Several of the men nearby nodded angrily.

'They're not hellburners,' said Juan evenly.

'You don't know that.'

'I've lived three times as long as you, Welshman. I've been at sea three times as long.' Juan was aware that many eyes were upon him now, so he spoke up. 'This is what I say. If they were hellburners, they'd have blown up long before now. They're ordinary fireships – no crews, no direction, easy to avoid if a crew knows what it's doing.'

'And does this crew?'

'Not one man of them, my friend. They've cut the anchor cables, like every other ship in the Armada. So what does that mean, d'you think?'

Spadaro, a more experienced seaman than Owen Gravell, spoke up.

'The formation's broken,' he said. 'The fleet's in no order.'

'And that's the least of it,' said Juan, one eye watching through the oar hole as the *Girona* began to move away from the limited threat of the English fireships. 'No anchors – that means no mooring, not here, not anywhere. No mooring means precious little chance of waiting for Parma to come out, even if we defeat the

English in the battle to come – for mark my words, my friends, the English will attack as soon as the sun is up.'

'Then what of us?' said Owen Gravell.

Juan had no answer. Instead, he took one last look at the English fireships, now drifting aimlessly and burning themselves out as the ships of the Spanish Armada began to sail away from them along the coast of Flanders. He shivered, despite the warmth of the August night.

It was as though someone had stepped upon his grave.

Twelve

Dawn.

Jack Stannard was at his now accustomed station in the fo'c'sle of the *Revenge*. All around the English fleet was advancing purposefully upon a fair south-westerly breeze, *Revenge* being the most leeward of the flagships. Ahead, only a handful of Spanish ships retained any semblance of a formation as they waited to receive the onslaught of their opponents; he recognised one of them from the previous actions as the flagship of Medina Sidonia himself. Behind them he could see the remaining ships of the Armada, all bearing away upon the wind, some of them dangerously close to the lee shore of Flanders.

The fireships had done their business as well as could have been expected. The great fleet was scattered, and now it was up to the oncoming English ships to put paid to it once and for all. The sense of anticipation aboard the *Revenge* was palpable, with men grinning broadly at each other as they went about their business. Sir Francis Drake, clearly visible upon the poop deck, was like a small boy, hopping from one foot to the other in excitement.

Yet amidst this colossal confrontation of two mighty fleets, the ordinary life of the sea went on; close inshore, a few small fishing craft were plying their trade as though nothing untoward was happening.

An idea occurred to Jack. But surely it was an impertinence? Surely Lord Howard and Sir Francis and all the other famous seamen of England would have thought of this? Surely they had better intelligence than he did? No, it would have occurred to someone else already, someone far greater than him. When all was said and done, he was nobody.

Yet Jack Stannard still felt that he was not serving his queen as well as he could. If he said what was in his mind, the worst that could happen was that he would be rejected out of hand, then derided mercilessly by the likes of Nicholas Fitzranulf. He could live with such slights, he reckoned.

What did he have to lose?

He made his way through the throng of men on the upper deck of the galleon and went up to the quarterdeck, where Lieutenant Bodenham was seeing to the affixing of even more swivel guns. The word was already running like wildfire through the messes: today's battle would be a close-quarters affair, closer than ever before, and was likely to be murderous.

'Mister Bodenham,' said Jack, 'I request an audience of Sir Francis.'

'Aye? Concerning what, Stannard?'

'A matter for his ears only, sir. Mayhap a matter of great concern to England.'

Bodenham glared at him critically, but he was too good an officer to dismiss out of hand the possibility that the deputy purser might have a case. He nodded, and Jack proceeded up to the poop deck, where he bowed before Drake, who was now somewhat more stationary.

'Well, then, Deputy Purser!' cried the admiral merrily. 'It appears to me that you've been finding the blood of

Dons more to your taste than inventories of biscuit. There should be plenty of the former for you today. Just make sure there's still enough biscuit when we get hungry. And beer! Aye, beer above all, eh, gentlemen?'

He directed his remark to the little gaggle of volunteers standing on the larboard side of the deck, who laughed dutifully. Jack was relieved to see that Fitzranulf was not among them.

'Fear not, Sir Francis,' he said, 'there'll be ample beer for us all to toast victory over the Dons.'

Drake clapped him on the shoulder. 'Well said, lad, well said! So then, what concerns you so much to bring you to me?'

'Sir Francis, do we have intelligence of Parma?'

Drake looked astonished. 'Parma? Intelligence of Parma? I wouldn't have thought that's your concern, Master Stannard.'

The admiral's face was darkening, and Jack wondered if he had made a terrible mistake in addressing him. Drake could change his mood in the blink of an eye; every man in the fleet knew that.

'No, Sir Francis. But... well, if we don't, I think there might be an opportunity to obtain it.'

Drake's expression still verged on the hostile. 'How so?'

'There are fishing boats yonder, Sir Francis, close inshore. The crews are bound to know the disposition of Parma's army – how ready it is to sail, exactly where the barges lie, all of it.'

'Perhaps,' said Drake, evidently thinking hard, 'but they're Flemings and papists, and no friends of ours. Besides, this is chiefly a Devon crew, and not one man of it speaks Flemish.'

'I do,' said Jack, confidently. 'I'm a Suffolk man, Sir Francis. Much of our trade is with Flanders – I've been on voyages there since I was nine or ten. I speak enough of their tongue to be understood, as I do with Frisian, High German...'

'Aye, very good, Master Stannard, very good. Very impressive. I am impressed indeed. Greatly impressed. Impressed beyond measure. But I'd remind you they're still our enemies.'

'Not so, Sir Francis. Most of the men of these parts hate King Philip as much as we do. They long to join their northern friends in their new republic. Many of them are as good Protestants as you and I.'

Drake was uncharacteristically silent. For a moment he looked across to Gray, the sailing master of the *Revenge*, who seemed to be nodding to himself. Drake stroked his beard, stared at Jack, seemed about to say something, changed his mind, walked away to look out to sea, then returned.

'If I venture upon this,' he said slowly, 'it seems I lose very little. Perhaps I lose you, Master Stannard, but I'm sure one of these fellows' – he pointed to the small group of gentlemen volunteers – 'can count as well as you. Mayhap, at any rate. Perhaps I lose a few men in a boat's crew, but that's a loss I can bear, even if their widows and children can't. But if you're right, and you can give me word of Parma... and if, as you say, those fellows yonder believe in the reformed faith, and aren't papistical vermin... Very well, Deputy Purser, you can have a boat and a crew. But methinks you need some fighting men too, in case you encounter the Dons, and you'll need a man to command them. Ho, Mister Fitzranulf, there!'

The man in question was just returning to the poop deck, and looked up at Drake's call.

'Please, Sir Francis, anyone but—' said Jack, softly and urgently.

'When you fight for your queen and country, lad, you can't choose who dies alongside you.'

Jack thought there was a hint of a smile on Francis Drake's lips, and a glint of mischief in his eyes.

-

Tom Stannard stood atop the white cliffs which stretched northward from Dover. He could see the distant flashes of gunfire, could hear the thunder of the cannon. All around him, people were cheering or praying, depending on their inclination. But Tom stood stock still, not really registering the dreadful event being played out upon the horizon.

He was numb. He could barely remember the voyage of the pinnace which brought him and most of the crew of the *Eagle* back to Dover during the previous night. The men had wished to stay and fight, but Bosun Laine of the *Rainbow*, presumably acting on Lord Harry's orders, had been adamant; the great galleons were already overmanned and could take no more supernumeraries. Besides, the men of the *Eagle* and the other seven fireships had already played their part to bring about a victory for England, Laine said. Now the business would be decided by the heavy cannon, by the skill and determination of Howard, Seymour, Drake, Hawkins, Frobisher and all the rest of the Navy Royal's brave seamen.

Despite the loss he had suffered and the lack of sleep, Tom found himself irresistibly drawn to the cliffs, the best vantage point ashore, and reached the summit just as dawn broke.

He still hoped against all hope that his fears for his eldest son were unfounded. Perhaps Adam had, after all, spoken the truth to Luke Fletcher, that he had come off with the fireship crew, that he was safe aboard one of the other ships in the fleet. But Tom knew he was clutching at straws. He recalled Adam as a baby, a silent, staring child, the pride of his mother and father until his strange nature became apparent and his two brothers came along to provide marked contrasts with their eldest sibling. He recalled Adam as a boy, always drawn to the rantings of the most extreme hedge-preachers, always critical of the sermons and ceremonies of the established Church, always speaking out, always offending people. He recalled above all the sight of his son's face in that alehouse yard in Dover, and the stream of abuse he had unleashed against his father in the cabin of the *Eagle*. What unfathomable depth of hatred had Adam felt against him, and what terrible madness had that hatred engendered? Adam knew better than most how harshly scripture condemned the sin of self-killing, yet he seemed to have chosen that road rather than look upon his father an hour longer. Did he think that the flames would somehow purge him of both his and his father's sins, that sailing to his death in God's holy cause against the legions of the Antichrist would earn him forgiveness when he came before the judgement seat? There was no telling what might have passed through Adam's mind. Tom could only pray that wherever he had gone, he was at last content.

Even if Adam was now at rest, would he, Tom, ever be? The dark thoughts crowded in on him, and one question troubled him above all others.

Had he ever loved Adam, or at least the Adam of recent years, a man who conflated love with sin, who so evidently hated his fellow men, and was thus difficult beyond measure to love in any kind?

As he stood upon the white cliffs, Tom Stannard could not answer that question to himself. Instead, he wished only that he could have asked Adam's forgiveness, that last time they were together. He wished he could ask him now, that Adam would somehow appear beside him, smiling as had done so briefly when he was a small child, and that all was well.

But in life or in death, Adam Stannard would not bestow such forgiveness; that much was certain. So Tom mourned alone, praying that he would not also have to mourn his youngest boy, Jack, somewhere away in the distant battle fighting for queen and country aboard Drake's *Revenge*.

-

The pinnace had its single sail set, Jack delighting in his first command, Matt Bradlow at the helm. Astern, the battle had begun in earnest. *Revenge* and several of the other principal galleons were engaged with Medina Sidonia and the small cluster of ships around him, the culverins and demi-culverins thundering as the fleet closed to engage, drums and trumpets adding to the cacophonous din. Drake had given him a crew of four, including Bradlow at Jack's request, and the sullen, green-faced Fitzranulf commanded four soldiers who were unused to small craft and seemed intent only on not spewing up their victuals. The pinnace was a swift, sturdy craft, a little larger than those in which Jack had learned to sail off Plymouth and then off Dunwich, and the south-westerly carried it rapidly towards the nearest Flemish fishing boats.

Jack was in his element. This was infinitely superior to being cooped up below decks writing and rewriting endless lists, and it was even better than manning a gun on *Revenge*, where he was merely one of many with such a role. It was clear, though, that the opposite was the case for Fitzranulf, who kept directing hostile glances towards Jack. Why did the proud gentleman volunteer detest him so? Perhaps there was time for an answer to that question, and for a little sport too, before they came up with the fishermen.

'A fine day for a sail, Mister Fitzranulf!' said Jack, cheerily.

He could see the distaste in Fitzranulf's expression. On the *Revenge*, safe among his friends, he might have replied with some barb, but here, he was at once at the mercy of Jack Stannard, the man entrusted by Drake with command of the boat, and had to set his own example to the soldiers he nominally commanded. So his response, when it came, was begrudging but neutral.

'If you say so.'

The pinnace lurched. The wind was strengthening, and coming round a little more northerly. Fitzranulf and the soldiers gripped the wale more tightly and looked around in alarm.

'A gentle breeze and modest swell, no more than that,' said Jack. 'Matt Bradlow, here, and I have sailed out of Dunwich into a hundred times worse.'

Bradlow nodded.

'You are welcome to it,' said Fitzranulf, bitterly.

'If you dislike it so, then what brings you upon it?' said Jack.

'All men of birth and honour should fight to defend their country and their queen,' said Fitzranulf, albeit reluctantly. 'The enemy comes by sea, *ergo* we must fight upon the sea. It would not be my choice.'

Jack considered this. At bottom, Fitzranulf's reasoning was essentially his own, although he was hardly a man of birth. Were they really so different, then?

'Only men of birth and honour?'

'We are bred to it,' said Fitzranulf. 'It is our calling, just as this strange domain of waves appears to be yours. Lineage is all, as my father says – he is Somerset Herald, you know.'

A wave broke over the bow of the pinnace, soaking all within. Fitzranulf scowled and wiped himself down.

A herald of arms, Jack thought. So that was why Francis Drake, whose saying that gentlemen should haul and draw with mariners was a byword, tolerated the presence of such an idle, cunning creature aboard his flagship. Jack recalled his father telling him that in England, every yeoman sought above all else to be a gentleman, and to bear a coat of arms; every gentleman sought to be a knight, and to marry a rich heiress; every knight sought to be a lord, and to establish a dynasty that would endure for centuries; while every lord sought to marry the queen. He knew from his own observation that the College of Arms, where Fitzranulf's father worked, was one of the keys unlocking such upward movement. He recalled how animated the knights and gentlemen of the Suffolk Sandlings had been when the heralds had come round on a visitation a year or so before. Dusty pedigrees were fetched out of old trunks, or, some said, forged in their entirety, to be laid hopefully before the heralds. So Nicholas Fitzranulf's presence aboard *Revenge* was explained at last. Perhaps Sir Francis Drake secretly hoped to become a lord, and pandering to one of the herald's sons might prove as efficacious a way of achieving that end as defeating the Spanish Armada or presenting the queen with a vast treasure in prize money.

They were closing the nearest of the fishing boats. The Flemings attempted urgently to hoist their single sail and draw in their nets, but this effort to preserve their catch doomed any prospect of escape. Jack went forward into the bow of the pinnace and, in halting Flemish, hailed the fishermen across the water.

'Ho there! We're friends!'

A huge ruddy fellow who was presumably the boat's skipper stood up.

'You speak our tongue?'

'I am Jack Stannard of Dunwich. I've often sailed to Sluis, Ostend and Nieuwpoort.'

'And I to your Lowestoft,' said the Fleming cautiously. 'You can't want our fish, Englishman, and we have no money.'

'I say we're your friends,' said Jack, 'and so we are. We come under the commission of Sir Francis Drake, vice admiral for the queen's majesty.'

The name had the desired effect.

'Drake? You know Drake himself?'

'I know him,' said Jack. 'He gave me this order in person, not an hour past.'

The fishermen chattered rapidly among themselves, their voices so low and fast that Jack had no chance of following what they said even if the wind was not blowing and the roar of guns did not provide a constant backdrop.

'Then what service can we do for the famous Drake?' said the huge skipper.

'We seek news of Parma's army. Is it ready to come out? If the wind changes, can it sail directly for England?'

The skipper spat into the water. 'Tell the great Drake this, Englishman. Tell him Michel Gilbertszoon Cobbaut says it. The Dons here have fretted for weeks that there was no word from their Armada. Then when word came at last, the Armada was hard behind it. So they're not ready, Stannard of Dunwich. They're still in their billets, all the way inland nearly to Bruges. They can't sail today, nor tomorrow, nor this week, nor next week. They're not coming out, that's what I say, and my word is good.'

One of the Flemings suddenly stood up, pointed off to the north and shouted something Jack took to be akin to 'Sail ho!'

He turned and saw a pinnace coming down upon a beam reach. A flag that was rather too large for the boat flew from its stern, and that flag was Spanish.

'Bring her about, Matt Bradlow!' cried Jack. 'Steer directly for *Revenge*, and God willing we can outrun her!'

'Aye, aye, Master Stannard!'

Jack turned back to the Fleming, who was giving orders to his own crew to run before the wind and return to their own harbour.

'Farewell, Skipper Cobbaut. My thanks, and those of my queen and Sir Francis, for your intelligence.'

The Flemish skipper waved. 'God speed, Jack Stannard of Dunwich. Tell Sir Francis from me that we'll pray for him to beat the Dons, and for your queen to come and make us free.'

The two boats parted, and the *Revenge*'s pinnace set off on her new course. But the Spanish boat was making good headway, and it would be a close-run thing.

-

The rumour swept like wildfire through the lower deck of the *Girona*.

'Moncada is lost!'

Juan was one of the first to hear the dreadful words. As was always the way of such things, the rumour quickly became harder fact, reported downwards from the upper deck. The *San Lorenzo*, *capitana* of the galleasses, had somehow gone aground in the mouth of Calais harbour, and the English were falling on her as though she were carrion. Men redoubled their prayers. First the dreadful fear of the fireships; now this – was God testing the Armada prior to its ultimate victory, or had he already delivered his divine judgement against them? In any event, the *Girona*'s oars were clearly not yet needed. The slaves could feel the vessel turning using its sails alone, and through his oar hole Juan caught glimpses of other ships and of the coast of Flanders beyond. He could guess what was happening: once again Medina Sidonia was deploying his better ships, including the three surviving galleasses, into defensive wings, or horns, to protect the weaker units of the Armada. But to what purpose?

Juan reckoned he knew this coast better than any other man on the *Girona*, better than almost anyone in the entire fleet. There was no harbour anything like large enough to receive so many ships, and the deep draughts of the *urcas* and the larger galleons would prove fatal in the shallow shoal waters that stretched all the way to

Denmark. Moreover, a few short miles would bring them within the seas claimed by the rebel republic of the Dutch, who could deploy yet another fleet into the fight against them. But if the Armada could defeat that fleet as well as the English, then perhaps Parma would be able to come out after all. The invasion, the great crusade to return England to the true and holy Roman faith, might still succeed.

Spadaro, as was his wont, was praying intensely and aloud, but now he had a new prayer on his lips, one that certainly would not have been sanctioned by Fra Gordillo or Captain Spinola. He was praying that the *Girona*, like the *San Lorenzo*, would be driven into the shallows, close enough to shore for them all to get to land. Perhaps he thought their ankle shackles would miraculously fall away if he prayed hard enough.

Juan closed his eyes and began his own prayers, albeit in silence. The aim of his devotion was not that dissimilar to Spadaro's, though there was one important difference. If the English had taken the *San Lorenzo*, as the rumour had it, then perhaps her slaves were already free men. If God willed it, perhaps an English ship would capture *Girona* too, in which case Juan could become Jack Stannard once again, return to Dunwich and die in his bed surrounded by his family, a man at peace. So he prayed for capture, and any English man-of-war or captain would suffice to make his prayer a reality.

Even Francis Drake.

Thirteen

The Spanish pinnace would cut them off, and there was nothing for it but to fight. Thankfully the Dons numbered roughly the same as Jack's little crew, and Jack was confident that Matt Bradlow was the better helmsman. But were Fitzranulf and his men equal to the armoured, grim-looking soldiers in the enemy craft? Jack stole a glance at Fitzranulf, whose face was white. Seasickness, or something else? There was no time for doubts. He reached into his canvas bag at the stern, drew his sword from its scabbard, then took out a wheel-lock pistol his father had once bartered from a destitute soldier in Bruges. Steadying himself on the thwart, for the sea was getting choppier by the minute, he loaded and primed the weapon.

The Dons were shouting now, bellowing oaths in praise of *El Rey Felipe* and Santiago. Fitzranulf, whose duty it should have been, showed no inclination to reply in kind, so Jack stood up, waved his sword defiantly and roared, 'God for England and St George! God for Elizabeth!'

One of the Spanish soldiers also stood, and casually levelled an arquebus directly at Jack. For a moment Jack was staring down the barrel of the gun, realising that the fellow was well within range, and thought his last moment on earth had come. He saw the gun spark and heard its report, but in the same instant a wave struck both boats. The Spaniard's shot missed by a distance, and the man himself, less accustomed than Jack to standing in a small boat on a rough sea and already unbalanced by the recoil of his gun, toppled over the side. There was a brief glimpse of his hand clutching desperately but futilely for the boat, then his armour pulled him under.

Good, thought Jack. A slight shift of the odds in his favour.

But now the Dons put their helm over to come beam-on to the English pinnace. There was still no order from Fitzranulf, who seemed frozen upon the thwart, and one of his soldiers turned imploringly to Jack.

'Choose your man,' cried Jack, using a command he had heard his father employ against a Scottish pirate, 'and slice his guts out!'

With that he levelled his pistol, waited for the next uproll, then fired at the Spanish helmsman. The kick of the weapon sent a pain shooting through his arm and shoulder, but when the smoke dispersed, it was clear that the shot had missed. The Dons now returned fire with a pistol and two arquebuses, but their aim was equally erratic. The distance between the two boats was closing rapidly, though, and it would soon be impossible for even the poorest shot to miss.

At last Fitzranulf stirred himself. He lifted his own pistol – an obviously expensive and immaculately clean affair – and fired at the fellow who seemed to be his opposite number, the officer commanding the Spanish soldiers. To Jack's astonishment, his ball struck the man in his left shoulder, spinning him round and making him scream.

Fitzranulf must have registered the looks on the faces of Jack and the other men in the boat, for he gave an uncharacteristically modest smile and said, 'Hares. Irish hares. Best target practice in the world.'

The Spanish officer was clearly enraged by his wound and yelled an order at his helmsman, who came up even closer into the wind to lay their pinnace alongside Jack's. Away to windward, great English ships were closing the rearguard of the Spanish Armada, but the sea might have been empty for all Jack cared. The only battle was here and now, and it was to the death.

Two of the Dons levelled arquebuses, and Jack, Fitzranulf and the rest ducked behind the wale to avoid the incoming fire. But it was a ruse. The two hulls slammed together, and without hesitation, two more of the Spaniards leapt across into Jack's pinnace, one of them driving a long dagger straight through the neck of one of Fitzranulf's men as he did so. As Jack stood, he saw the other soldier coming straight for him. He could not outfight a man whose sunburned, scarred face suggested a veteran. He fell back, hoping others would come to his aid, but they were all engaged with their own battles. Blades clashed within and between the boats.

Jack had to act. If he did not, the advancing leering Don would go through him and cut down Matt Bradlow – and if he killed their helmsman, the entire crew would be lost, along with the intelligence it had gleaned, and the mission would be in vain.

Jack thrust at his opponent, but the Spaniard deftly swayed back, parrying as he did so, then swiftly executed a slashing cut that bit across Jack's right arm, causing him to grunt in pain. Once again he backed away – and tripped over the thwart, falling heavily against Matt Bradlow's legs. He looked up and saw Bradlow smile.

'For Dunwich, Master Jack,' he said, handing him his reloaded pistol.

Jack took the gun, levelled it and fired. At a range no greater than the height of a man, the force was sufficient to penetrate the Spaniard's breastplate. The Don looked down at the hole in his armour, at the red trickle emerging from it, and then fell dead to the deck.

But the battle for the pinnace was going badly. Two of Fitzranulf's soldiers and one of the sailors were dead, a second sailor badly wounded, and two Spaniards were pressing Fitzranulf himself right into the bow. Jack's sometime foe seemed to be wielding his sword competently enough, but his face was wet with tears and there was a damp stain at his groin.

'One chance, Matt,' said Jack.

'I see it, Master Jack. Ready about!' he shouted. 'Lee ho!'

With that, he put the tiller hard over. The pinnace pulled apart from the Spanish boat, the sail flapping uncontrollably as the hull went through the wind. The speed of the manoeuvre surprised both the Spanish helmsman and the Dons within the English boat, who had lost the support of their comrades and were facing a half-dozen reinvigorated Englishmen, who pressed forward against them. Both sides could see that the odds were now overwhelmingly in favour of Jack's men, for on its new tack the pinnace was rapidly closing a large English galleon, coming down fast upon a wind that was increasingly north-westerly. It was not the *Revenge*, but the banners of St George streamed from its tops and staffs. The helmsman of the Spanish pinnace, seeing that his cause was now irretrievably lost, put his tiller over and bore away, abandoning his fellow Dons to their fate. They, seeing that all hope was gone, flung their weapons to the deck and raised their hands in surrender.

Fitzranulf stepped forward, grinning like a cat.

'My first victory!' he cried. 'The day is mine, by God!'

Jack exchanged a glance with Matt Bradlow. They both smiled.

-

Willing hands helped Jack, Bradlow and the other men from the pinnace up onto the deck of the galleon. Fitzranulf came last, but he had taken a minor cut across the palm of his hand and struggled to grip the rope ladder.

'You, fellow!' he cried to a simply dressed mariner with distinctive red hair. 'Help me up here!'

The man looked at his shipmates around him, grinning broadly to one and all. Several of them laughed.

'Damn it, man,' said Fitzranulf, 'where's your captain? I'll have him flog you for disobeying a command from a superior!'

The red-haired man merely chuckled.

Jack saw a young, very well-dressed fellow with a fussy beard, clearly a gentleman but also something of a peacock, step forward and look over the ship's rail at the struggling Fitzranulf. A thought came to him – perhaps this was *Elizabeth Bonaventure* or *White Bear*, in which case this might be one of the young earls, Cumberland and Sheffield, who commanded those ships. He was keen above all to present his intelligence of Parma to this galleon's captain as soon as possible, then return to the *Revenge*. But the thought of presenting himself before such a high dignitary as an earl of England unnerved him in a way that talking almost as an equal to Sir Francis Drake did not.

'Well now,' said the peacock and putative earl, looking downward, 'and who may you be, sir, to tell the captain of this ship his business?'

'Captain? I am Nicholas Fitzranulf, gentleman volunteer under Sir Francis Drake.'

Finally Fitzranulf managed to haul himself onto the deck with his good hand. As he did so, he scowled malevolently at the red-haired mariner, then essayed an extravagant bow to the man he assumed to be the captain.

The peacock looked at him gravely, then burst out laughing.

'Mister Fitzranulf indeed. Well, well, you've given us all good sport this day! You see, I am not the captain. I am Sir Charles Blount, like yourself a gentleman volunteer, serving here aboard the *Rainbow*. That' – he pointed to the redhead – 'is the captain. Mister Fitzranulf, I name to you the most noble and honourable Lord Henry Seymour, Admiral of the Narrow Seas fleet by commission of the queen's most excellent majesty.'

–

A few minutes later, in the great cabin of the *Rainbow*, Seymour donned a rich scarlet gown that put his lordly status beyond any doubt at all. Talking was difficult, for the ship was alive with the sounds of battle; drums beat, trumpets blew, guns were run out, men shouted and cheered, for the English fleet was closing rapidly on the fleeing Armada and would be within range in a matter of minutes. Even so, Seymour listened gravely to Jack's intelligence, signalling to his clerk, the only other person in the cabin, to note this point or that.

When Jack had finished, the admiral looked closely at the young man standing opposite him.

'You have done well,' he said. 'I witnessed your fight in the pinnace. Your courage will be reported to the Lord Admiral and Sir Francis in the same dispatches that take them word of Parma, and the boat that goes to *Revenge* can carry you back so that you can receive Sir Francis's approbation in person. You have done your queen and country great service this day, John Stannard.'

'Thank you, my lord.'

Jack's heart could have burst with pride. To have done notable service for his queen and country... It was all he had ever wished for. To have witnessed the humiliation of Nicholas Fitzranulf in nearly the same moment was a gilding of the lily.

'But tell me. You are a Stannard of Dunwich? Son, perhaps, to Thomas Stannard of that town?'

'I am, my lord. My father captains the *Eagle of Dunwich*, under your command.'

Seymour appeared to be struggling to find words.

'Then you must prepare yourself for dire tidings, John Stannard, and pray to God for strength to bear them.'

With that, Seymour told him.

Fourteen

Juan was in Hell.

Fra Gordillo always talked of Hell in his homilies. According to him, it was a place of eternal pain and anguish, of flame, of sulphur and brimstone, of Satan's infernal army torturing each and every sinner, of Lucifer's whores flogging every lost soul, whether repentant or unrepentant. But no words of any priest, not even the Pope, could ever conjure a vision as terrible as the reality the slaves of the *Girona* were living through. One English ship after another came into Juan's limited view, their great guns spitting hellfire from their barrels, the stench surely more than equal to the sulphur and brimstone of the dark realm. The range was closer than it had ever been in the previous engagements, and the hull of the galleass shook as it both took hits and responded, the recoil of its guns rattling the timbers so hard that it seemed the vessel would split at its seams. Everywhere on the deck, men were screaming, crying, praying. Adil the Moor was bowing his head incessantly towards where he assumed Mecca ought to be, while Spadaro fingered his paternoster so desperately that his fingers began to bleed.

All around, ships were suffering. The *Girona* and her two surviving fellow galleasses, *Napolitano* and *Zúñiga*, the most nimble vessels in the entire Armada, were evidently being ordered hither and thither to relieve whichever ship seemed to be taking the worst pounding. For hour after long hour, the slaves stayed at their oars, sometimes called upon to row by an urgent beat of the drum, sometimes ignored as the vessel steered under sail alone and the guards went above to reinforce the men on deck. In either case, there was no call now for the singing voice of Juan Estandar; the Most Fortunate Armada had no song left to sing.

Juan could not make out which ships they were trying to support, for the wind had got up even more, the sea was choppy, and the smoke from the constant gunfire obscured much. Even so, those he was able to glimpse momentarily were evidently in dire straits. There was a galleon of the Levant squadron, riddled with shot from stem to stern, its masts and rigging in ruins, men running about its decks trying to put out small fires. An hour or so later, the *Girona* came up to an *urca* that was listing, clearly holed below the waterline, a large red stain that could only be blood plainly visible on its side. Juan glimpsed at least two ships well to leeward of the fleet, seemingly disabled and certain to run aground on the vast sandbanks of the Flanders coast. He saw one of the Biscay ships completely surrounded by four English galleons, which blasted away at her with impunity until she sank before *Girona* and other reinforcements could reach her. The screams of her doomed crew carried over even the relentless barrage of cannon fire to reach the ears of Juan and his fellow slaves.

All the while, though, the *Girona* herself escaped serious punishment. The ability to deploy the oars enabled her to get out of trouble easily, taking courses that no ship under sail alone could possibly follow, while the English seemed intent on hunting down the largest and most prestigious targets. Knowing his fellow countrymen,

Juan reckoned that this was because they expected them to contain richer plunder than a mere galleass, where the lower deck was filled with pitiful slaves rather than gold or silver bullion. He was sipping foul water from a jug being passed around the deck during a brief respite when the thought came to him that this would be true above all of his old rival Francis Drake, the tales of whose avarice had grown with his legend.

'*La Venganza*! The dragon is coming!'

The cry from the upper deck seemed to have been conjured by his very thought. The *Girona* began to turn to windward, still under sail alone. As she did so, Juan saw a galleon he recognised as the *Regazona*, her hull and rigging shattered by the English man-of-war that had just been lying alongside her. But that ship was now moving away and turning to engage the *Girona*.

Like the lookout above, Juan recognised the English ship from their previous encounter, further down the English Channel. It was the *Revenge*, and Francis Drake.

-

All around Jack Stannard, Englishmen were cheering and singing. The mighty Spanish Armada was in complete disarray, some of its best ships shattered, sinking or driven aground. At long last the English were getting close enough to make their superior gunfire count – close enough, in fact, to be even within the range of arquebuses, to see the faces of individual Dons on the decks of the ships they attacked, to hear their enemy's shouts, screams and prayers clearly across the water. The *Revenge* was like an avenging angel framed in timber, moving over the sea brandishing a fiery sword, and that sword was in the hand of the half-man, half-devil who stood upon her poop deck, laughing ecstatically and waving his gleaming blade as each shot struck Spanish timber or Spanish flesh. Taking their cue from Francis Drake, the crew of *Revenge* were like men possessed, firing faster than they ever had done, revelling in each triumph as a Spanish man-of-war or transport ship tried frantically to break away from the engagement.

It was a time of glorious victory, of an ecstasy surely akin to that which each of them would experience in Heaven. Yet in the midst of it all stood one man who did not share in the furious elation around him. Jack fired his gun, shouted encouragement half-heartedly to the men around him, and watched as the Dons suffered, but he felt nothing. It was as though he was somehow a prisoner in a different body, and that body was moving without his order.

His mind, though, was still filled with the awful words Lord Henry Seymour had spoken.

Adam was dead.

Dead in battle, dead aboard a ship; Adam, his brother, the least warlike and least nautical of them all. Dead seemingly by his own hand; Adam, his brother, the most God-fearing of them all.

Jack could not comprehend his own thoughts. He knew he should feel naught but grief, and some part of what he felt was grief indeed, or so he believed. But he had other thoughts too, and they were not worthy ones. Had he ever loved his brother? When they were children, Adam had bullied him and Peter mercilessly, until the ever-to-be-remembered day when Jack was at last old enough and big enough to unite with Peter to turn on their eldest sibling. When he was older, there was Adam's relentless castigation of Jack's supposed sins, his endless, pompous, tedious discourses from scripture to demonstrate that the two younger Stannard brothers were certainly damned.

'Are you well, Master Jack?'

He became aware of Matt Bradlow's voice. He had told Bradlow of his loss, and although he had expressed conventional sympathies, Jack knew that Bradlow could be counted among the many Dunwich men who, over the years, had come to detest Adam Stannard.

Time to put grief, or whatever it was that Jack truly felt, to one side.

'Well enough, Matt Bradlow.'

He lifted his eyes from the deck, where they had been fixed for God knew how long, and looked all around. The *Revenge* was moving away from its most recent opponent, a big flagship from one of the Armada's Italian squadrons, and the brief respite provided an opportunity for men to rest, drink ale and eat some bread and cheese. At every point of the compass, ships flying the flag of St George were battering their opponents, always staying just far enough out of range so the feared Spanish troops had no opportunity to board. Everywhere, too, the sea was filled with the carnage of battle. The waters between the ships of the two fleets were filled with wreckage – spars, great chunks of timber, torn remnants of sails and flags, ropes and tackle, the bloated, bloodied bodies of dead men still floating upon the surface, seabirds feasting greedily upon their carcasses. Small boats braved the open water, carrying orders between flagships, just as one had carried Jack from the *Rainbow* back to the *Revenge* earlier in the day. The sea was even rougher than it had been then, the wind north-westerly and blowing strongly, giving yet more of an advantage, pressing the Dons ever further towards the deadly coast of Flanders. Adam Stannard would have taken it as convincing proof that God truly was on England's side.

There were shouts from the poop deck, men pulled hard on ropes to shift the sails, and the bow of the *Revenge* began to turn. It seemed that Francis Drake had selected a new target, and Jack saw it at once. A galleass, this time, flying the banners of Naples. Relatively unscathed, by the looks of it.

Francis Drake and the *Revenge* would alter that.

-

Tom Stannard arrived in Sandwich in the middle of the afternoon, having taken four hours to walk there from Dover. All the while, he heard the distant rumble of gunfire. The English fleet was engaged in a battle to the death with the Spanish Armada, that much was certain. But Tom had no thoughts of what victory or defeat might bring. Adam was gone, his ship was gone, and the only thing he could think of was to get home, to get back to Dunwich, to pray for his lost son in St Peter's church as he had once prayed there for his lost father. There had been talk in Dover of a ship lying at Sandwich that was bound for Lowestoft and then Hull, and Tom intended to buy passage aboard her if he could.

As he neared the south gate through the town wall, though, he could see that it was guarded by a half-dozen sturdy fellows with a variety of weapons, two of them clad in breastplates and one other in a battered rusting helmet.

'Ho there, fellow!' cried the one in the helmet, evidently the leader of the small troop. 'The town's closed. Go back to where you came from, or on to Margate for all I care!'

'Is that a fit welcome for a fellow Englishman who's been with Lord Harry Seymour's fleet?'

The fellow in the helmet frowned. 'Lord Harry's fleet is over yonder,' he said, waving his hand vaguely towards the distant gunfire. 'Why ain't you with it? Deserter, are ye? Traitor to your queen and country?'

One of the men with him lowered his ancient-looking bill towards Tom.

'For God's sake,' he protested, 'I was master of the *Eagle of Dunwich*, taken up as a fireship for the attack on the Dons at Calais!'

'Fireship?' said the leader, open-mouthed. 'There was a fireship attack?' He looked at his companions in arms. These were clearly no fighting men, merely a rag-tag local watch. God alone knew what Parma's veteran regiments would do to them, or to the thin, ancient, crumbling walls of Sandwich.

'There was,' said Tom. 'I'll tell you of it, and give you coin to buy ale, on condition you then direct me to the *Swallow* of Lowestoft.'

As he told the story, and even more so as he walked through the streets of Sandwich a few minutes later, it occurred to Tom that he could have told his audience anything at all and they would have believed him. Indeed, for all the town's bovine guards knew, Tom could easily have been a Spanish spy, or else one of those inveterate English papists, like his sister, who wished the Armada to succeed. But he was plausible, he smiled, he gave each of the guards a coin, and in a trice he was within one of England's Cinque Ports, once the bulwarks of the kingdom's defences.

Somehow he doubted if a Spaniard could have got within the walls of Cadiz quite as easily.

-

The larboard demi-culverins of the *Revenge* belched flame and iron. Jack saw at least a half-dozen shot strike the galleass, mainly in her sails and rigging. The Spanish vessel was lower in the water than the English galleon, and the range was now so close that Drake's gunners could not depress their barrels sufficiently to fire into the hull. The galleass replied, but its rate of fire was slower, and although its guns were able to fire into *Revenge*'s hull, they were fewer and lighter than their English opponents. But the upper deck of the galleass was lined with heavily armed and armoured Spanish troops, and their arquebus fire was intense. One of the men next to Jack took a ball directly in his forehead. As he slumped back, Jack went to support him, stooping just in time to feel the rush of another arquebus ball pass his shoulder, through the space where his head had been a moment earlier.

No time to mourn Adam now.

'Hold your stations, lads!' he cried. 'Hold, and give them a taste of English fire!'

He took up one of the arquebuses stacked against the base of the foremast, already primed by two of the ship's boys, steadied himself on the wale, selected a black-clad target and fired.

A miss, dammit – and the fellow seemed to be a priest, too, casting benedictions over the troops around him. How Jack wished to send a papist to hell to atone for his brother's death, and a priest would have been doubly suitable.

The hull of the *Revenge* shook once more as the great guns fired again. Part of the starboard quarter of the galleass seemed to burst into a shower of splinters. Three bodies were flung into the air, seemingly suspended there for a moment before falling into the sea. But once again the damage to the Spanish vessel was relatively minor, and with the wind in the wrong quarter to go through the favoured figure-of-eight manoeuvre, Drake responded by having the *Revenge* fall away a little to leeward, opening the range.

The gun crews reloaded with all haste, then knelt expectantly by their guns, many of them looking astern for the order from Drake. The admiral seemed unusually still and silent, as though he was in prayer.

At last he looked up and called out to his men.

'This is for all those good Englishmen who have perished at the hands of King Philip's minions! Wait for the downroll, boys, make every shot count, and send the Dons to Hell! Steady… steady… *Give fire!*'

-

The ball struck the starboard side of *Girona*'s oar deck, instantly killing the man who occupied the equivalent place to Juan on that side. A large shard of timber flew across the deck and drove into the chest of Spadaro, who was thrown against a bulkhead. He was quite evidently dead before his body settled on the deck. A fellow three rows forward of Juan got to his feet and turned round, revealing that the left half of his face was missing. The man next to him screamed as he grasped at the bloody stump of what remained of his left arm. Juan went to Spadaro and made the sign of the cross over his body.

'One blessing, at any rate,' said Owen Gravell, putting a hand on Jack's shoulder, 'he's free of this now.'

'True,' said Juan, fighting away the tears. 'The harshest kind of freedom, though.'

An under-officer whom Juan did not recognise came onto the deck, attended by half a dozen soldiers. Was Cala dead, then?

'All hands!' cried the officer in a strong Galician accent. 'Clear the deck of dead and wounded, then stand by to deploy oars!'

With that, the upper deck guns of *Girona* fired in retaliation, shaking the entire hull. The broadside was more ragged than that of the English, Juan thought. He could see the *Revenge* through the great hole in the starboard side, and it seemed as though the galleass's fire had not damaged her at all. Perhaps Drake really was protected by Satan and witchcraft, as the more superstitious of the Dons had it.

The soldiers moved up and down the deck, striking out at those they considered to be too slow in shifting the corpses and the wounded into positions where they could not interfere with the rowing. Juan shuffled back to his place, but the officer came across to him. He was a young fellow in his middle twenties, of an age with Juan's grandsons Adam and Peter Stannard.

'You are the one called Estandar? The old man who sings?'

'I am he, *señor*.'

'Captain Spinola's direct order, *anciano*. You are to sing—'

The *Revenge* fired again. By some fluke, or perhaps by the dark forces that watched over Francis Drake, a great shot entered through the newly made hole in the *Girona*'s side. One moment the young officer stood close by Juan; the next moment he did not. Or rather, his upper body did not. His legs and the bottom part of his torso remained upright for the briefest of instants, a hellish mass of entrails spewing out, before falling to the deck several feet from his upper half, which had been driven against the larboard side.

There was a moment's terrible silence as soldiers and slaves alike looked at the dreadful sight. Then, without a word, the slaves resumed the business of hauling the oars outboard.

Juan wondered if he should send word to Captain Spinola to find out exactly what he was meant to sing. But the captain would have more important priorities, and Juan already had a song in his mind.

-

'Damned cheats!' yelled Francis Drake. 'Stay and fight like honest men!'

The galleass had deployed its oars and was hauling in its sails. Its bow turned slowly north-west, directly into the wind, where the *Revenge* could not follow it. For a fleeting moment it was directly stern-on and an ideal target for a raking broadside. But most of the gun crews on *Revenge* were still reloading after their last salvo, and only two demi-culverins were able to fire in time. Both shots struck home on the fragile stern of the galleass, but without supporting fire, they did little harm. Slowly but inexorably the galleass pulled away and was soon out of range of the English guns.

Drake shouted a few more oaths but was then all business again, giving the orders for the *Revenge* to turn to leeward. There were many more tempting targets within the desperate defensive wall of the Spanish Armada, and nearly all of them were not equipped with oars.

As the galleass rowed away, directly into the wind, and just before it moved out of hailing distance, Jack Stannard heard the strangest sound. Through the noise of battle, the blowing of the breeze, the cracking of sails, the swelling and breaking of the sea, the shouts of men – through all of it, he could just hear a single voice carrying across the water from the enemy vessel. It was a man singing. His words seemed to be in English, and the tune was well known to Jack. Strangely, though, it was a song he had only ever heard sung in Dunwich or the immediate vicinity.

Magnus the emperor,
He came to Dunwich town,
There he set his mighty throne,
St Felix, pray him crown!

Jack looked around and chided himself. It could only be a trick of the wind.

Fifteen

Meg stood naked in the principal room of Sir Nevill Bourchier's house. The man himself was absent, as was only proper, but she could still sense the malevolent eyes and ears of her sister, somewhere not very far away.

Three women circled her, assessing her as though she were a prize heifer at a mart. She had expected the jury of matrons; her aunt Agatha had once been inspected by one, very many years before. The purpose of the procedure was to examine the suspected witch for telltale scratches or other marks that would supposedly prove that the Devil had fornicated with her, or else that satanic imps had suckled blood from her breasts. Meg knew all that, and mocked it. But nothing could have prepared her for the shame of standing naked before these three unknown women, all of them well dressed and evidently respectable goodwives or matrons, as the law demanded. None of them had given their names, for a suspected witch was exempt from social niceties. Two of them were older than Meg: the one who seemed to be the leader was short and round, with a shock of frizzed white hair, while the other was taller and stooped, and had straight hair that still contained ample traces of its original dark brown. The third woman was much younger, no more than thirty, with a kindly face that a certain kind of man would find beautiful. She was very quiet, perhaps overawed by the occasion or by the two older women.

'You have a good body for a woman of your age,' said the short woman. Meg made no reply. 'Aye, the Devil would still enjoy taking that body, I don't doubt.'

'Are we just going to look at her?' asked the younger woman, and Meg wondered if she had misjudged her.

'No,' replied the short woman, 'it is our duty to search her thoroughly. Everywhere, remember.'

Meg took a breath, for Agatha had warned her of this.

Fingers began to prod at her flesh, pulled her ears to check behind them, tugged at her hair to examine her scalp, then lifted her eyelids to examine their undersides. The stooped woman made her open her mouth and looked within, then probed at her tongue and the sides and roof of her mouth, making Meg gag. The short woman lifted her breasts, moving closer to look at them very closely. The younger woman examined her feet, then her legs, then her private parts, pushing Meg's thighs and buttocks aside.

Meg lost track of time. She could bear the humiliation before these women whom she did not know and would probably never see again, but the thought that Mary was certainly watching from some concealed place, gloating over her shame, was nearly too much to bear.

At last the three women moved away, still looking at her appraisingly.

'You bear no marks,' said the short one. 'We shall report as much to Sir Nevill.'

She and the stooped woman began to move away, but the younger one remained where she was, staring intently at Meg, who was unable to avoid her gaze. Now that she studied her features closely, she could swear that the woman reminded her of someone…

'Wait,' said the young woman. Her colleagues turned and looked at her curiously. 'No marks? On a woman of this age, who has lived roughly upon a heath for many years? Let's not be so hasty. Sisters, I ask you this – would not the Devil, the king of Hell, cunningly conceal his marks upon the body of his favoured concubine? We all know his satanic power. Would he not be able – aye, likely – to make any marks upon this witch's flesh disappear for the duration of our examination?'

The two older women looked at each other uncertainly.

'That is madness!' said Meg, unable to restrain herself any longer.

The younger woman smiled. 'Proof of the Devil's intercourse with you is madness? You condemn yourself, witch. Sir Nevill will be delighted to obtain such clear evidence to send up to the assizes.'

Meg looked again at the implacable face of her adversary. The features were so familiar…

'What is your name, Goodwife?' she asked.

The younger woman laughed. 'It is not for you, the accused, to ask me my name. And anyway, it will mean nothing to you, the name of Goodwife Martha Cawston.'

'But what was the name of your father?'

Martha Cawston's expression remained merry, but there was a sudden coldness to her eyes.

'I think you know who my father was, Margaret de Andrade, formerly Stannard.'

With that, she turned, joined her fellow matrons and left the room, leaving Meg to snatch for her shift. But as she covered her nakedness, she nearly fainted from the shock of her discovery.

The eyes were the same, as were the cheekbones. She remembered the last time she had seen those features: on a man's face, amid the ruins of the Dunwich Blackfriars some twenty years before. The face was that of her family's bitterest enemy, Stephen Raker of Southwold, a man in whom that town's ancient hatred of Dunwich was united with a very specific hatred of the Stannard family, especially Meg's father Jack. For another twenty years before that, Jack Stannard had been responsible for the execution of Raker's father.

No, there could be no doubt of it. Martha Cawston was Stephen Raker's daughter.

-

Perhaps I truly should have been a soldier, thought Peter Stannard.

Admittedly, the conditions in the camp at Tilbury left much to be desired. There were too few tents, so like most of his fellows he was compelled to lie upon the open ground. The food provided by the quartermasters was beyond description, and men with the wits and skill to catch rats and rabbits were looked upon as gods. The ale stank.

Then there were Peter's fellow soldiers. If this was the last defence against Parma, he thought, then Englishmen might as well start learning Spanish. Cut-throats and cripples seemed to form the backbone of the army. The regimental colonel was a chinless young courtier who appeared not yet to have begun shaving. He was rarely seen, and most of his captains seemed to be cut from similar cloth. There was one veteran, though, a man who had fought in Flanders under the Earl of Leicester himself. Peter made every effort to avoid this officer, who would be able easily to expose his tale of having fought at Zutphen and seen Sir Philip Sidney die.

As it was, the sergeant with immediate responsibility over Peter, Bennet Barnes and the four-score others in his company was an amiable old fellow from Norfolk who had never been outside his native county before and seemed to regard Tilbury as the end of the earth. He was impressed by how Peter wielded a weapon, little realising that his expertise derived from play-fighting upon the stage, and by his ability to declaim an order, an easy matter for an actor accustomed to keeping the attention of an audience. So in short order the fictitious Peter Dowling found himself with an acting rank of corporal, the actual holder of that rank lying in one of the sick tents and like to die.

If only his brothers could see him now, Peter thought.

He and Bennet Barnes were attempting to train a score or so of the least likely soldiers in basic pike-craft when he became aware of a loud cheering at the other end of the camp.

'What's afoot, d'you think?' asked Barnes.

'Mayhap the Armada's been sunk,' said Peter. 'Mayhap we can all go home.'

'Amen to that, Corporal Dowling, amen indeed.'

A boy was running towards their part of the camp, bawling something about the queen. Peter reached out, grabbed him by the arm and swung him round.

'Well then, lad,' he said, 'what's the news? What's this of the queen?'

The boy, a thin, mouse-haired child, was breathless but excited.

'The queen's coming! She's coming downriver in her barge! She'll be here today!'

'What's your authority, boy?'

'Authority? What authority's needed? It's what they're saying over by the fort, so it must be true!'

The boy shook himself free from Peter's grip and ran off, shouting again that the queen herself would be there among them that very day.

'Is it true, d'you think?' said Bennet Barnes.

'Aye, it's true,' said a woman's voice. 'That's what they say among the camp followers, and they know the truth of everything.'

Peter turned and was astonished as never before. There stood his Arabella, as large as life, smiling impudently at him. She was attracting a fair measure of attention from the troops over whom Peter had nominal charge. Men nudged each other, grinned, and made obscene gestures with their fingers. Bennet Barnes's jaw hung low.

Peter went to her, took her by the arm and led her out of earshot, to a chorus of loud and lewd advice from his men.

'Great Christ in Heaven, woman, what are you doing here?' he demanded in a low voice.

'"Oh my love, what pleasure bursts in my heart to see you stand before me." I'm happy to see you too, Peter.'

'This is a dangerous place!'

'From what I've seen thus far, the only danger to me might come from a drunken young blade who can't keep his prick within his breeches. I'm well used to fending off that sort, believe me. Besides, I reckon there's less danger here than there'd be if I'd stayed in Bromley. Enough folk at the palace knew of Henry Ballard's lust for me.'

'I thought you'd go to London.'

She grinned. 'And miss my chance to see the queen?'

'But you're among the camp followers, woman! Base whores! Lewd wenches!'

'Oh, men,' she said impatiently. 'A woman is a camp follower so she must be a whore. I expected better of you, Peter Stannard. Most of them are respectable goodwives, following their husbands into danger. Aye, there are whores enough, it's true, but they don't need to parade their wares – few of the men have enough coin to pay for them anyway. So I've taken to your trade, and am acting a part.'

'What, the part of a whore?'

'Hardly. The respectable and demure wife of a sergeant under Sir John Norreys. You've taken my name, so I've taken yours.' She essayed a curtsey. 'Goodwife Stannard at your humble service.'

'You brazen doxy! Pray you don't get found out. For one thing, there really is a Sergeant Stannard, albeit not under Black Jack. My uncle Harry. He's one of the yeomen, and likely to be among the queen's guard.'

'Better yet, then,' said Arabella. 'It seems I play the part of your aunt. Well, nephew, shall we stand here and talk all day, or find a quiet place where we may commit incest?'

Nonplussed, Peter followed her.

-

Juan Estandar stood upon the deck of the *Girona*. He did not look at her consorts in what had once been named the Most Fortunate Armada. Those that were left, those that had not perished in the waters off Flanders as *San Lorenzo, San Mateo* and *Maria Juan* had done, were now in good formation again, but they were heading north, every inch taking them further from any prospect of uniting with Parma's army and landing it in England. Nor did Juan need to look astern, southward, at the distant sails of the English fleet – still in pursuit after forcing the Armada away from the shores of Flanders. He did steal a glance at Captain Spinola, pacing his quarterdeck. Like Medina Sidonia and his lowliest powder boy, they both knew the unspoken truth that was now common knowledge in every mess in every ship in the Spanish fleet. The only course left to the Armada was to attempt to return home to Spain, but the English and the prevailing south-westerly winds prevented them from turning back to take the most direct and relatively easy passage by way of the English Channel. No, only one route lay open to the Armada now, and that was by way of the north coast of Scotland and the west coast of Ireland.

As Jack Stannard, Juan had sailed those seas, and knew what awaited the Spaniards. He doubted very much if Medina Sidona, Spinola and the rest of them did.

For now, though, his eyes and thoughts were turned elsewhere. *Girona*, being so versatile, was one of the guard ships assigned to the windward flank of the Armada, and as such was westerly of the rest of the fleet, well within sight of the English coast. Juan screwed up his eyes, wishing that somehow he could project his sight several miles to see the shore more clearly. He prayed that Gordillo, Cala or any other of the other petty gods of the *Girona* would not interrupt him, for he needed to concentrate more intently than he had done in twenty years.

Was that tiny, distant dark shape upon the land Orford Castle? Two windmills north of it, though. Had they been there when he last sailed this so-familiar coast, over twenty years before? He could not remember.

Still the Armada edged northward, nearly beam-on to the stiff breeze from the south-west. A beacon was blazing near what could only be a church tower – was that Aldeburgh?

Juan could feel his heart beating faster in his chest, and he began to recite the *Ave Maria* to himself.

There was the cliff. He was sure of it; on this coast, the coast of his native Suffolk, there was nothing else it could be. Dunwich Cliff, as familiar to him as the backs of his hands. It looked different. Had more of the town gone, then? But there – yes, there, that could only be the tower of All Saints! It still stood, thanks be to God, but of course, it was so far inland that it would stand until Doomsday, even if the rest of his home town was lost to the sea. All Saints. Beneath its shadow, his beloved Alice slept for eternity, God rest her beautiful soul.

Juan realised he was weeping. He had not wept in twenty years, but in his heart he was with Alice, he saw Tom and Meg as children once again, and he thought he could hear the bells of all the lost churches, deep beneath the waves…

'The nest of viperous heretics will still fall.' It was Fra Gordillo, standing behind him. How dare such a creature destroy Juan's moment? Destroy his precious thought of his dear Alice? 'It will take another year or two, maybe even ten, but the king will build another Armada, a mightier Armada. By then, Juan Estandar, even you will be long dead and unable to sail with it, to be a curse upon it, to prevent its glorious and inevitable triumph!'

Juan turned. The priest's expression was a snarl, his eyes wide with pure hatred. There was nothing Juan wished to say to such a creature. Instead, he weighed what he was about to do. Thomas Ryman would have disapproved, he was certain of that.

Suddenly, but with extraordinary force for such an old man, he punched Gordillo full on the chin. The priest staggered back and fell to the deck. As the nearest soldier lowered his halberd towards him, Juan grinned. The long years had fallen away. He was Jack Stannard of Dunwich again. He had seen Dunwich Cliff and the tower of All Saints, he had been with Alice in his thoughts and within sight of her burial place in body, and he had struck a blow for his country.

Now, at last, he could die, and die a happy man.

Sixteen

The queen.

Elizabeth, by the Grace of God. Gloriana. The Virgin Queen.

For Peter Stannard, she was a distant glint of sunlight upon a well-polished cuirass. His regiment was about halfway back in the massed ranks of the army, well behind the veteran regiments, and all he caught were occasional glimpses through the forest of helmets, pikes and arquebuses. The queen had arrived the previous day, made a perfunctory review of the troops around the fort and the church upon the hill, then retired to a local gentleman's house, where she spent the night. That morning, there had been a demonstration from some of the best regiments – Peter's, of course, not being counted among their number – with cavalry, musketeers, pikemen, billmen and archers mounting mock attacks to demonstrate how they would destroy Parma's veterans. It was all very noisy, drums and trumpets adding to the din of the mock battle. Perhaps the queen was impressed by it, but those in the newly raised units, who could see hardly anything, merely spent the morning getting bored.

Once the display was done, Elizabeth rode through the lines of her regiments, getting ever closer to where Peter and his companions were shuffling into some semblance of attention. At last he could see her clearly. She was riding upon a white horse, the sword of state borne before her by the Earl of Ormond. She wore a silver cuirass over a white jacket, and had pearls in her hair. Behind her came a page carrying a cushion, upon which was a silver helmet with white plumes. Alongside her rode the earls of Leicester and Essex, her former and present lovers if the more scurrilous rumours aired around the campfires were to be believed. Leicester, the commanding general of the army, looked very ill, his face white and lined with pain. Red-coated guards flanked the royal party, and Peter assumed that one of them would be his uncle Harry, the only one of his father's half-siblings for whom he had any time. Two Stannards in attendance upon England's queen; had there ever been such a day in the family's history?

And had there ever been such a queen? Men talked of Cleopatra, the Empress Theodora, Eleanor of Aquitaine, Isabella of Castile, but he doubted if any of them could have appeared as glorious and as martial as Elizabeth of England did that day at Tilbury.

This was theatre at its purest, and Peter was looking upon a sublime mastery of it.

The royal party halted; the queen seemed to raise herself up in the saddle, then lifted a gloved hand. It was clear she was beginning to speak. Peter strained to hear, but it was difficult. Only those in the front few rows stood a chance of hearing her clearly. Behind that, there was the inevitable low hubbub of a crowd of Englishmen assembled together, even though the regiments were meant to be at attention. No man actually spoke – the sergeants and corporals, including Peter himself, were strict on that, but their own murmured orders and imprecations probably created more noise than if they said nothing. Then there were the sounds of men shuffling from foot to foot, of clanking scabbards, of farting and belching, of the south-westerly breeze cracking flags and tent canvas.

So Peter Stannard listened as hard as he could and caught some words, sometimes even parts of sentences. It did not help, of course, that the queen was a woman and thus not able to project her voice as well as a man could, especially a man trained to the stage. But her words were clearly making an impression on the soldiers in the front rows, who were rapt.

At last she settled back into her saddle and rode on, to unrestrained cheers from those in the front ranks.

'What did she say?' said one man in Peter's troop.

'Couldn't hear a fucking word,' said another.

A memory came unbidden to Peter Stannard. He recalled lying in bed with Arabella at the Bell in Bromley after one of their first and particularly vigorous bouts of lovemaking. She was explaining how much she loved the theatre, and actors, and the very art of acting. She bemoaned the fact that she could not be an actor herself, as she longed for nothing more.

'No woman may perform upon the stage,' said Peter, with more loftiness than befitted his entirely naked state.

'Oh nonsense,' said Arabella. 'I know of one woman who does precisely that, and plays a man to boot.'

'Really. Oh really. And who, pray, is this unnatural abomination? This empty codpiece strutting the boards? This brazen strumpet who somehow avoids the gaze of the Lord Chamberlain?'

Arabella grinned. 'Why, the queen of course. Does she not act upon the greatest stage of all, and play the part of a man – of a king?'

The men around Peter were still complaining about hearing nothing of what the queen had said. An idea came to him. True, it was bold and impudent, but he had faith in himself. Until the last year or so, he had always taken women's parts and performed them more than credibly if Rob Wasdale was to be believed. Well then. If the queen could play a king, Peter Stannard could play the queen.

'Good fellows!' he cried. 'Brave soldiers of England! Hearken to me, to Corporal Dowling!' He raised his voice as though declaiming to the highest gallery during a downpour.

'Who's that jackanapes?' shouted one fellow.

'Hear me, my friends!' said Peter, raising his hands to silence his audience. 'I have especially keen hearing – aye, notably good! It's been a gift since birth. I heard the queen's words, as God is my judge! Be silent, and I will repeat what she said!'

He saw a number of men, including captains and sergeants, looking at him suspiciously, but the army was no longer at attention and the rear ranks were already dispersing back to their makeshift quarters. Bennet Barnes, standing close by, was looking at him incredulously.

'Go on then!' cried another of the corporals.

Peter saw a powder barrel over by one of the pieces of field artillery and climbed onto it. More and more men turned to look at him, and their ranks fell silent. It was a larger audience than that which the queen had actually addressed, he reckoned.

'These are the words of our queen! This is what Elizabeth, sovereign lady of England, has said in this place, on this day!'

'Get on with it!'

Peter paused for dramatic effect, his eyes scanning his audience and demanding perfect silence. He took the deep breath essential to his delivery. Then, very quietly so that all would need to strain to hear, he began.

'My loving people! We have been persuaded' – the 'royal we', always important to remember when playing royals – 'we have been persuaded by some that are careful of our safety to take heed how we commit ourselves to armed multitudes, for fear of treachery; but I assure you I do not desire to live to distrust my faithful and loving people. Let tyrants fear!' There were cheers at that. Peter raised his right hand to hush the crowd and continued. 'I have always so behaved myself that, under God, I have placed my chiefest strength and safeguard in the loyal hearts and goodwill of my subjects; and therefore I am come amongst you, as you see, at this time, not for my recreation and disport, but being resolved, in the midst and heat of the battle, to live and die amongst you all; to lay down for my God, and for my kingdom, and my people, my honour and my blood, even in the dust.'

Now the cheering was unconfined, men shaking their weapons triumphantly in the air. Peter smiled. If Parma came now, these men would drive him back into the sea in minutes.

He raised his hand again. There was an immediate hush, which enabled him to speak more gently, slowly turning his head from side to side to look into the eyes of his audience.

'I know I have the body of a weak, feeble woman,' he said. Tellingly, only one fellow sniggered at that, and he appeared to be in drink. 'But I have the heart and stomach of a king, and of a king of England too, and think foul scorn that Parma or Spain, or any prince of Europe, should dare to invade the borders of my realm; to which rather than any dishonour shall grow by me, I myself will take up arms, I myself will be your general, judge, and rewarder of every one of your virtues in the field.'

Another burst of cheering. He could see that some men had tears in their eyes, and that more and more of the troops in the rear rows who had been drifting away were coming back, the news having apparently spread of this singular corporal's claim to know the exact words the queen spoke.

'I know already,' Peter continued, 'for your forwardness you have deserved rewards and crowns, and we do assure you on a word of a prince, they shall be duly paid. In the meantime, my lieutenant general shall be in my stead, than whom never prince commanded a more noble or worthy subject…'

There were no ribald comments about the quite obviously dying lieutenant general, Leicester, and his alleged sport in the queen's bed when they were both younger. Peter Stannard had his audience in the palm of his hand. Time to raise his voice and build to the final peroration.

'…not doubting but by your obedience to my general, by your concord in the camp, and your valour in the field, we shall shortly have a famous victory over these enemies of my God, of my kingdom, and of my people!'

The roar could be heard in Flanders, or so it seemed to Peter. The stamping of feet and pikestaffs on the ground seemed to make the very earth shake. Men crowded around him, tears streaming down their cheeks. Two insisted that he climb upon their shoulders, and when he had done so, they carried him triumphantly through the massed ranks. Amid the blur of faces, Peter noted only a handful of individuals. There was Bennet Barnes, looking at him as though he was the risen Christ. There was a black-cassocked clergyman of about his own age who seemed to be writing frantically with a pencil in a small leather-bound notebook. And there, at the back of the crowd, was a small gaggle of women that included Arabella in its ranks. She had her arms folded in front of her and was looking at him as though he were a naughty child caught in the act of stealing something.

No matter. Peter Stannard knew he had just delivered the greatest performance of his life, and that he would never have such an audience again.

-

The distant bell of Tilbury church tolled five of the afternoon. Peter Stannard's regiment had just finished a late meal of barely edible broth, and yet more drilling would shortly commence. As men ate, there had been much talk of the queen's speech as relayed by their very own corporal. Most had been enthralled by his performance and complimented him on it, but a few claimed that he had made up the words, while others, generally the older sort, expressed regret that Elizabeth did not have rather more than just the heart and stomach of a king, longing for a man to lead them into battle as Harry the Fifth had done at Agincourt. Peter was tired of such carping and even of the congratulations of those who had revelled in his, or rather the queen's, words. He longed for nothing more than to create a plausible excuse to go off in search of Arabella and seek out a more comfortable location for fornication than the small space between barrels of bread and cheese that they had appropriated on the previous day.

Out of the corner of his eye he saw a sudden flash of red and heard a gruff voice growl, 'Make way there!' A firm hand grasped his shoulder and swung him round.

'You,' said a square-faced, grey-bearded, heavily built man of forty years or thereabouts, attired in a morion helmet and an immaculate red tabard adorned with the royal lion crest. 'Impersonating the queen, eh? Men have been hanged for less, Peter Stannard.'

The men around the campfire stared open-mouthed at the spectacle, then frowned at each other on hearing this newcomer address their corporal by an unfamiliar name.

Peter met the newcomer's uncompromising gaze.

'Well met, uncle,' he said.

Seventeen

'You're damnably lucky, lad,' said Harry Stannard to his nephew as they walked through the camp. 'Everyone around the queen was in good spirits after the success of her speech, and my Lord of Essex reckoned that if you'd conveyed Her Majesty's words to even more of the army, so much the better. If the words you spoke truly were hers, of course. Essex's chaplain was meant to be writing it down but got caught short, then found himself trapped in the throng on the way back from the jakes. So he copied down your speech, because he was closer to you than to her. But what you said was what she said word for word, was it not, nephew?'

'Word for word, uncle. Upon my honour as a Stannard.'

Harry Stannard made a strange kind of snorting noise. 'Aye, well, the honour of the Stannards has been a movable feast over the years. Even more so in my grandfather the leper's day and before, or so I was told. But as I say, you're lucky, lad. Lucky that I heard your voice from a distance when you were being the queen, and recognised it. Lucky that I heard the great ones talking about this insolent corporal. Lucky that I sought you out before anyone else did.'

'I'm grateful, uncle.'

'As you should be. But you of all men a soldier, Peter Stannard? How did that come to pass, eh?'

Peter considered telling him the truth, but he did not entirely trust Harry Stannard. The brood of his grandfather's second wife was cut from a very different cloth to the two children of the first marriage. Instead, he simply shrugged.

'I could tell you it was to do my duty for queen and country, but I doubt you'll believe that. No, it was a woman.'

Harry laughed. 'Ah. Of course it was. The reason why half the army is here, I reckon. Running away from this woman of yours, or trying to impress her with warrior airs?'

'More the latter than the former.'

'Well, you'll have little hope of making an impression. The word is that the army'll be discharged shortly, maybe even in a day or two. The Armada is sailing north, they say, away from England. Parma won't come out now, and Burghley won't want to pay us for a minute longer than he has to. If he pays you at all, that is. The most recently raised regiments will be the last to be paid, that's for certain. The way it always is in the army.'

'That's of no concern, uncle. If the threat's past, mayhap the theatres will reopen in September.'

'The theatre. God in Heaven, my father was disgusted enough when my brother George set up for a lawyer. A good thing he perished in the Indies rather than see the disgrace you've brought upon the family.' Harry Stannard spoke good-naturedly, but Peter knew there was real meaning in his words.

'A better thing, then,' said Peter, 'that my brother Jack does honour to our grandfather's name at sea, while Adam does his best to ensure we're all saved before the celestial throne. Even if he thinks I'm a lost cause.'

'Adam – he's a strange one. He'll come to a bad end one day, just like your aunt.'

'My aunt? Mary or Meg?'

'Not Mary, that's for certain. She's in a rich man's bed, so that dear sister of mine is well content. No, Meg. You've not heard? Of course not – how could you? She'll be on trial for witchcraft at the Suffolk assizes in a few weeks' time. Strong evidence against her, your aunt Mary says, and she should know because she procured much of it. You look surprised, nephew. But she's sailed close to the wind many years, has Meg. You know she favoured the late Queen of Scots over her present majesty in her great tent yonder? Made plenty of enemies in her time. She'll hang, I reckon. I blame my father. Meg was his favourite; we all knew that from the moment we first drew breath. He indulged her in everything. Meg, singing, and telling tales, the three great loves of his life after your grandmother died. He never loved my mother, that much is certain.'

Peter was astonished and horrified in equal measure. He had fond memories of his aunt Meg. A year or two after his mother died, when he was six, his father moved the family back from Plymouth to Dunwich, where the Stannard affairs were in considerable disorder after the loss of his grandfather, the elder Jack Stannard, during the disastrous voyage of Hawkins and Drake to the Carib Sea. From then on, Meg had largely brought up him and his brothers. Even when he was nine or ten, Adam was offended by her cheerful reliance on doctrines that could not be found in the dour Geneva Bible, but the two youngest boys loved her beyond measure. She encouraged them to question, to think for themselves, and above all to be free in their hearts and spirits, even when the cares of the world weighed in upon them. When Peter announced his intention to join the company of travelling players who passed through Halesworth and the Sandlings one summer, and whose performances utterly enthralled the youth, it was Meg who convinced his father that he should follow his dream. Every winter when the theatres were closed, Peter returned to his home town and sat in his aunt's little cottage upon the heath, listening again to the tales of ancient Dunwich handed down to her by her father and his father before him, tales that were just as enthralling as they had been the first time he heard them.

He realised that his uncle was talking about those same tales, and his thoughts returned to the present.

'Oh, my father – your grandfather – was a great one for stories, as I say,' said Harry. 'The battles he'd fought in. How he saw the old king, Harry the Eighth, and watched the *Mary Rose* go down. About the old friar who taught him to fight, who'd fought on Flodden Field and at Pavia, or so he said. About all the illustrious men he'd known, or claimed to have known. Walsingham. Can you believe it? Sir Francis Walsingham, the queen's spymaster. The most feared man in England. He was meant to have summoned my father to a meeting in London, to have given him some mission or other. Beggars belief really. But even if it was true, what did it all avail, eh, nephew? My father probably ended up being buggered to death by some Spanish milord in the Indies, mayhap even by the Grand Inquisitor himself. What's left of Dunwich will be under the water before you're in your grave. And as for my dear half-sister, your aunt… well, the only miracle is that she wasn't taken up as a witch or a papist long since. So let her be, Peter Stannard. Let her be.'

But the younger man was only half listening. His grandfather had indeed been a great one for stories. Peter could hardly remember the elder Jack Stannard, but his father had often talked of him, and the old man's tales were as familiar to the young actor as the words of an oft-performed play.

Peter took a perfunctory leave of his uncle, and smiled to himself as he walked away. He would not take up Harry Stannard's parting offer of familial cheese and ale by the Yeomen of the Guard's camp fire. Nor, come to that, would he be rejoining his own regiment, especially not now that some of them had heard his real name. Hundreds of men were deserting the army every day, and that night, Peter would become one of them, taking Arabella with him. Most of those running from the colours had little idea of what they would do or where they would go, beyond the ungainsayable conviction that the army was a living hell and that anywhere, anything, would be better.

Peter Stannard was not one of these. On the contrary, he now had a very precise plan of where he would go, what he would do, and who he would do it with.

Eighteen

The man who will live forever lived still.

The wrongdoers' cell on the *Girona* was a tiny space right forward on the orlop deck, hard upon the ballast. It was impossible for a man to stand upright. Juan wished that one of the soldiers who had witnessed his assault on Fra Gordillo had run him through there and then. To die there, in sight of Dunwich – to die quickly – that would have been suitable indeed. But no, Bosun Cala came on deck just as Gordillo started screaming for the soldiers to strike down his assailant, and insisted on naval discipline being followed. So Juan was removed to the cell, but he expected at any moment to be dragged from it and either hanged from the yardarm or simply thrown over the side. Surely Gordillo would want revenge, in the form of a token trial and as rapid a dispatch as possible of his assailant? And when that death came, as it soon would, Juan could expect only the worst pains of purgatory and hellfire for all eternity. He had assaulted a priest, surely one of the very greatest sins. He would burn in agony forever, there could be no doubt of it.

But it would have been worth it.

He lost track of time, of whether it was day or night. Strange; they should surely have come for him by now. The Armada had to be continuing northward, though. The galleass had not made a major change of course;

the waves breaking on the bow, a few inches from Juan's head, were still following the same pattern. There had been no more fighting, that was certain. His only contact with other human beings came twice a day, when one of the ship's boys came to bring him some scraps of food and a little water, and to take away the pail of his waste. Then, one time, he heard someone approaching the cell a short while after one of the boys had been. Gordillo, perhaps, come to gloat? Come to lay out in precise detail the manifold horrors that awaited Juan's immortal soul? He steeled himself.

'Well then, Jack Stannard,' said a familiar Welsh voice, 'you've made quite the story for yourself now.'

'Gravell? How aren't you chained on the oar deck?'

'No call for the oars, for there's an abundance of wind. But there's certainly a call for skilled seamen who can help with the repairs, so many of the Dons are being killed in the battle or now laid low with the bloody flux.'

'They'll punish you if they find you here.'

'Mayhap,' said Gravell. 'Best they don't find me then, I'd reckon.'

'What news, man?'

'None. We still go north at the pace of the slowest ship. The English still follow. And you still live, my friend.'

'For now.'

'For the voyage. Seems Spinola was all for executing you according to the law of the sea – striking a superior, you see. No shortage of witnesses. If he'd had his way you'd already be victual for the fishes. But Gordillo – well, once his rage at you subsided, he sang a different song. Demanded you be kept alive, in fact. Said it's nothing to do with the law of the sea; he's a priest so it's the law of the Church that applies, says you must come to trial before the Inquisition when we get back to Spain.'

'Back to Spain? That'll be weeks away. Maybe months.'

'If it ever happens. There might be another fight with the English, or we might all be sunk in great storms – we've both sailed northern seas, Jack Stannard, we know what they're like, but these Dons don't, God help them. They think there are vasty sea monsters ahead, but you and I know there's enough horror in those waters without need of them.'

'I needed such cheering, Welshman.'

'Ah, but didn't you know we Welsh are known for our cheeriness, Stannard of Dunwich? I'll wager, though, that Fra Gordillo will never see you burn in an *auto-da-fé*.'

There was more to that than the Welshman knew, Juan thought. Regardless of what happened to the Armada, the Inquisition took months even to begin a case, and years to end it, as he knew from personal experience during his time in Mexico. He would be dead of old age long before he could be bound to a stake atop blazing faggots.

'Mayhap one day we can toast your winning that wager over good Suffolk ale, Owen Gravell,' he said as merrily as he could.

'Amen. But I'd best go now, before any of the Dons find me here.'

'Aye, best indeed. God go with you, Welshman.'

'And with you, Jack Stannard. Go on living, old man.'

'That seems to give me no difficulty, when so many find it impossible. God works in mysterious ways, my friend.'

But Owen Gravell had already gone.

Meg dreamed of Juan. Her long-dead husband was no longer the beautiful young man who had lain beside her so briefly so very long ago. In the dream, he was a much older man with a greying beard. He was clad in armour, and he was standing in the prow of the flagship of the Spanish Armada. Then, somehow, he was within her, but it was as though he was ravishing her instead of caressing her gently as once he had done. The armour was gone and he was naked, as was she. The flagship was gone, too, replaced with a legion of writhing sea monsters who hissed and spat at her. Then—

'One of them sort of dreams, eh, me nabbity?'

She woke and saw the pitted face of the crone called Purton, one of her fellow prisoners in the bridewell of Bury St Edmunds. She groaned as the truth of her situation came back to her. They had brought her there that morning, fettered and manacled, past the fallen ruins of the great abbey, into this nasty, mean building next to the tollhouse and abutting the town wall. She and Purton were the only women in the damp, stinking prison, and both of them were accused of witchcraft. One of the men across the way had made a lewd comment as Meg was bundled into the cell, but his fellows swiftly hushed him; no man in his right senses wished to incur the wrath of two reputed witches.

Her case had proceeded rapidly after the judgement of the jury of matrons. Too rapidly, in fact: it was almost as though Sir Nevill Bourchier, or rather her half-sister Mary, had made special arrangements to ensure that the grand jury was already sworn when the matrons reached their verdict, ensuring that her case could be sent up to the assizes without delay, and before any members of the jury – or, indeed, Bourchier himself – could have any second thoughts about the matter. The campaign against her was deeply conceived, that was certain. Mary Stannard had shown no compunction in turning to the Stannards' inveterate foes the Rakers once before, years earlier, so recruiting one of that family to the jury of matrons to ensure it damned Meg was well within her sister's capabilities.

''Ere,' said Purton, 'whadye think of this, eh? One of the gaolers, the fat sottish one, says that the assize is to be held by Wray himself. Imagine! If I'm to be sentenced to hang, me nabbity, I'm glad it'll be at the hand of a famous judge.'

'Wray?' said Meg. 'Who's Wray?'

'Don't ye know naught in the Sandlings? Sir Christopher Wray, the Lord Chief Justice of England, no less. Used to be Speaker of the House of Commons. A great man, me nabbity, a very great man. What an honour, eh?'

Now Meg recalled the name. Six or seven years before, the Jesuit priest Edmund Campion had been arraigned before Wray. To Meg, Campion and the other missionary priests who sought to keep the flame of the old faith burning in England were heroes – nay, saints in all but name. Yet the noble Campion was condemned by Wray as a common traitor and hanged, drawn and quartered at Tyburn Tree. When the news reached Dunwich, she wept for a day.

Still, Goody Purton, the self-confessed witch, was right in one sense. It would be an honour indeed to be sentenced by the same tongue that had spoken the words to condemn the blessed Campion. Consoling herself with that thought, Meg turned over and tried to get back to sleep, hoping that the dream of her Juan would return.

-

In truth, the sickness had begun in the English fleet even before the terrible battle off the coast of Flanders. A day or two before, Jack Stannard had heard of three or four men who were supposed to be sweating, fatigued and spewing, but he, like most, attributed this to men working nearly every hour of every day in the summer's heat, getting hardly any sleep and eating poorly, if at all. One or two had the quickshits, but that was always the way aboard a ship and was always blamed on the victuals, thus upon the purser, thus, aboard *Revenge*, upon Jack.

The doubts began to develop in Jack's mind thanks to his nominal superior, Martin Jeffrey. The purser had remained in his cabin for most of the voyage up the Channel, especially during the fights; Jeffrey was not a man renowned for, nor capable of, martial valour, and no man, not even Jack, thought anything of it. On the rare occasions when he saw him during those days, Jeffrey was sweating and complaining that his head, arms and legs gave him pain, but then that was his accustomed condition and was a consequence of the constant proximity of a bottle to his sea-bed. But then, on the morning after the battle off Flanders, when it was clear that the Armada had turned away from that coast and was fleeing northward, Jack went below and found Jeffrey groaning pitifully, his tiny cabin stinking intolerably from a bucket that seemed to contain both bloody shit and vomit. The fat man's invariably red face was as pale as a ghost and soaked in sweat.

'I'm dying, boy,' said the purser of *Revenge*.

'That cannot be, sir,' said Jack. 'You are as healthy as Sir Francis.'

'Dying, I say! Get me the surgeon.'

'The surgeon, sir, or another bottle?'

'Damn your blood, Stannard, no bottle. I've not been able to touch a drop of drink these two days. And the endless noise – what's a battle but a way of denying an honest man his sleep? Oh Jesus—' He turned and spewed over the side of his sea-bed, only partly finding the bucket at his side.

Jack left him, and was thoughtful. Martin Jeffrey not drinking for two days? The notion was as unlikely as bread without cheese or man without woman. Perhaps the purser really was ill. Jack decided to fetch the surgeon after all, but by the time they returned to the tiny, putrid cabin, Martin Jeffrey was dead.

-

'Purser Stannard,' said Sir Francis Drake. 'How does it sound, eh?'

'I hadn't considered it, Sir Francis,' said Jack.

'Not considered it? You Suffolk men are strange beasts. It's a promotion, man. Acting, by my warrant alone, but a promotion all the same. More pay, if that parsimonious old bastard Burghley ever decides to unlock the treasury chest and pay the money due to us. I wouldn't make plans to buy a farm in Dunwich based on that slender hope, my friend.'

'As you say, Sir Francis.'

Drake was sitting upon his favourite carved oak chair. It bore a passing resemblance to the throne of some eastern potentate, Jack thought. For his part, the new purser of the *Revenge* remained standing.

'I do say. Purser is a useful position, Jack Stannard – useful to he who holds the office and to his captain. All those monies that pass through a purser's hands. All those notes of credit. A purser need not depend on the pittance the queen promises to pay him on that far-off day when unicorns roam the earth again. You have opportunities, my friend.'

'I… I don't know what you mean, Sir Francis.'

'Great God, did original sin never reach Suffolk? Martin Jeffrey might have been a sot with scrambled wits, but he understood the world a thousand times better than you, lad. Now, he and I had an arrangement, you see. "Drake's portion", we called it. A half of all proceeds devised by the purser to be paid directly and in coin to myself. I expect the same arrangement to continue under your long and beneficial tenure of the office, Jack Stannard.'

'But Sir Francis—'

The admiral raised a hand. 'That is all upon the matter, Purser. Now, is there anything else?'

Jack took a deep breath. 'We are low on all victuals, Sir Francis, even biscuit and cheese. Our supply of stockfish is almost exhausted. We're already on short allowance, but I fear we'll have to reduce even that within two or three days. Can we not revictual from Hull or Bridlington?'

Drake looked at him with astonishment writ large upon his face. 'Revictual? We're still in pursuit of the Dons, boy, or hadn't you noticed? Still upon God's work. Besides, d'you think Burghley will gladly honour our credit for any victuals we demand? Oh, they'll be glorying in our victory, him and Walsingham and Leicester and all the others about the queen, but now they'll want nothing more than to see the back of us as quickly as possible so they don't have to call upon their precious coffers for a farthing more.'

'But the men are already weak and exhausted, Sir Francis,' Jack protested. 'If they don't have proper sustenance, even more of them will surely die. The sickness, this bloody flux, is taking more of a hold by the hour.'

'Oh, a surgeon as well now, Purser Stannard? Or a physician, perchance? No, you don't understand the world at all, my friend. So consider this. The more men who die, the more readily the victuals will go round those who live. The more men who die, the lower the call upon the treasury when payment falls due. So they all – Burghley above the rest – *want* the men of this fleet to die.'

Drake stood, walked to a small table hard against a futtock and poured himself a cup of wine.

'But surely, Sir Francis, the queen would never permit such a thing!'

Drake turned and looked at him, a half-smile upon his lips.

'I know the queen, Jack Stannard. I flatter myself that I have come to know her quite well. Her Majesty detests spending money, unless it's upon jewels for herself. So return to your duties, Purser, and consider this question as you do so. Do you really think Burghley would act as he does if Elizabeth didn't at least wink at it?'

Nineteen

Juan was now accustomed to his confinement. In many respects, it was more comfortable than some of the places he had known in the last twenty years; better, certainly, than the stinking hole in the ground in Mexico where he had spent so many months. Being right in the bow, he was tossed by the motion of the ship more than he had been on the oar deck. But here at least he did not have scores of snoring, farting, weeping men all around him. True, the space was too confined for him to lie down, but he could make himself reasonably comfortable against the first knee timber of the hull. The cell was also less damp than he had expected; Spanish caulking was surprisingly effective, it seemed, and the bow was the part of the hull damaged least by the near-constant firing of the great guns, which had shaken some of the planking further aft very nearly apart. Best of all, he did not have to experience any more of Fra Gordillo's dire homilies, nor the personal abuse of the priest himself, who had not deigned to venture forward to his assailant's cell. No doubt Gordillo was licking his lips at the prospect of presenting his case against Juan before the Grand Inquisitor himself, the heir of Torquemada, and then watching the old Englishman burn upon the pyre. At any rate, he had not come to torment Juan, and for that small mercy he was grateful.

All of this, though, was offset by the absence of even the faintest glimpse of sunlight or the surface of the sea, and by the lack of human company. Owen Gravell never returned – presumably the repairs had been effected and the slaves had returned to the oar deck. The boys who came with food twice a day said nothing, presumably under strict orders not to engage with the prisoner. Juan attempted to engage with them three or four times, then abandoned the effort. Gradually he made his peace with the darkness. It did not matter whether his eyes were open or closed; he found he could conjure up images of his Alice, of his children, and of his old mentor Thomas Ryman. He was back in Boulogne again with the Genoese Valente, in Africa with Bruno Santos Cabral and Francis Drake, on countless voyages on countless seas. He sang all the songs he could remember, from '*Sumer is Icumen In*' to old King Harry's own song, '*Pastime with Good Company*'.

If this was madness, Juan thought, then it was not the living hell that all men assumed it to be.

One day, though – he assumed it was another day, but it might not have been – he sensed that one of the boys was lingering a little longer than usual outside the bulkhead that sealed his cell, having passed food through the tiny hatch and exchanged pails.

'Are you still there, lad?' said Juan, not expecting an answer; but it was good to try his normal speaking voice again, rather than only singing.

There was no reply, and after a little while longer, he heard steps receding up on the deck. The next time, though, his attendant stayed a little longer still. Juan asked him no question, but instead began to sing 'King John and the Bishop'. He heard shuffling followed by a cough, so he fell silent.

'Fra Gordillo said in his homily that you are in league with the Devil,' said a low, childish voice with an accent that Juan could not place. 'He says you are a sorcerer. That is why you cannot die. But the Holy Inquisition will purge you in the flames of *auto-da-fé*, he says.'

'And you believe that?'

There was a long pause.

'Fra Gordillo says it, and he is a priest, so I ought to believe it. But I saw you on deck, before the battles, and you did not look like a sorcerer to me. You just looked like a very old man.'

'That's all I am, lad. A very old man.'

The boy seemed to consider this.

'Fra Gordillo says you are a traitor to Spain, too.'

'I'm English, lad. England's at war with Spain. That's not treason, whatever Fra Gordillo says.'

The boy did not reply, and Juan heard the receding steps again.

The next time he came, Juan attempted to converse with him, but the lad said nothing. Perhaps it was a different boy. He could not know. But the time after that, the boy lingered once again behind the partition that sealed Juan Estandar from the rest of the world.

Then, without warning: 'My name is Sabino Ibaiguren, but I am called Sabi. I am a Basque, of Donostia in Guipúzcoa. Some men call us Basques traitors too. Some call us heretics. Whatever we are, we are not afraid of sorcerers. But I do not think you are one, for if you were, you could easily escape from your cell. So you are either a very bad sorcerer or just a very old Englishman.'

'Well now, lad, you speak more sense than many priests I've known. I am pleased to have your acquaintance, Sabi.

My name is Juan… No. My name is Jack Stannard, of Dunwich in Suffolk.'

There was a pause.

'That is a strange name. But if you are an Englishman, Jack Stannard of Dunwich, tell me this – many of the men, even the officers, say that Francis Drake is the Devil, and that is why we have lost these battles. If he is the Devil, is Fra Gordillo right about you, and you are in league with him?'

Juan laughed. He could not remember when he had last done that.

'Oh, Francis Drake is not the Devil, and I would verily be in league with the very Devil himself before I would ally with Drake. I know him, you see. I have talked with him. I have sailed with him.'

There was a childish gasp, audible even through the timbers.

'*You have sailed with El Draque?*'

'That I have. Shall I tell you of it, Sabi?'

The boy did not demur.

–

On a warm summer's evening, Tom Stannard finally returned to Dunwich. He had hired a horse in Lowestoft, where the friendly master of the *Swallow had* landed him, and ridden by way of Blythburgh. The familiar road, coming into the town at the Bridge Gate by way of the ruins of the old leper hospital where his grandfather had spent his last years, should have lifted his spirits, but it did not. Instead, he was returning home with a heavy heart, without his eldest son.

On an impulse, he dismounted by the crumbling walls of St James's hospital and went within. He remembered coming here as a child to see his leprous grandfather, and being frightened beyond reason of the old man. The horror of his appearance was one cause of his fear, but not the strongest; no, that was the strange air of malevolence that seemed to pervade whichever space the elder Peter Stannard nominated. By his own choice, Tom would never have given one of his own sons the name of that dreadful decayed creature, but it had been the name of his wife's father, who still lived when the child was born, and Catherine was adamant upon the matter.

He looked around at the overgrown wreckage of the leper hospital. Even its chapel was open to the elements, and there was no sign that any human being had ever occupied it, let alone his grandfather. He had thought of offering up prayers for Adam here, in greater privacy than either of Dunwich's surviving parish churches would be likely to afford, but there was no trace of God's presence in this place any longer.

There was a movement behind him.

He felt a chill, half expecting to turn and look upon the ghost of the first Peter Stannard.

'Master Stannard. Tom.'

A familiar voice and a familiar face. Tom breathed deeply.

'Francis Birkes,' he said. 'Well met.'

The joint bailiff of Dunwich, a man nearly twenty years Tom's junior, gave a slight bow of his head in respectful greeting. 'Aye, well met. I noticed you upon the road and saw you come in here.'

'I have a great burden, Francis, and thought this place could give me a little relief from it. But I was mistaken. Naught here but ruins and memories.'

'A great burden?'

Tom took another deep breath. 'Adam is dead.'

Birkes gasped. '*Dead?* What, in the Armada fight?'

'Aye, in the Armada fight.' The lie came easily, and Tom realised that it had to be the story he maintained from now on with all and sundry. Adam Stannard, who if truth were told had been widely disliked in Dunwich, died heroically fighting the Dons. It was all that had to be said.

'May God comfort you and yours, Tom.'

'My thanks. Now I'll make for the heath, I think, to tell my sister—'

Francis Birkes raised a hand. 'I wish I wasn't the one to have to tell you this, Tom, but you have a double burden. Let me tell you of your sister Meg, and of what your other sister has done.'

-

The atmosphere in the English fleet was strange. By rights, the men should have been triumphant. The defeated Armada would not – could not – turn back now, so the English sailors should have been anticipating their return to home and hearth, the acclaim of their family and friends, and the payment of the substantial sums of coin due to them. They were the men who had saved England, the men who had triumphed over the Don and kept Parma and the Inquisition at bay. Aboard *Revenge*, though, only Francis Drake seemed to see things in this way. He paced the deck furiously, sometimes breaking into a little jig, always wearing a broad grin on his face. He shared jokes with the meanest cabin boys, and toasted his men from the poop deck, drinking fine claret out of Venetian glass.

Almost no man in the ship shared his mood. All were aware of the number of their shipmates who were already dead and of those who were dying. Every healthy man wondered if or when he would succumb to the bloody flux. The Medway and the prospect of better air and victuals ashore still seemed as far away as Cathay. Obtaining the pay to which they were entitled seemed even more distant.

Jack Stannard was one of those who could feel nothing triumphal about their situation. He avoided the upper deck, and the admiral, as much as he could. True, the air between decks was even more fetid than usual, but it seemed preferable to the alternative. He busied himself with his inventories, observing that the gap between the victuals available and the number of mouths they had to feed was widening in a manner precisely inverse to that generally witnessed by pursers of the queen's ships.

He was lost among his numbers when Tom Rayment, one of the ship's boys, found him. Jack's heart sank, fearing a summons from Drake. But it was not. It was the least likely of all summonses.

He went down to the orlop deck, where the dying were laid out; the better sort on rough pallets, the rest simply lying upon the deck to live out the last pathetic minutes of their lives. It took his eyes a few moments to adjust to the darkness, his nose rather longer to adjust to the stench. He looked around, and finally saw the unnaturally pale, sweat-drenched face of Nicholas Fitzranulf. The man already looked like a cadaver. His ribs showed through his soaked shirt, while his cheekbones had become so pronounced that he resembled a death's head.

Jack went to his side and knelt down. Fitzranulf's eyes remained closed, and he wondered whether his foe was already dead. Why had he been summoned? Did Fitzranulf wish to apologise before he died? Did he wish to beg forgiveness for his unjustified and inexplicable hostility?

Jack looked round for the surgeon, then remembered the fellow was already dead. The only one left to attend to the dying was a common seaman from Bristol who had once served as an apothecary's apprentice. The man was at the far end of the deck, and seemed himself to be sweating and trembling.

When Jack turned back, he saw that Fitzranulf's eyes were open and upon him.

'Stannard,' said Fitzranulf in little more than a whisper. 'John Stannard.'

'Say what you have to say, Fitzranulf.'

The dying man closed his eyes once again, and for a moment Jack thought that whatever he had intended to say was lost. But then Fitzranulf tilted his head slightly, opened his eyes and spoke again.

'Look at you,' he said, very slowly and quietly, struggling for every breath. 'Look at you, a nobody from a place eaten by the sea like a canker. Look at Drake, a farmer's son. Walsingham, a lawyer's brat. Nobodies rule in England now, as long as they have enough money. Men of mean birth. Name and lineage count for naught.'

'You lie there in your state. I kneel here in mine. Name and lineage seem not to have dictated our conditions.'

Fitzranulf coughed, and Jack thought his enemy's bowels might have loosened too.

'I fear Heaven,' said Fitzranulf. 'The preachers say that all men are equal there.'

Jack was fast losing patience with this, the self-pitying last words of a man he detested. Besides, he wanted to be away from this deck of death, in case he too finally succumbed to the sickness.

'Why did you summon me to see you, man?' he demanded.

Fitzranulf managed a terrible smile, even as the sweat poured from his brow.

'For this reason,' he said, raising himself as much as he could. 'Come closer, Jack Stannard, that I might whisper it.'

Jack hesitated, but stooped down as far as he thought he dared.

'Ha! So you've fathomed it, then. Yes, bean counter, you're right. I see the fear in your eyes. God willing, I've already infected you with this flux. If not I, then all of us down here, forgotten by you and Drake and the rest of them.' He coughed, although in truth it was no more than a dry, rasping stammer. 'If there's any justice left in God's world, you mean, undeserving, low-born *nothing*, you'll follow me into the deep before the week is out. Think on that as you start to get the sweats and the shits, John Stannard of Dunwich.'

Twenty

'The English have gone, *Jaun* Jack,' said Sabi, using what he had told Juan was the Basque word for 'mister'. 'No sails astern anymore.'

In the darkness within his tiny cell, Juan frowned to himself. If the English had gone, did it mean that the Armada was no longer a threat to England? Surely that must be the case. Was there any other possible explanation? Perhaps Parma had taken advantage of the absence of the English fleet to cross the Channel. Perhaps England was already Spanish, and the Armada would be able to come into safe harbours within a matter of days. But for that to be so…

'Where are we, Sabi?'

'On *Girona*, of course, *Jaun* Jack.'

'No, where is the Armada? Do you know?'

'I've heard some of the officers talking. They say we are off the coast of somewhere called Scotland. The Frit of Furt, or some such name.'

The Firth of Forth, upon the east coast of Scotland. Juan had a sudden memory of sailing into that broad haven over forty years earlier, in the war fleet of King Henry the Eighth. Of the battle he had fought off Leith, and the sight of Edinburgh burning.

'Scotland is a country, Sabi. It has its own king.'

'Is it friendly to King Felipe, *Jaun* Jack? Will we go there? Will we go ashore and be treated well?'

The *Girona* had not altered course, so she, and thus the rest of the Armada, had to be continuing northward. Besides, Juan knew from Owen Gravell and others that the old beheaded Queen Mary's son was now king in Scotland and wished for nothing more than to succeed to his kinswoman Elizabeth of England's throne. So he would hardly wish to offend the so-called Virgin Queen, and nothing could be more certain to do that than for King James to give safe haven to the Spanish Armada.

'No, Sabi,' he said finally, 'we will not be going ashore in Scotland.'

Even through the planking that divided them, he could hear the lad sigh.

'I have had enough of the sea, *Jaun* Jack.' Sabi sounded almost tearful. 'I want to be ashore again, and home in Donostia. I want to be dry. I want to be warm.'

'Put your faith in God, Sabi. If he wills it, you'll return home. But it'll be a long while yet, lad.'

-

For a woman who was undoubtedly destined to hang, having confessed to *maleficium*, to blighting the crops of an entire village near Beccles, and to possessing no fewer than three infernal imps, which did her bidding while pleasuring her night and day, Goody Purton was a remarkably cheerful, ever-grinning creature.

'*Carpe diem*, that's what I always say, me nabbity. We've been granted these days we wouldn't otherwise have had. We should make best use of them, I say.'

Meg looked around the damp walls and floor of their bare cell and wondered how exactly they could make any better use of their time. But in one sense, Goody Purton was right. The Suffolk Assizes had been delayed, Sir Christopher Wray having taken longer than expected at Buckingham, Bedford and Huntingdon, the consequence being that the noble judge had not yet even reached Cambridge, let alone commenced the assizes there. No doubt the delay was something to do with the alarm caused by the Spanish Armada, although to Meg's disappointment, it seemed that any prospect of deliverance from that quarter had vanished. Even in the Bury bridewell, both turnkeys and prisoners knew of the great battle off the coast of Flanders and that the Dons were running northward. Meg had had no word of any of her family – of her brother Tom, commanding the *Eagle of Dunwich*, or of her nephews Adam and Jack, also with the fleet. She did not worry for Peter; the last place the most irreverent of the three brothers was likely to be found was in any army or navy. But as she reflected upon it, she knew that her biggest regret was that not one of her closest, most beloved kin would know she had gone to the gallows until long after the event had happened. None of them would see her in court, none of them would see her swing.

No, it was a pity that the high-and-mighty Sir Christopher Wray was delayed. Meg wanted to get it done, to have her day in court. She would not confess and provide Sir Nevill Bourchier and his whore, her sister, with an easy triumph. She would face her accusers before a true English jury, and she would at least put up a fight before she was taken to the gallows.

She was a Stannard. Fighting was what Stannards did.

'A game, then,' she said to Goody Purton, smiling suddenly as she did so. 'Name as many emperors of Rome as you can, not counting Byzantium.'

The old woman looked at her as though she had just sprouted horns and a tail.

'Emperors? Don't know no emperors, me nabbity. No emperors in Saxmundham. What's wrong with Crambo or Hoodman Blind?'

-

One by one, the great galleons and carracks of England wore ship, adjusted sail and set their new courses. With the wind south-westerly, it was a relatively easy matter for them to come round and start to sail back the way they had come. They were off the Firth of Forth, or so Lieutenant Bodenham said; somewhere over the horizon to the west, the young King James sat within one of his palaces, no doubt hoping and praying that the English fleet off his coast would not seek to repeat history and decide to cap its triumph over the Armada by randomly slaughtering some Scotsmen, burning Edinburgh and generally doing those things Englishmen had always done to amuse themselves in Scotland.

Jack Stannard stood on the fo'c'sle, observing the scene around him. Once, he would have thrilled at the sight; now, he felt nothing beyond a desperate desire to be home. But where was home? Dunwich, whence his family hailed and where he had spent most of his life? Plymouth, where he had been born and where he had stayed with his long-dead mother's family before taking ship in the *Revenge*? At first, he had regarded the ship as his home. He loved it, he honoured Francis Drake, he served the queen. When and how, exactly, had he come to doubt all those articles of faith?

It was two days since they had buried Nicholas Fitzranulf in the ocean deep. In truth, burial was too grand a term for it; Fitzranulf's body had been bundled over the side with a dozen others, with no ceremony of any kind. Drake, who should have conducted such a service, wanted to avoid all contact with the infected. He was seen less and less on deck, confined to his cabin by his own choice. Poor Fitzranulf, who had thought himself so far above everyone else, to be just one more shrivelled corpse committed to the deep without even the semblance of a Christian burial.

Nicholas Fitzranulf.

Jack had thought much of the man's last words and his last act. God willing, Fitzranulf's attempt to kill him by infecting him with the bloody flux had failed thus far; Jack remained stubbornly healthy, even as more and more men of the *Revenge* fell ill and died. The Irishman had been a failure in that as in so much else of his life.

Yet were they really so very different?

Fitzranulf had died cursing what England had become – at any rate, what he believed it had become. And the more he thought upon it, Jack could only concur with him. Not because men of ancient blood and lineage were ignored, for Fitzranulf was surely wrong about that. A Howard commanded the Navy Royal, a Seymour was one of his deputies, and few lineages in the world were more illustrious than those two, let alone in England. No, that had been the bitter, desperate, jealous fantasy of a man whose family had fallen far below what it had once been, and if that line contained many more scions like the dead Nicholas, then it was hardly a surprise. But money was all, greed was all. In that, at least, Nicholas Fitzranulf had been right.

Jack looked away to the west, towards the invisible shore of Scotland, to where the prince his countrymen named as King Jamie Sext sat upon his little penniless throne. Now that the Armada was defeated and the prospect of King Philip's daughter being installed as England's Queen Elizabeth the Second was gone for ever, King James appeared ever more certain to be the next English monarch. If God granted him his allotted three score years and ten, Jack Stannard would probably live most of his life under that unknown foreign king, who was about his own age. Would things be any different under James Stuart? Could they be any worse? Would men like Francis Drake still hold sway?

His brother Adam and his enemy Fitzranulf were dead. Perhaps they were the fortunate ones.

Part Three

Look and bow down thine ear, O Lord, from thy bright sphere
behold and see,
Thy handmaid and thy handiwork amongst thy priests
offering to thee,
Zeal for incense reaching the skies,
Myself and sceptre, sacrifice…
He made the winds and waters rise
To scatter all mine enemies.

Poem written by Queen Elizabeth I, set to music by William Byrd and performed at the thanksgiving service for the defeat of the Spanish Armada, St Paul's Cathedral, 24 November 1588

Twenty-One

The first storm struck the *Girona*. Juan braced himself as best he could, but the bow of the galleass bucked, reared, pitched, yawed, rose and fell like dice shaken in a cup. He vomited and vomited again until there was nothing left. The very hull seemed to be screaming in agony, the timbers groaning as though they were human limbs being pulled apart by mighty pincers. The impact of what had to be colossal waves made the bow shudder. He could hear the wind howling and screeching, cold blasts seeming to penetrate right through the hull timbers to blow directly into his face. In the brief moments of respite, he could hear other sounds from further aft, and knew they were the screams of sailors, soldiers and slaves alike. He had no idea how long it lasted, but it had to be hours.

Then, very slowly, it eased. He knew the signs from when he had stood at the helm or been lashed to a mast, judging the passage of a storm from one of his own ships. The movement of the hull became very slightly less crazed, the noise of the wind and the hammering of the waves just a little less loud and incessant.

He must have slept, for when he woke, the sea was still choppy but nothing out of the ordinary. He tried to wipe some of the vomit off the rags he wore, the same rags he had been wearing when he hit Gordillo, but he knew it was a hopeless task. And then, astonishingly, there was a familiar voice just outside his cell.

'*Jaun* Jack? Are you alive?'

'Sabi! Yes, I live. As do you, it seems. Thanks be to God!'

'I was scared, *Jaun* Jack. I have never been so scared.'

'But you have lived and come through your first great storm. You're a true seaman now, lad.'

Sabi seemed unconvinced. 'Men have died,' he said. 'Not just of the storm – there's disease all through the ship, and hunger and thirst. They've reduced the rations again, just half a pound of rotten biscuit, a pint of water and half a pint of wine for every man each day, nothing else. They're throwing bodies off the deck even now.'

'The slaves at the oars too?'

'They say so, but I haven't been down there.'

Juan wanted to know if his friends like Owen Gravell and Adil still lived, but it would be dangerous for Sabi to try and find out.

'And where are we, my friend? Do you know?'

'I have not heard anyone say what the places are called. But there are coasts on both sides of us now – I saw high cliffs when I was on deck a little while ago, the greatest of them on the large island to northward. There are towers on the coast to the south.'

It sounded like the Pentland Firth. Juan had sailed through that strange, confined, vicious channel on some of his early Iceland voyages with his father, so very long ago. If he was right, the isles called Orkney lay to the north and the north coast of Scotland itself to the south. Soon, and no matter what further troubles awaited it, the Armada would be turning south-west and setting course for Spain. But what was left of the Armada?

'Are the other ships still in sight, Sabi? Is the Armada still together?'

'Some of them are in sight. De Leyva is right astern of us, and they say the duke is still with us too. But I've heard men say that many ships were scattered in the storm, and God knows where they are.'

Juan remembered the charts he had studied countless times over the years, the very charts his father had first taught him to understand. It sounded as though the ships with *Girona* were indeed going through the Pentland Firth, but if the storm they had weathered was southwesterly, as it surely had to be, then others might have been forced northward, to take their chances between Orkney and Shetland. Juan had seen the coasts of those isles, and wondered how many galleons or *urcas* or galleasses might have come to grief on them.

'I have some biscuit and water for you,' said Sabi. 'Shall I take your pail away for emptying too, *Jaun* Jack?'

Despite himself, Juan knew that he was smiling.

'No need, Sabi. It emptied itself during the storm.'

-

Very slowly, the great ships of England were towed, warped and sometimes sailed up the broad, winding channel of the Medway. They should have been returning in triumph, thought Jack Stannard, with cheering crowds thronging each bank. Instead, they came back to their moorings off Chatham in gloom and silence, like a fleet defeated. Some of them, like the *Bear*, had barely half their men left. None of them still had captains aboard. The Lord Admiral left the *Ark Royal* at Sheerness, Drake, Hawkins, Seymour and the rest following him in short order. They were going to court to be feted as the heroes of the hour, while the real heroes still languished and perished in the pestilential hulls in the Medway. Drake had not bothered to say farewell to his men, not even to his officers. Bodenham passed on to Jack a verbal command to make up his accounts for the voyage and forward them to old William Borough, the Clerk of the Ships. But unless fresh orders came, Jack was then discharged from the ship.

The *Revenge* emptied. Jack watched as the great guns were unloaded into barges, then taken off to the ordnance yard. The stores followed in short order, then the men, the sick going first. Jack was pleased to see that Matt Bradlow was one of the last to leave. Perhaps Dunwich men were immune to the sickness that had devastated the fleet; it was a hope to cling to.

'Well, Matt,' he said as they stood in the nearly empty waist of the *Revenge*, 'where are you bound now?'

His father's old shipmate grimaced. 'God knows, Master Jack. There's talk of a mighty fleet going against Spain next year, so maybe I'll seek a place in that. Or I might return to merchants' voyages again – I'll see what berths offer in London, and if that fails, mayhap I'll go back to Dunwich to see if any of your father's ships are setting out. First, though, a few of us are going to Greenwich Palace to petition for our pay. Some of the lads from *Ark* and *Victory* too, that I know of.'

'Petition? What, petition the queen herself?'

'Hardly that; she'll not see the likes of us. But Burghley, who has the purse anyway – he's the man we want.'

Jack recalled what Drake had said of Lord Burghley, and doubted the petitioners' prospects of success. A thought struck him. Surely the petitioners would stand a better chance if they were supported by an officer? It was a bold thought, and his father would surely counsel against it if he were present, but Jack considered that he had nothing to lose. He had seen enough of the queen's service to know that he wanted no more of it. He certainly did not wish to depend on the good graces of Sir Francis Drake for advancement. His father would be disappointed, but not greatly so; he had always envisaged Jack ultimately returning to Dunwich and succeeding him in charge of the Stannard ships, warehouses and trades, the sojourn in the Navy Royal being but a way for Jack to learn sea business and make connections that might prove valuable to the family. Did it matter, then, if someone as high and remote as Lord Burghley, a man who would surely never even have heard of Dunwich, took umbrage at Jack Stannard aiding worthy men in a righteous cause?

He called after Matt Bradlow to tell him that he would accompany the petitioners to the royal palace at Greenwich.

Twenty-Two

Sir Nevill Bourchier revelled in being content. His large oak chests groaning with coin gave him contentment. The continuing success of his ventures in trade, notably his lucrative monopoly over glove-making, gave him as much contentment again. His knighthood from the queen, thoroughly deserved, gave him especial contentment. He had imagined that the purchase of a pleasant estate near the coast in Suffolk, and his acceptance into local society as a justice of the peace, would be contenting beyond measure.

Then he encountered Mary Stannard, scion of a local family that seemed to have money.

At first her willing body brought great contentment indeed to his pintle, largely redundant since the death of his wife three years earlier. But it swiftly became clear that the brazen wench's ambition went far beyond being a mere bedfellow. She desired fine clothes. She demanded jewels. She hinted at marriage, subtly at first, then ever more stridently. Above all, though, she insisted that he collude in her scheme to destroy her hated half-sister.

Sir Nevill agreed to all this with the sole exception of marriage, at which he yet baulked. He was besotted with her, and as far as he could see, her much older sibling was clearly a witch, and a papistical witch to boot, so she deserved the full weight of the law against her. Yet as the summer wore on and the terror of the Armada grew more real, Mary became ever more hysterical. She railed against the iniquities of the law – its slow pace, epitomised by the tardiness of the circuit judge in reaching Suffolk, and above all its irritating requirement for evidence. She seemed to think that her word alone ought to be sufficient to condemn her sister to the gallows without further ado. Although Nevill Bourchier was a novice in the law, he knew that such things might happen, perhaps, in less blessed countries like France or Spain, but they most certainly did not happen in England. When he said this to his mistress, though, she raged and spat at him, crying bitter tears all the while, while in the intervals between her outbursts she assumed even more airs and graces, playing the part of the great lady she most certainly was not.

In truth, then, Sir Nevill was already starting to think of discarding her. Even if the inevitable demise of her hated sister might make her happy for a few short days, no doubt she would then find some other cause to berate him about.

Such thoughts were very much on his mind, and were spoiling what should have been a pleasant supper at the splendid house set aside for the visiting circuit judge. Bourchier and several other justices of the peace for the county of Suffolk who were involved in bringing cases to court on the morrow had been invited to sup with that most eminent judge, Sir Christopher Wray, and he had been determined to make an impression upon a man who could potentially do much to further his ambitions. Above all, he fancied taking a turn as high sheriff of Suffolk, which would be a mighty distinction indeed for a man who was born the son of a mere tanner, the most pungent and thus most despised of trades.

Yet Bourchier was not content at the supper. He was not content because he suspected that he shared his bed with a malevolent harpy who would make his days ever more miserable. He was also not content because there were unsettling rumours that an eminent personage had arrived in the area incognito, supposedly in the company of two of his daughters, supposedly to inspect an estate he had recently purchased in these parts. The name of this personage was one that filled all Englishmen who knew it with fear…

'I was enquiring, Bourchier,' said Sir Christopher Wray, whose previous words Sir Nevill had evidently missed entirely, 'whether you're certain the case you're bringing tomorrow won't present any difficulties.'

Bourchier recovered himself quickly. 'Oh, none at all, Sir Christopher. The grand jury had no doubt that the case was strong enough to come before you, and the verdict of the jury of matrons—'

'I place little weight upon what a gaggle of women says, Sir Nevill.' Wray smiled thinly. The Lord Chief Justice of England was a small man with strange, pale features and pronounced cheekbones. He spoke quietly and in a broad Yorkshire accent, but his words somehow possessed unchallengeable authority. 'If a woman bears marks,' he continued, mockingly impersonating a woman's voice, 'she is a witch. If she does not bear marks, she is a witch. England has surely moved beyond such idle superstition. We rightly ended the swimming test – sink, drown and you're innocent, float, survive and you're guilty so you're killed anyway. We ended the scratching test – have the victim scratch the suspected witch to draw blood, and if the victim recovers from their malady, the suspect is guilty. Who was to say that the victim would not have got better anyway, or that they were lying about the symptoms improving? No, we are better than that, Sir Nevill. We have moved beyond fanciful popish superstitions. We are not Spain, after all.'

'Umm – quite so, Sir Christopher.'

Bourchier had not expected such strange thoughts from such a senior judge, and that, too, brought him ill content. Earlier in the evening, he had even heard Sir Christopher tell a fellow justice that not every woman accused of witchcraft was guilty, and that he had presided over as many acquittals as convictions. The times were disordered indeed.

These thoughts were still weighing heavily on Sir Nevill Bourchier's mind when he left Wray's quarters to make his way back to the house where Mary Stannard would be waiting for him, probably to castigate him for some supposed failing. It was late, and his hand went to the hilt of his sword. But the streets were quiet, and after all, Bury St Edmunds was not London—

The two men emerged from a side alley, blocking his path. He realised that a third had come up behind him. The two ahead were strapping fellows, one older than the other. They were clad entirely in black.

'Sir Nevill Bourchier,' said the older of the two in front.

'I… I shall summon the constable, and the night watch…'

'They are the other side of town, Sir Nevill. They will not bother our business here.'

Bourchier's limited reserves of resolve and bluster disappeared.

'I have coin,' he said.

'No doubt you do, Sir Nevill, but we have no interest in it. Nor does our master. He merely wishes to see you, and has sent us to escort you to him. The night is dark, and there might be dangerous men hereabouts.'

'Who is your master?'

Even in the darkness, Bourchier could see that the older man was smiling grimly.

'Oh, I think you know who our master is, Sir Nevill. I think you know very well.'

Sir Nevill Bourchier felt strangely as though all the blood in his body was draining towards his feet.

Twenty-Three

For one brief moment before waking, Juan dreamed he was young again, in his bed in his house in Dunwich, with Alice lying beside him. Then he woke, and realised he was still in his pitch-black confinement in the bows of the *Girona.* He stretched as much as he could to bring a little life back into his desperately aching limbs.

He had not even the first idea of where they were. For what must have been days on end, there had been nothing but relentless storms. The galleass pitched and rolled, Juan spewed and prayed for death. But still God mocked him and kept him alive.

Sabi had not returned. Juan had been attended instead by the other boy or boys, who said nothing. He had asked if Sabi was dead, but got no reply. Now, though, they were evidently in an anchorage of some sort. The hull rose and fell with the tide, but otherwise the water lapped gently against the timbers, and this had finally allowed him to fall into a deep and lengthy sleep.

It had to be Ireland, he reckoned, but he had no idea of where on that lengthy and dangerous coast they might be. He heard the unmistakable sound of boats bumping up against the hull, and dimly heard distant voices that sounded Irish. If he was right, then for now, at least, the *Girona* would be safe.

He heard the familiar sound of light steps upon the deck, a boy's step, then the pause as the boy listened out for any sign to suggest that the ancient man within the cell was still alive.

'*Jaun* Jack?'

'Sabi! I'm glad to hear you, my friend. I feared you were dead.'

'They put me with the helmsman, *Jaun* Jack, all the way down the coast of Scotland. The storms were so terrible, they had to relieve him every half-glass. So each man had to have a little food and wine ready for him the moment he came off watch, and they had me and Alfredo from Naples do duty attending upon them.'

'An important duty indeed, Sabi. And *Girona* is still here, so the helmsmen must have done well.'

'It was terrible, *Jaun* Jack.' The lad's voice was quivering. 'Even if I live for as long as you, I don't wish to know such horrors again.'

'I pray that you won't, lad. But tell me – where are we?'

'I have heard some men say that it is a harbour called Killybegs. A strange name. It is in Ireland. The people help us, even though I've heard men say that Ireland belongs to Queen Elizabeth.'

'The Irish hate the English, Sabi. They're good Catholics, so yes, they'll help us. But sooner or later the English will send troops out of their garrisons. Are any of the other ships with us?'

'None. Only we lie here. I've heard talk that the Irish speak of other ships in other harbours, but I don't know which. No man knows how much is left of the Armada, *Jaun* Jack. Fra Gordillo says we must all pray even harder to be delivered. He says God is testing our faith.'

'That's what priests always say, Sabi. But yes, Fra Gordillo is right about one thing: we must all pray for deliverance. We must pray that the captain and the men can get *Girona* to sea again before the English arrive. And then, my young friend, we must pray that we can somehow get back to Spain.'

'That's a lot of prayer, *Jaun* Jack. And prayer doesn't seem to have helped the Armada much thus far.'

'Don't let Fra Gordillo hear you say things like that, Sabi, or he'll lock you up in here too and then haul you before the Inquisition if we ever get back.'

'Yes, *Jaun* Jack. As you say, *Jaun* Jack.'

-

Greenwich Palace was a relatively modest affair, Jack thought. True, there was an impressive range along the river front itself, all red brick with towers, turrets and battlements, but the buildings behind that were low and plain. He had seen Whitehall many times, and had also seen Richmond and Hampton Court on a river voyage when he was a boy. He had even seen Nonsuch, the astonishing confection that seemed nothing less than a fairy fortress mistakenly deposited in the midst of Surrey. Greenwich seemed no match for them. Yet its location on a great bend of the Thames, with all the shipping of London moving up- and downstream past it, gave it a peculiar quality and grandeur.

There was already a large crowd at the landward gate of the palace as the twenty or so men of the *Revenge* came down the hill from the Black Heath to join them. Men and women alike were clamouring for admittance, many of them waving their petitions hopefully in the air.

There were beggars galore crying out for alms, some of them undoubtedly wounded soldiers or sailors. Inevitably, there were whores and hawkers in abundance, as well as those sorry creatures who spent the best parts of their lives outside mighty buildings hoping to catch a glimpse of the great and the famous.

Jack and Matt Bradlow pushed their way through the crowd to address the corporal commanding the red-tabarded guards on the gate.

'Ho, Corporal!'

'Ho yourself. Sailors, be you? Got enough of them inside already. Drake, Hawkins, all the captains from the Armada fight. Get along to Deptford yard, they'll serve you bread and ale over there.'

'These are men of Sir Francis Drake's ship, the *Revenge*, and I am the purser, John Stannard. We seek to petition the most noble Lord High Treasurer of the kingdom.'

'Burghley?' The man laughed. 'I wish you good fortune of that, John Standard or whatever you said your name was.'

'We are Englishmen who have ventured our lives for the queen,' cried Matt Bradlow. 'We have fought the Armada. We have *beaten* the Armada. We seek only what is due to us.'

The corporal shook his head. 'You think they' – he jabbed a finger towards the palace – 'want to be reminded of such things here and now? They're mounting up for a great hunt, friend. A hunt to celebrate defeating the very same Armada. The thrill of the chase now, then roasted venison tonight, washed down by the best French wines. You and your friends here play no part in that scheme, I can tell you.'

Bradlow looked at Jack in despair.

'If not Burghley,' said Jack, 'then perchance Lord Harry Seymour will see us and receive our petition.'

'Seymour? You've not heard, then. He lies sick – like to die, they say. Caught the bloody flux at sea. Pity. A good man, that one, like all his kin.'

Jack felt as though he had been hit hard in the stomach. Seymour, who had been so kind to him when relating the death of his brother, who dressed like a common seaman and took part in their songs and games. Modest Seymour, the very opposite of Francis Drake. With Seymour dead and the likes of Howard, Hawkins and Wynter surely too ancient for much more command at sea, the Navy Royal would be left in the hands of the braggarts and the vainglorious, of the Drakes and the Nicholas Fitzranulfs. It was not a prospect that appealed to Jack Stannard.

The inner gates of Greenwich Palace opened, and a large hunting party appeared from within. First came the hounds, loping grey beasts, accompanied by their handlers, then the horn blowers, then the first of the riders, clad in hunting green, all mounted on splendidly groomed steeds. Jack recognised the Earl of Cumberland, the strutting young prince of the north, then Drake, Lord Sheffield, and a half-dozen other commanders. They were heavily outnumbered by the landsmen, of whom Jack recognised only a few. But one was unmistakable, the vast white beard betraying the venerable age that made him a most unlikely huntsman. Yet he sat well upon a horse, for he was a Lincolnshire man and thus born to the saddle.

'Burghley,' said Jack, in no more than a whisper.

A troop of royal guards fanned out from within the outer court, clearing the petitioners and the rest of the gaggle at the gate to make a path for the hunting party. They poured through, seemingly oblivious to the cries for alms, for receipt of petitions, for relief from a hundred and one griefs and injustices. The men of the *Revenge* pressed forward, but the red-coated halberdiers held them back.

As Burghley approached, though, Matt Bradlow broke away from the rest, found a gap between two of the guards and ran forward, taking hold of the bridle on the Lord Treasurer's horse. The beast whinnied frantically and very nearly threw its elderly rider. Jack saw clearly the two expressions that passed over Burghley's features in no more than a moment: first fear, then rage. He spurred his stallion forward, the speed of his reaction taking Bradlow by surprise. He released his grip on the bridle a fraction too late. The frenzied surge forward of Burghley's horse knocked him off balance, and he went under its hooves. His body seemed to bounce off the hard, dusty road, then fell directly under the hooves of Lord Cumberland's horse, following close behind Burghley. The remaining riders avoided Bradlow, who was lying still on the ground, but not one of them halted and dismounted to see how he was. At last the rear of the hunting party rode out of the gate, and the men of the *Revenge* rushed forward to attend their fallen shipmate.

Jack knelt down. It took him just one brief glance to see that Bradlow's neck was twisted at an impossible angle. A man of Dunwich, a man who honoured Jack's father, a man he had come to regard as a friend. Matt Bradlow, who had survived countless voyages and the fight against the mighty Spanish Armada, who had avoided the terrible fever that had decimated the men of England's navy, had died instead under the hooves of horses ridden by the queen's chief minister and one of the kingdom's greatest lords.

Jack stood and looked towards the distant hunting party, disappearing over the ridge of the Black Heath with horns blaring and hounds barking excitedly.

He himself was no great horseman, but he had ridden long and hard many times on Dunwich Heath and elsewhere in the Sandlings. So he had sufficient experience to reckon that Cumberland had had sufficient time to steer his mount to the side of Matt Bradlow.

The noble earl had deliberately chosen not to do so.

Twenty-Four

The courtroom was full. As Meg and her fourteen fellow prisoners were led in, shackled together as was customary, there was a brief, awed hush. Then the jeering and catcalling began, notably towards the bewildered young man who was accused of murdering a popular local girl. The victim's mother sobbed, but the friends and family members around her spat and howled at the accused, calling down God's judgement upon him.

Meg looked around, but there seemed to be no familiar faces. Bury was a long way from Dunwich, though, and none of her close family – none, at any rate, of those who loved her – were anywhere nearby. She did not even know whether her brother and her favourite nephews still lived.

No, she was wrong. There was one familiar face, that of Sir Nevill Bourchier, who looked surprisingly uneasy. Of his doxy, her sister Mary, there was no sign. True, there was a soberly dressed woman sitting upon the same bench as Sir Nevill, her face concealed by a veil, but she was clearly with the equally well-attired young woman by her side. Could the veiled woman be Mary, or perhaps Martha Cawston, sometime Raker? But the build seemed wrong for both of them.

Meg chided herself for making too much of it. She knew, for she had sometimes been one of them, that there was a certain kind of person, particularly women, who loved nothing better than an assize day. A sudden confession, a dramatic accusation, the exposure of a false witness, the passing of a death sentence – each or all of this could excite a woman to pleasurable ecstasy, Meg had once believed.

Now, though, her thoughts were filled with nothing but fear. Before she came to court, she had nearly convinced herself that the case against her would be dismissed out of hand as flimsy beyond measure, or that her own skill with words would destroy the testimony of her unknown accusers. But there, actually inside the courtroom alongside her fellow accused, all of her confidence fell away. She looked at the gaudily painted royal coat of arms upon a shield above the judge's vacant bench, the lion and the red dragon supporting it, and realised that the full majesty of the so-called Queen Elizabeth's law was about to be deployed against her. She was naught but a pitiful old woman, entirely at the mercy of this far more dreadful force.

An usher beat a gavel, and the court fell quiet.

'Silence, I pray you, and all rise for the most honourable and most learned Sir Christopher Wray, Chief Justice of her blessed Majesty's Court of Queen's Bench, Lord Chief Justice of this realm of England!'

A side door opened to admit the illustrious judge. Meg was surprised at how small and pale he was, but otherwise Sir Christopher Wray was a sight to strike terror into the heart of any malefactor. He was clad in a voluminous robe of remarkably bright scarlet trimmed with ermine. Around his neck was a large gold chain of office, gleaming in the summer sun that streamed through the windows of the courtroom. He wore a simple black cap upon his head. He went to his large high-backed chair, turned, and looked out over his courtroom. For a moment he stood impassive, directly beneath the royal arms, as if to emphasise that there and then, in that place, he was the living embodiment of royal authority. He looked across at the row of accused men and women, and seemed to stare directly at Meg for a moment. Then he sat down, and those in the courtroom drew breath.

Meg was in the middle of the row, and would be the eighth case of the day. Goody Purton sat a few spaces away and would be fourth. The alleged murderer of the local girl would immediately precede Meg.

The panoply of the law unfolded. Meg's belly was still twisted with fear, but her natural curiosity and interest in the doings of her fellow human beings slowly got the better of her.

Each defendant was unshackled in their turn, then led before the judge. The witnesses stepped forward to give their evidence, and sometimes the judge, sometimes the accused themselves, asked them questions, which the law insisted upon calling interrogatories. From time to time, whichever justice of the peace had brought the case to the assizes might come forward to clarify a point of fact, but otherwise, no person other than the judge, the defendant and those who accused him or her took a part in the proceedings. No person apart from the defendant spoke on their behalf. Meg had once heard that the late Queen Mary, of blessed memory, had proposed to allow witnesses for the defence, but the suggestion had been rejected out of hand as being entirely un-English.

In each case, the jury of a dozen men listened, debated briefly, then returned their verdict. From the voices of each successive jury foreman, and the look of his fellow jurors, Meg reckoned that those who sat in judgement upon their peers were almost entirely poor, illiterate fellows, many of whom clearly had difficulty remembering what had been said a few minutes earlier. But it would not have made any difference if they had the witnesses' original written depositions laid before them, Meg thought; they would not have been able to read them anyway.

The first three cases were straightforward. One old man was accused of buggery, convicted, and sentenced to hang; from beginning to end, his case took no more than twenty minutes. A sturdy, defiant fellow was accused of horse theft but acquitted by what was clearly a partial jury, a suspicion alluded to heavily by Sir Christopher Wray, who nonetheless did not see fit to overturn the verdict as he was entitled to do. A strange dark woman was accused of impersonating an Egyptian, one of those wandering folk who told fortunes; she was sentenced to hang and responded by screaming and raging, calling down curses upon the head of the Lord Chief Justice, who merely looked at her silently and curiously.

Then came Goody Purton.

She had confessed to her supposed crime, although during all their weeks together in the bridewell, Meg had never managed to establish why she should do such an unaccountable thing. Now, at Wray's prompting, she repeated her written confession as best she could, to gasps and cries from those assembled in the court.

'About two years last past,' she said, 'there appeared to me in a field near Lavenham a creature resembling a large black dog, which spoke to me and desired me to give it my soul, in which case I'd have the power to do whatever I wished.'

If that be so, thought Meg, *why did this dog not give you the power to escape?*

'To this I consented, and allowed the dog to suckle my breast. Some weeks later, I begged a pedlar for some pins, but he would not give them to me. The black dog appeared to me again and asked what I wished done to him. "What can you do?" I said. "I can lame him," said the dog. "Go on, lame him then," I said. The pedlar went no more than three hundred yards before he fell down lame.'

There was a great gasp at this, but Meg's thoughts were quite otherwise. *Satan, prince of darkness, surely has the power to strike down kings and potentates. Why then would he limit himself to inflicting a limp upon a pedlar in Suffolk?*

'I killed a child of Richard Trenchard of Long Melford by means of a picture of clay,' said Goody Purton, to further gasps.

'Interrogatory,' said Wray. 'Why did you kill him, and what are these means you speak of?'

'I was passing Trenchard's house on the way to the mill,' she said. 'He shouted at me, "Get off my ground, you whore, you witch, I'll see you hanged!" So I says, "Go hang yourself!" Past the next hedge, the black dog appears to me and says, "Be avenged on him!" So I makes a picture of clay in his image, dries it, sticks a pin in its heart, then burns it. And Trenchard's young boy falls ill, and in half a year he's dead.'

Several of the women in the courtroom burst into tears, but Meg's emotions worked very differently. *Would not the stabbing and burning of a clay image of Trenchard kill him, not his son? And kill him swiftly, not by a lingering illness?*

There was more – a confession to the killing of a cow, another of charming milk into butter – but the substance of the case was already decided. The jury's verdict was a formality, as was the sentence of death by hanging, which Wray passed in a tone as easy as if he were buying an apple.

As she was taken down, Goody Purton looked directly at Meg. She was grinning broadly, as though she were strolling through a meadow with a lover.

That will be my fate very soon, thought Meg, and her fear returned in full measure.

-

A costermonger accused of cheating honest folk by providing dishonest measures was sentenced to a whipping, after which, and to much excitement and murmuring in the courtroom, the alleged murderer of the local girl was brought forward. He was a tall, bold fellow who evidently knew a little of the law, for he exercised his right to challenge twenty potential jurors before he could object to no more. It was clear to Meg, and probably to every other person in the courtroom, that he could have challenged every man in the kingdom until doomsday and still not found a jury more inclined to acquit him.

The trial unfolded with an air of inevitability that was apparent to all but the defendant. The parish constable swore to the discovery of the body, stabbed in the belly and left for dead in a field outside the town. He had subsequently searched the defendant's hovel and found a knife stained with fresh blood. A physician testified to the presence in the girl's womb of an unborn child, a revelation that brought on sobs from some of those present. The girl's father, a respectable yeoman farmer, said that the accused, a ne'er-do-well, had been pursuing his daughter relentlessly for a year, forcing his way upon her and thereafter demanding that she marry him even though he was drunk, a braggart, and a notorious thief and liar. Both a goodwife and a thatcher of unimpeachable repute testified to seeing the defendant running down the lane from the field in question, his hands and shirt bloody, the knife discovered by the constable in his hand.

Throughout all this, Sir Christopher Wray sat silently upon his judge's bench. His strategy was apparent to every person in the court who had any modicum of intelligence, for the accused man seemed to be intent on condemning himself out of his own mouth. He questioned the parish constable, calling the man a drunk and suggesting firstly that he had never found any body at all, then changing to propose that the constable had discovered the body of a totally different girl, despite her father having identified her. He denigrated the physician, calling his skills and practices mere witchcraft. He claimed the eyewitnesses were mistaken, that it was not him they saw, that he had been at an alehouse in Newmarket at the time in question and that several unnamed boon companions, now strangely vanished from the district, could testify to this. Above all, he raged at the girl's father, denouncing him as a liar, a sodomite and a papistical traitor.

At this last charge, Sir Christopher Wray's patience evaporated.

'I think,' he said calmly, 'we have all heard enough. Good men of the jury, I ask you to retire to consider your verdict.'

The jury did not even go through a semblance of retiring. They sat where they were, whispering to their foreman, who spoke the word 'Guilty!' loudly and with some relish.

The murderer's confidence vanished in the blink of an eye. He let out a loud and terrible scream, then fell to his knees, sobbing and wailing as Wray pronounced sentence. He would not or could not get to his feet, and was dragged from the court.

One of the gaolers from the bridewell came over to Meg, unlocked her fetters and led her into the middle of the room.

It was her turn, her case, her arraignment as a witch.

Twenty-Five

Even within his putrid cell in the bows of the *Girona*, it was apparent to Juan that something markedly serious was afoot. There were shouts from the deck above, the sounds of far more men than usual treading the timbers, bangs and jolts as something – what, he could not tell – was either brought aboard or lifted off.

'*Jaun* Jack!'

'Sabi! What news, lad?'

The boy sounded breathless. 'I can't stay – they'll be down here any time now.'

'Who, lad? Who'll be down here?'

'The new men! We're taking aboard men from ships that have been lost, or that are too badly damaged to make the voyage home. *Rata Encoronada* especially, and *Duquesa Santa Ana*. Many men, *Jaun* Jack!'

'How many men, Sabi?'

'Too many to count! Maybe a thousand or more. And great men! De Leyva himself is aboard – I just saw him! Imagine it, the famous de Leyva, a man intimate with the king, and I've breathed the same air as him. And he has his following with him – sons of every great noble line in Spain, they're saying up above. What a tale to tell my children one day!'

Despite himself, Juan could only smile. But he was enough of a seaman to know that the arrival of so many men aboard *Girona* could mean only one thing.

'Sabi, have you heard any men talking about where we're going? Are we still bound for Spain?'

'I heard some of the officers talking,' said the boy, 'and some of them mentioned Scotland. Why would we be sailing for Scotland, *Jaun* Jack?'

'It makes sense, Sabi. If we've taken on all these other men, we can't make the passage to Spain. But Scotland is a short voyage. Its king is neutral, and God willing, he'll allow us to cross to his other coast, there to find ships to take us to Flanders. And from Flanders, Sabi, you'll be able to get home to Spain.'

Juan Estandar kept his other thought to himself; namely, that the ports of the east of Scotland would also contain ships trading to London, Norfolk and Suffolk. If he could somehow escape while they were ashore in Scotland, he might yet return to Dunwich after so many years.

There were noises astern. Loud voices were getting closer.

'They're coming, *Jaun* Jack. There'll be men quartered all along this deck, right up to your bulkhead. I may not be able to get through to talk to you again.'

'I shall miss you, my young friend. God willing we'll both go ashore safely in Scotland, and I'll be able to see what you look like at long last.'

'I'd like that too, *Jaun* Jack. Until then, may God be with you too.'

'Amen to that, Sabi. Amen indeed.'

–

'Culprit,' said the clerk of the court, 'do you plead guilty or not guilty?'

'Not guilty,' Meg said in as firm a voice as she could muster.

There was a murmur of anticipation around the courtroom. Most witches confessed before they came to trial, as Goody Purton had done; it was relatively rare for the evidence in a case such as this to be heard in the open court. And witch trials were always especially enjoyable, full of a heady mixture of the supernatural, village jealousies, and outright sexual perversion. Their only shortcoming was that England no longer permitted the burning of convicted witches, immolation being infinitely more pleasurable than a mere hanging.

'Culprit,' said the clerk, 'how will you be tried?'

'By God and my country,' said Meg, knowing those were the words she was meant to use.

She did not bother challenging any of her potential jurors. They had the same sullen, bovine faces as those in the previous cases, and she recognised none of them. There would be no men of Dunwich or Sandlings so far from home, that was for certain, but the presence of the erstwhile Martha Raker among the jury of matrons made her wonder whether her opponents had somehow devised a jury of Southwold men, who were bound to convict her even if the Virgin Mary herself came down from Heaven there and then to testify on her behalf.

The clerk turned towards the crowded benches, looking particularly across to where Sir Nevill Bourchier sat next to the two mysterious women.

'If any can give evidence,' he said, 'or can say anything against the prisoner, let him come now, for she stands upon her deliverance.'

There was no movement in the court. Meg kept her eyes on Bourchier, who was evidently agitated beyond measure. At last he rose from his place.

'May I have leave to approach the bench, m'lord?' he enquired of Wray, his voice no more than a nervous, stuttering whisper that few but Meg and the judge could have heard.

'It is irregular, but yes, approach, Sir Nevill,' said Wray.

Bourchier stepped close to the judge and whispered urgently in his ear. Wray turned to look at him several times, his accustomed mask of placid detachment slipping into frank astonishment. He asked several questions, which made Bourchier even more discontented. He was now sweating profusely, and grumblings of impatience were coming from several quarters of the courtroom.

At last Bourchier withdrew and resumed his seat. Wray looked directly at Meg, and there was something in his eyes she did not understand. If he had not been one of the greatest men in England, and she naught but an old crone accused of witchcraft, she might have sworn that the expression she saw in them was fear.

Wray began to address the courtroom.

'It seems,' he said, 'that the anticipated witnesses for the prosecution have not appeared.' There were gasps galore, and even a few audible cries of 'No!' 'We have their written testimonies, but it is a firm principle of English law that such testimony, even if sworn before a justice of the peace and weighed previously by a grand jury, as opposed to the petty jury that sits here today, cannot be admitted in a court of law. Here, before God and myself representing the queen's most excellent majesty, only spoken testimony can be admitted, so that the accused may look into the eyes of their accusers and challenge them for the words they utter, not any others.'

Bourchier looked more uncomfortable than ever, glancing frequently at the women by his side.

'It is also a principle of English law,' Wray continued, 'that if no prosecution witnesses appear, the accused must be acquitted.'

More cries of 'No!'; the people of Bury St Edmunds evidently did not want to be deprived of a good witch trial.

'However,' said Wray, 'it seems the testimony of an additional witness was presented to the grand jury but did not form part of the indictment sent up to this assize. It is uncommon, but precedents for admitting such witnesses are known. I myself have presided on such occasions. Clerk of the court, admit the witness.'

The clerk nodded, went to the side door of the court and opened it. The witness entered, and now it was Meg's turn to gasp.

It was Mary, her sister.

Twenty-Six

The two women stared at each other. Meg tried to remain calm, but it was difficult. Mary was dressed modestly, a rarity for her, and clearly wanted to present an image of a demure and respectable maiden, but her features seemingly could not resist assuming an expression of triumphant smugness.

'Your name, parentage and condition?' demanded the clerk of the court.

'Mary Stannard of Dunwich, spinster,' said Mary confidently. 'Daughter of John Stannard, merchant and shipmaster, and Jennet, maiden-named Barne.'

Sir Christopher Wray looked at her.

'Barne? That is an uncommon name.'

'My lord, my late mother was kin to Sir George Barne, who was Lord Mayor of London in Queen Mary's time. Thus I am kin to his son, the present Sir George Barne, who was Lord Mayor last year.'

There were nods among the knowledgeable, and one man whistled.

'Impressive,' said Sir Christopher Wray. 'Most impressive. I have met the present Sir George. But tell me – you are Mary Stannard, daughter of John Stannard of Dunwich? Isn't the accused a daughter of the same man? Are you, then, the defendant's sister?'

'Half-sister, my lord. Yes, to my eternal shame, I am.'

More gasps and whispers in the courtroom. This was promising to be quite the highlight of the day, outdoing even the murder case. It was permissible under the law for children to testify against their parents in cases of witchcraft, and for such evidence, usually inadmissible in other kinds of case, to be accepted. But it was rare indeed for a witchcraft trial to depend upon the testimony of one adult sibling against another.

'Well then, Mistress Stannard, we shall proceed with your testimony once the clerk of the court has administered the oath. Culprit, you may of course question the witness against you. Remember, too, that you may make a statement of your own at the conclusion of her evidence.'

He nodded to Mary, who momentarily seemed entirely dumbstruck. Then her old self-assurance returned, and she swore the oath to tell the whole truth. Meg smiled; the whole truth was a notion as alien to Mary Stannard as the sweeping plains of Muscovy.

Then she began.

'The culprit yonder, Margaret de Andrade, has long been reputed a witch, and to have used sorcery and charms.'

'Interrogatory,' said Meg, who had noted the formal method of legal questioning from the previous cases. 'Reputed by whom?'

Mary seemed momentarily abashed that her word could be doubted, even by her sister. But she collected herself immediately.

'By many good folk of Dunwich,' she said. 'I name Richard Jephson, whose cow was made sick by the culprit. Then I name Hannah Fawcett, whose boy child died after the culprit's ministrations. I name Hugh Cuddon, who was cursed by the culprit in the hearing of many in All

Saints church in Dunwich and died of a fall from a horse eight months later. There are many others, my lord.'

Misrepresentation, thought Meg. Old Dick Jephson's cow was notoriously scrawny as a consequence of its owner's neglect. Goody Fawcett's child was sickly from birth, and not even the finest physicians of Padua could have saved him, even if his sottish mother had not dropped him head first onto a stone floor. Above all, Stannards had been cursing Cuddons, and the reverse, since the dawn of time. But she held her peace for the time being.

'Interrogatory,' said Sir Christopher Wray. 'This is all presumption and hearsay, Mistress Stannard, although such can, of course, be admitted as evidence before the law. Is there, though, a matter that you yourself witnessed?'

'There is, my lord.' Mary puffed herself up. 'My late mother, the kinswoman of the notable Sir George Barne aforesaid, was done to death by the accused.'

'Interrogatory,' said Meg. 'How, pray, did I accomplish that?'

'You – that is, the culprit, the accused – were always hostile to my mother. You conspired her death. You made a clay model of her and stuck pins in it. I saw it in your cottage. And my mother suffered for many months with stabbing pains and boils all over her body, after which she died in agony.'

'I tried to lessen your mother's pain,' said Meg angrily. 'The Lord knows why, after all the wickedness and spite she bestowed upon me!'

'Culprit,' said Wray, 'save such counterblasts for your statement at the close of the trial!'

'There is worse, my lord,' said Mary, now preening herself like a peacock. 'The culprit has an unnatural gift with numbers and the art of counting, so much so that she has always kept the ledgers and accounts of our brother's affairs. This is not a right and proper thing for a woman.' There were many nods and murmurs of agreement in the courtroom. 'She has also been renowned as an inveterate papist and recusant, hostile to the queen's most excellent majesty. Why, she even married a Spaniard—'

'The culprit is not on trial for popery or treason, Mistress Stannard,' said Wray, interrupting her.

Mary seemed not in the least abashed. 'Very well then, my lord. But there is a further matter, and it is a weighty one. It is universally known that the town of Dunwich was once mighty indeed, nearly as great as London, but that it has been blighted for many years by the advance of the sea. It is common knowledge that this has been accomplished by the malevolence of the family of Stannard. The accused's aunt, my aunt, was always reputed to be a witch. Her father, our grandfather, was a leper and thus obviously cursed by God. So it went on, back through the generations. I thank God every day that I have been spared such a contagion in the blood.'

'Your thanks to God are commendable, mistress,' said Wray, 'but they are *ultra vires*. Inadmissible.'

'Interrogatory,' said Meg swiftly. 'Do you claim then, sister, that I and our aunt and grandfather before me – aye, and countless generations of Stannards before that – are responsible for the decay of Dunwich, and its loss to the sea? Even when our ancestors were but common foretopmen or ploughmen?'

There was utter silence in the courtroom. Those present were relishing the spectacle of two sisters battling each other like street cats.

'It has been said by many of good repute,' said Mary, without the least apparent shame. 'There is one more matter of which I have direct knowledge, my lord.'

'Very well, mistress, you may speak it.'

'The culprit yonder has also bewitched me. She has caused me grief these many years. She has inflicted on me a sickness in the heart. She has—'

'Interrogatory,' said Meg. 'Where is the proof of this sickness? You look uncommon well to me, sister.'

Mary's jaw fell. Her mouth opened and closed, but no words came. Her eyes blurred, though, and her cheeks reddened. Then she leaned towards Meg as though making to attack her.

'You made me barren!' she screamed.

The shock in the room was akin to that felt by those witnessing a beheading at the moment when the axe cuts through the neck.

'You bewitched me! You cursed and shrivelled my womb! I know you have a clay image of me! I know it! I know it!'

Meg could see Sir Nevill Bourchier blushing, and knew precisely what she had to say.

'Interrogatory. How can you know you are barren, sister, when you have never been married, and thus have never lawfully lain with a man?'

Mary stared at her, utterly dumbstruck. There was a stifled laugh from somewhere in the courtroom, while a few of the goodwives present were nodding and smiling at each other. Mary made an inaudible remark.

'Speak up, Mistress Stannard,' said Wray, 'that the clerk may record your response.'

Mary seemed very close to tears. 'To this interrogatory,' she said, 'I cannot say more than what was aforesaid.'

'Very well,' said Wray. 'You may stand down. The witness is dismissed. Culprit, you may now make your statement in your own defence.'

Meg nodded her head, took a deep breath, then addressed the jury.

'It is true that I am a healer,' she began, in as modest a voice as she could muster, 'and have been reputed as such for many years, having learned the business from my aunt. It is also true that my family has enemies in Dunwich, even from within its own ranks' – she glanced at Mary, who had gone to sit on a side bench – 'for we prospered in a time when the town decayed, and there are many who resent that. But there are many more who love us. For each of the names uttered by my sister, I can give ten more who have been helped or healed by my doing. As for her testimony, I ask you how unnatural it is for one sister to bring such charges against another. Why has she done this now, I ask, when my brother is away fighting for queen and country against the dread power of Spain? It is true that I have always had a facility with numbers and have been of use to my brother and our father before that. Yet this is not witchcraft, I say, but a gift from God! I am innocent, and crave the mercy of this court. Amen, amen, amen.'

She was nearly in tears, but Sir Christopher Wray was already speaking the familiar words he had uttered at the conclusion of each of the day's earlier cases.

'Good men of the jury, you have heard what this witness has said against the prisoner. You have also heard what the prisoner has said for herself. Have an eye to your oath, and to your duty, and do that which God shall put in your minds to the discharge of your consciences.'

Meg was led from the courtroom to await the verdict. No more than five minutes could have passed before she was brought back in. She was confident; surely the jury would see through Mary's spiteful, self-interested accusations. But as she returned to her place, she sensed that something was not right. She heard whispers, and feared that some seemed to be coming from the jury's bench.

'Papist bitch.'

'Don-fucker!'

'Knowing numbers is proof of a witch, I say.'

She turned to face the foreman of the jury, whose eyes seemed fixed firmly to the ground. Her body felt cold, as though she had stepped onto Dunwich Heath in her shift during a December blizzard.

'Foreman of the jury,' said Wray, 'you will look directly at the prisoner. You hold her life in her hands, so you will weigh well what you say.'

The foreman complied, albeit with evident reluctance. Meg could see something in the man's eyes. Was it pity? Contempt? Apology? Disgust? All of those? Whatever it was, there could be no doubt of what it portended.

'Foreman of the jury,' said the clerk of the court, 'have you reached a verdict upon which you are all agreed?'

'We have.' The foreman's voice was strained.

'Upon the dread charge of witchcraft laid against her, does the jury find the defendant guilty or not guilty?'

The foreman looked at Wray, then at Meg, then spoke, his voice barely more than a whisper.

'Guilty.'

Twenty-Seven

Meg's knees failed her, and one of the gaolers had to lunge forward to grasp her before she fell. There were gasps, exclamations and not a few cheers in the courtroom. She glanced up and saw the look of utter triumph on Mary's face. A couple of rows behind her, though, Sir Nevill Bourchier's expression was curious, and he was glancing urgently at Sir Christopher Wray, trying to catch the judge's eye and finally succeeding.

Wray gestured to the clerk of the court, who struck a gavel to demand silence. Slowly the hubbub died away, and the eyes of the Lord Chief Justice of England scanned the entire courtroom before finally settling upon Meg.

'Culprit,' he said, 'the jury has delivered its verdict, and by its strict and awful nature, my next words should be to ask you if you know any reason why I should not pronounce sentence of death upon you, now a convicted witch. Hanging by the neck until dead. That is the prescribed sentence for the verdict here spoken.'

Mary nodded vigorously.

'But it is an established principle of English law that if a jury reaches a verdict that is patently wrong and unsupported by the evidence, then a learned judge may overturn it.' A great gasp went up, but Wray raised his right hand to quell it. 'I have heard the same evidence as the jury. Unlike them, I find it based entirely upon the malice of one person against another – aye, of one sister against another.'

There was uproar in the court. Mary Stannard, who had been so exultant a moment earlier, looked as though she had been turned to stone. For her part, Meg no longer knew where she was, or what words were being spoken. Her stomach was a void, her mind a tumult. The foundations of her life had been swept from under her, like the sea undermining the base of Dunwich cliff.

The clerk of the court demanded order, finally obtaining a semblance of it, and Wray continued.

'I have no doubt also that the jury's verdict has been grounded principally upon matters that are of no relevance whatever to this case. *Imprimis*, I refer to the charge of popery against the accused – but this is not upon the charge sheet.' Several in the jury looked to the floor, but others glowered. '*Secundus*, I refer to the fact that the accused bears a Spanish name, and was married to a Spaniard. The name one bears is not a crime in England, no matter how strange it may sound to the ears of some, and I pray it never will be. Nor is guilt conferred upon a party by the place of their spouse's birth. To suggest otherwise is an abomination, contrary to the law both of realm and of God.'

There were murmurs in the room, but Wray was inexorable now.

'*Tertius*, I refer to the objection some seem to have to a woman who is skilled in the art of mathematics, for such it is called. To that, I will say only this. I have been present when the queen's most excellent majesty has been discoursing of astronomy and other learned matters with erudite professors of the universities, and their discourse was beyond me, the Lord Chief Justice of

England, because it was conducted entirely in Greek, a tongue in which I am not fluent. I ask then, does any man here condemn their queen for her learning, simply because she is a woman?'

He looked around the courtroom, and Meg saw many men and women alike avert their eyes.

'Thus,' continued Wray, 'I exercise a judge's time-honoured prerogative under the law of England and overturn the verdict of the jury. It is null, and it is void. The accused is acquitted of the charge against her.'

-

The *Girona* was under way. In his pitch-black confinement in her bows, Juan could feel the hull beginning to move, could feel waves starting to lap on the beak-head. But the galleass was much deeper in the water than usual. He could hear, could even smell, the scores of men crammed into the space just behind the bulkhead that confined him. No matter how tightly they were packed, though, they remained a goodly way from his cell. Perhaps they thought the sounds from behind the bulk-head came from some sort of ghost or devil; perhaps they had heard that the man imprisoned there was a heinous traitor who had struck a priest, undoubtedly damning him to the terrors of hellfire, and did not want to imperil their immortal souls by getting close to him. Perhaps, though, it was simply the smell that must have been emanating from the makeshift prison.

Sabi did not come, and neither did anyone else. Juan had evidently been forgotten and would rot where he was, long before the *Girona* reached the coast of Scotland. He tried calling out, hoping that one of those quartered nearby would take pity on him, but none replied and none engaged with him. It was likely in any case that no man would willingly share his already constrained allowance of food and water with a wretch who was locked away like a rabid dog. Besides, if there really were over a thousand men crammed into the *Girona*, their rations could only be pitiful, even with any fresh supplies obtained from the Irish.

Perhaps, though, it would not be starvation that finally carried off *el hombre que vivirá para siempre*. For two or three days, Juan had been feeling increasingly feverish, and he knew he was sweating profusely. His limbs ached even more than usual, and he was shivering. He had only his own urine to drink. His sleep, such as it was, became a succession of strange visions, faces from the past seeming to pass before his eyes. His beloved Alice. Thomas Ryman. His cousin Simon Bulbrooke, who had been cut down by the French at Boulogne over forty years before. Francis Drake, though God alone knew why he of all people should appear in such a procession. Juan's father Peter, the leper of Dunwich, was present too; there could be no escaping the old man's malevolent influence. And there was William Seaward, the last priest of St John's church in the town, his final moments forever imprinted on Juan's mind as Dunwich Cliff collapsed beneath his feet, taking with it the doomed rector and the entire east end of the building.

It was time, Juan sensed. Time to join them all.

–

The previous evening, Jack Stannard had taken the coast road from Ipswich, going by way of Hollesley to Orford.

There he encountered a shipmaster he knew, an old friend of his father's, and allowed the fellow to ply him with tankard after tankard of good ale at an alehouse in the shadow of the church. Jack began to tell the story of the fight against the 'invincible' Armada, and gradually acquired an audience. More and more men moved closer, and listened in awe to his tales of the fights in the Channel, of the fireship attack at Calais – he did not mention the loss of his brother – and the dreadful battle off the coast of Flanders. At first there were nods of appreciation, even a few bursts of applause. But as he took the story forward, and told of the disease ravaging the fleet, and all the deaths, more and more men frowned or muttered, and a few began to move away.

Then it began.

'I call you liar!' cried one large drunken fellow with a vast broken nose. 'You wasn't there if you're spewing forth such nonsense! Sir Francis Drake and all the rest of our noble captains – heroes, every one of 'em! God bless 'em all!'

There were loud cheers at that.

'I was there,' said Jack indignantly. 'My father and brother were there too, with the *Eagle of Dunwich*. Some of you will know our name, that of Stannard.' A few older men nodded. 'My brother Adam perished, God rest him. I was on *Revenge* under Drake, and will swear to it upon the Bible. And Drake is not what you think he is. Let me tell you of Sir Francis Drake—'

'Nah,' said sot-nose, 'you won't speak a word against Sir Francis, you little Dunwich runt! Drake's a true English hero, that he is, and if you say otherwise, I'll beat you until the blood comes out of your eyes, boy. God for England!

Elizabeth! St George! Francis Drake! Fuck the Dons and all naysayers!'

Even though he was well into his cups, Jack was still sober enough to realise that the mood in the alehouse was against him. He had been there, he had fought, he had seen it all, but none of that mattered. The men of Orford did not want to hear the truth, only the legend that was already being born in taverns and alehouses all over England.

He made his excuses to the shipmaster and stumbled out into the night air. There was enough of a moon for him to find his way, so he set off northward along the shore. He found a fisherman upon the Alde who was willing to take him across to Aldeburgh, whence he continued onto the levels of Minsmere before climbing the ridge beyond. Sometime in the middle of the night, he reached his aunt Meg's cottage upon Dunwich Heath. It was empty, the door open to the elements and the contents scattered across the floor. Jack had sobered up several hours earlier and felt a sudden surge of dread. Where was she? What had happened?

He pressed on across the heath and then onto the cliff, through the old defensive barrier of the Palesdyke and into the long-abandoned part of the town, past the ruins of the long-gone monasteries and the still extant bulk of All Saints church where his grandmother lay. Onward as a glorious dawn was breaking, along Maison Dieu Street to the familiar door. There he knocked, expecting a long wait before anyone answered, but it was unbolted immediately.

His father, who had evidently not slept that night, stared out suspiciously, taking a moment to register who was standing before him.

'Jack,' he said. 'Oh sweet Christ, Jack, my boy! One of my sons has come back. God be praised, God be praised!'

They went to each other and embraced, each sobbing plentifully on the other's shoulder.

'Father,' said Jack after a minute or two had passed, 'I went by way of Aunt Meg's cottage. What's happened?'

'Come in and rest, son, and I'll tell you. Though you'll find it as hard to believe as I did.'

'Tell me now, Father. How can I rest until I know?'

Tom grunted as though he were in pain. 'Aye, well – your aunt's on trial at Bury assizes, this very day. Charged with witchcraft upon the word of your other aunt, Mary.'

'Bury? Then why aren't you there, Father? Why aren't you with her?'

'Come and rest, Jack; take a pot of ale with me, and we'll eat some bread and cheese. Then I'll tell you the other half of what's befallen my sister, although God knows, I find it hard enough to believe. But it's the better half of the tale, son. Trust me on that. By far the better half.'

–

Meg stepped into the open air outside the court, blinking desperately against the unexpected light.

After so very long locked away in dark cells, the sheer brilliance of the day was perhaps the greatest shock, even though it was a dull grey day under a leaden Suffolk sky. But the purity of the air was almost as much of an assault on her confused senses. No more than a few distant open sewers and piles of dung polluted the otherwise fresh, glorious atmosphere. They were more than offset by the kinds of smells she had not experienced for many months:

fresh fish upon a hawker's stall, the smell of newly washed linen drying in the breeze, perfumes from the stalls that served the richer and more fragrant ladies of the town. She breathed in deeply several times, revelling in the moment.

And people were ignoring her. In court, and trudging in shackles along the road from Dunwich to Bury so many weeks before, she had been the centre of attention, pointed at, jeered at, but always an object of interest. Now, though, people walked, ran or rode past her, all going about their business and all engaged in their own conversations, not one of them taking the slightest notice of her.

She was free.

She looked around, but none appeared who could explain what had happened. There was no face she recognised, not even a hostile one; of her sister Mary, there was no sign at all. Bewildered, she began to walk, but she did not know the town and had no idea of her direction.

Then she turned a corner, lifted her eyes and smiled. She knew exactly where she must go.

Increasing her pace, she made for the towering crumbling walls ahead of her. This, she knew, had once been one of the largest and richest abbeys in the entire kingdom, where for many centuries the blessed Benedictines had prayed, provided schools and hospitals, and served the people with humble obedience. Then King Harry the Tyrant, to satisfy his insatiable lusts for money and the bodies of women who were not his lawful wife, brought them all low. England had not been the same since, she thought as she entered the ruins. Now it was a meaner, harsher land, where people lived in suspicion of each other and where ever-stranger distortions of God's teaching were disseminated every day. Meanwhile a bastard and usurper, the daughter of a whore, reigned over all, aided and abetted by an avaricious clique of self-serving mountebanks.

There was a sound behind her, and she turned.

The two women who had sat next to Sir Nevill Bourchier in the courtroom stood a few paces from her, the one still veiled. Behind them were four men clad in black, apart from the livery they bore upon their chests, a blazon of arms she did not recognise. They were armed with large knives in their belts and appeared terrifying beyond measure; the few children who had been playing in the far recesses of the ruins when Meg entered them were now nowhere to be seen.

'Widow de Andrade,' said the unveiled woman, whose curling brown hair emerged from beneath her coif.

'Who are you?' demanded Meg, fearing that she might verily have gone from the frying pan to the fire, as the old saying had it.

The veiled woman looked around, seemingly checking that no other eyes were upon the scene and that no ears could hear what transpired. Then she peeled back the veil.

'Hello, aunt,' said Peter Stannard, grinning.

Twenty-Eight

'You have played a dangerous game,' said Meg to her nephew, who was now attired in manly garb, very much a dashing young blade upon horseback as their party rode away from Bury St Edmunds. 'Pray that he whose name you have taken in vain does not hear of it.'

'I think he has more important concerns, aunt,' said Peter, who had his hand in that of the young woman he had introduced to Meg, much to her astonishment, as his intended, Arabella Dowling by name.

They were all mounted, riding on one of the quiet back roads that ran across High Suffolk towards the sea.

'Judge Wray might tell him,' said Meg.

'Wray doesn't know and never will, if Sir Nevill plays the part we demanded of him.'

Meg shook her head. She was still astonished beyond measure at all that her nephew had told her, and could barely comprehend that the little boy whose cuts and grazes she had spent so much time cleaning and bandaging, seemingly so very recently by her recollection, was now grown into this cunning Machiavel. They might have shared the same name, but she had never once thought of this Peter Stannard, the roistering dreamer, as being cut from the same cloth as his great-grandfather.

Bolder than her grandfather, though, and even than her father. She felt sure that neither of them would have dared do what this Peter had done; indeed, she still found it difficult to believe.

'After I learned of your plight from Harry,' he had told her, a few miles earlier, when they were sure they were clear of the traffic to and from Bury, 'and he reminded me of an encounter your father once had with a gentleman of uncommon fame, I went to London to recruit the company. They called me a madman—'

'Aye, and still do!' cried an old man who had been introduced to her as Will Hetherington. The rest of the men around them laughed.

'But I was a madman offering coin.'

'Coin? I've never known you to have any coin, nephew.'

'Not my own, of course. I pledged Stannard coin. I know what pride you take in balancing the family's books, aunt, but I reasoned you would not object in this case.'

'How much?'

Just for a moment, Peter looked abashed, and once again resembled the little boy he had once been.

'We can talk of that later, when we reach Dunwich. But actors have no other employ in these times, and these fellows consented readily enough.'

There were nods and growls of agreement.

'Well then,' said Meg, 'it seems I am as constrained as I was in gaol!'

'Hardly, aunt. But then it was a case of ensuring you were acquitted at the trial. It was easy enough to send word to Dunwich to make sure the witnesses suborned by Mary did not appear at the assize – feeble creatures, easily gulled and easily bought. But we also needed to ensure that you would be acquitted even if Mary herself appeared as a witness, which I knew she might after I learned she'd testified to the grand jury. We knew we couldn't rely on any petty jury – country dullards, all of them, and we couldn't know who'd be chosen. So our only hope was to ensure the judge would acquit, no matter what verdict the jury delivered. It would be impossible to approach Wray directly, of course – too high by far, and he was bound to know the man whose name I intended to employ. So our only chance was to get Bourchier to convince him, and to do that, I had to turn Sir Nevill himself.'

Peter paused to take a swig from his leather pouch, and as he did so, Arabella Dowling smiled tenderly at him.

Ah, now that is love, thought Meg. *That's what I felt all those years ago, for such a very short interval.* She looked at Arabella more closely, then smiled to herself. The girl was with child; she was sure of it. A new Stannard!

'So I sent two of our men ahead,' said Peter. 'Landon, there' – an eager young fellow waved at Meg – 'and Smith. They went through the alehouses and taverns of Bury, spreading the rumour that one of the greatest men in the land was coming to the town incognito to inspect a new estate he'd bought in the area. Of course, such a rumour could easily be dismissed – it's an old trick of some of the boldest rufflers in London. But when word went round that the great man was accompanied by two of his daughters, and that he had taken one of the best houses in the town even at assize time, when the prices are raised so high – and more so when the two daughters were seen in Bury market, attended by liveried servants, even though one was veiled because her face was said to be scarred by the smallpox – well, it had to be true, didn't it? So Sir Nevill already knew of the rumours long before he received his summons, which was delivered in a manner bound to strike fear in his heart.'

'I've come to know Sir Nevill Bourchier,' said Meg. 'He did not appear to me as a credulous man.'

Peter laughed. 'Trust me, aunt, as we here all know well enough, any man is credulous if confronted by a good enough actor. And my friend Rob Wasdale there is certainly that.'

Lord Carnforth's Men cheered, and Wasdale raised a hand in acknowledgement, nodding to right and left as he did so as though milking the applause from an audience. Then, brazenly and to much laughter, he blew a kiss at Meg.

'Add the blackening of his beard and hair, dim candle-light, long shadows playing upon the wall, and in the role of the most feared man in England – here was the man Sir Nevill expected to see, and like all men, he saw only what he expected. Why, he even saw the two daughters of common report in the hall as he was led in, so why would he doubt? Rob can swear upon oath that he never gave that man's name, so he was not impersonating him. Sir Nevill simply assumed it was him.'

'I have just left a court of law, nephew,' said Meg, 'where I witnessed several cases before my own, and I am not convinced of that defence.'

'He never saw Rob's face properly, aunt. He certainly never saw mine – no one in Bury saw that, and remember, neither you nor Mary recognised me in the court. As for the rest of these good fellows, my friends… Without turning on your horse, aunt, could you put your hand on your heart and describe each of them to me? No, that's always the way. Actors have two faces: the one they're playing at the time and the one they usually wear, their true face. Everyone who sees them perform remembers the one; no one remembers the other. Most people have middling faces, middling builds and middling minds. Actors, though, can appear as gods or giants in one moment, and be naught but shadows the next.'

'You always appear as a god, my love,' said Arabella, merrily and loudly, drawing much ribaldry from the company.

'No man anywhere on the London stage can put on a tone of menace as well as Rob Wasdale,' said Peter, to more cheers for the renowned actor. 'So there was poor Sir Nevill, sitting in near darkness just a few feet from a man whose reputation he believed to be ferocious, and who then started telling our knight just how displeased he was at hearing how the Widow Margaret de Andrade had been arraigned before the assizes on a trumped-up charge of witchcraft; a woman whose father had once carried out a most important mission on his behalf, and was lost in the service of England, a hero to his queen and country. He told Bourchier in no uncertain times that he was to inform Wray to overturn all charges against her, and even if the matter went to a jury, she was to be acquitted, else the man sitting there in the darkness would be most displeased. I confess, aunt, it was a desperate plan. Even I didn't have entire confidence in its success. But then... Rob, you were in the room. Tell my aunt what happened!'

Rob Wasdale rode up beside them. Meg certainly would not take him for a god or a giant, but the big man had an air about him, beyond any doubt. For some reason he reminded her faintly of Stephen Raker, her family's implacable foe.

'Well,' said Wasdale, 'I hoped he'd be afeared – I wouldn't have been playing my part properly if he hadn't been. But then he starts weeping, and before long he's crying out too, swearing every blasphemy upon God's earth. Then he starts berating your sister, saying how she was naught but a mere whore and a dell, how she'd bewitched him – aye, that was the word he used – and how he wished to be rid of her, good and all. But she was set upon testifying before the court, and he knew that nothing he said or did could turn her from that course. So I spy a chance, even though I had no opportunity to talk it over with your nephew here. I says to him, "Well then, Sir Nevill, even if your hussy gives her evidence, you must convince the judge to discount it. And if the jury proclaims the widow guilty, you must overturn the verdict." See, mistress, I knew a judge could do that; saw it happen to my brother a few years back, though that time the jury found him innocent and the judge thought him guilty as sin. Which he was, but that's by the by. So I tell this Bourchier that if he does this, I'd be grateful to him, and that the likes of Lord Burghley would hear of it too. I told him he'd be a fine candidate for High Sheriff of Suffolk, one day soon. He dried his eyes then, stopped snivelling and looked as if a mighty weight had been taken from him.'

Meg recalled the strange moment in the courtroom when Sir Nevill had suddenly approached the judge's bench and engaged in an urgent discussion with Sir Christopher Wray. So that was the upshot: Mary would testify, but although the jury might be taken in by her feeble accusations, Wray knew what they did not, namely that the witness was utterly unsound. And if Bourchier should feel inclined to backslide, well, he had the two supposed daughters of his midnight phantom at his side to strengthen his resolve.

'You played your part well, Master Wasdale,' she said. 'I am grateful beyond measure to you.'

The actor-manager of Lord Carnforth's Men smiled broadly.

'Aye well, lady, I was glad to do it, for young Peter's sake, for the coin he's promised us, and now that I've met you, for your sake, too. Besides, it'll be quite a tale to tell my children, if I ever find where I've left them.' The actors around them roared with laughter. 'A glorious tale indeed. You can keep your Tamburlaine, and your Harry Fifth, and your King Arthur. I'll always look back on the night when I played Sir Francis Walsingham.'

Twenty-Nine

The *Girona* was lost.

Juan, still imprisoned in his makeshift cell, could feel the terrible motion of the hull as fearsome waves struck it beam-on. Men on his deck were screaming, others praying desperately to the Virgin and all the saints. The word must have come down from the helm only a few minutes before, but it had already reached the bows. Men were yelling that the jury rudder, which must have been fitted in the place called Killybegs, had given way. In this sea, and with the wind westerly, that could mean only one thing. The galleass was being driven inexorably onto the rocky coast of the very north of Ireland, with no chance of salvation.

Juan felt nothing but relief. He was sweating even more profusely, and the pain in his muscles overwhelmed him. Drowning would put a swift end to it, and he longed for that. It was how his old friend and mentor Thomas Ryman had perished when the *Mary Rose* went down over forty years before, and Juan would be pleased to join him in his watery grave. He offered up a prayer; not for himself, but for all those, known and unknown, he was leaving behind.

Then the ship struck the rocks.

There was a colossal impact, louder than the greatest thunderclap he had ever heard, and the entire hull shook.

He heard timber shatter, heard screams astern of him, and waited for the end to come.

The galleass seemed briefly to right itself – a trough in the waves – but as it did so, the floor timbers below Juan seemed to fall away. He had a momentary thought of drowning in the sea, rather than in his cell, and another of his head being dashed against a rock, but as he reached out, instinctively and desperately, his hand caught something, and despite the pain gripping him, he held fast. The rain was driving into his eyes, but he recognised his saviour at once. He was in a bed of kelp on a small shelf of rock in a great cliff that towered above him.

The man who will live forever lived still.

He turned and saw that the hull of the *Girona* was already a good distance away. There were many large and jagged holes in it now; a rock must have torn open some of the bottom timbers furthest forward in the bows, providing him with his miraculous escape. Those men further astern, where the ship's draught was deeper, had had no such fortune. The *Girona* was being broken apart by the huge waves pushing it time and again against what seemed to be a towering spine of rock protruding into the ocean from the cliffs to what could only be the south.

Men's screams could be heard even above the roaring wind. Were Owen Gravell's among them? Were Fra Gordillo's? Were poor Sabi's?

Juan clung to the kelp as each successive wave broke over him. It seemed as though the storm would endure forever, and he was not sure how long he could maintain his grip. He was tempted to let go, to fall into the sea and perish swiftly, but some strange, perverse force made him hold on. Gradually, though, almost imperceptibly at first, the force of the waves diminished; the wind was easing and the tide was on the ebb. A watery grey dawn broke in the east, illuminating the dire scene before him.

The *Girona* was gone, the largest remnant of the hull sinking before his eyes. All around, the sea was full of the detritus of the lost galleass: broken timbers, huge pieces of sail cloth and rigging, and worst of all, the bloated bodies of hundreds of dead men. Perhaps Alonso de Leyva himself and the flower of Spanish nobility who had accompanied him were among them. It was impossible to distinguish any individual, with just one exception. Far off, towards the point of the huge groyne of rock on which Juan lay, was a corpse attired in an unmistakable green and gold chasuble.

He was free of Fra Gordillo at last.

As the new day took a proper hold, he began to consider making an attempt to get ashore. He could not remain where he was indefinitely, and despite his fever and the pains that seemed to scream from every bone in his body, he knew that he had to get to land, to try to find shelter and warmth. There seemed to be no more than a handful of other survivors from the *Girona*. He could hear two or three men calling to each other, much further out on the strange talon of rock, and he could see a brace of others on the beach to the south-west, who must have been carried ashore on some planking that miraculously washed up in a safe place. It was certain that none of them could be from the oar deck; apart from himself, only men on the upper deck or very close to it were likely to have survived. So they would be Spaniards, and the huge influx of new men onto the ship meant he was probably unknown to them. Whoever they were, though, they were hardly likely to treat him kindly if they came upon him.

Old and sick as he was, Juan had one advantage over the few other survivors of the *Girona*. The bows had struck nearest the shore, so he was very close to the mainland. The cliffs had broad green ledges, falling away to the rocky groyne and the sea all around; if he could only reach them, he could surely work round to the eastern side long before any of the others could get there. He began to haul himself up on the kelp, losing his footing several times but always managing to hang on, and finally found himself on a more level platform above the tidal line. He pulled himself as upright as he could and began to walk towards the shore proper as casually as if he was strolling upon Dunwich Cliff.

Through the wreck and the hours spent clinging to the kelp, he had been sustained by an overwhelming urge to live, even though he had spent the moments before the *Girona* struck the rocks praying urgently for the same fate as Thomas Ryman. Now, though, with a gentle breeze blowing and a dull sun beginning to appear, he became more aware of his ailments. Every step was painful; he was stooped and limping, and his eyes filled with his own sweat, which he had constantly to wipe away.

Despite this, he murmured prayers for the souls of those on the oar deck who had become good friends – Owen Gravell; the Moor Adil, despite his being a heathen; Spadaro, who was already surely with God. But he wept and mourned above all for Sabi, the young friend whose face he had never seen; the boy who would never have the life he should have lived.

The more he mourned, the more the anger grew within him, fed by the fever that was consuming him. The Most Fortunate Armada, the Invincible Armada; whatever it was called, it had been doomed from the beginning. The insufferable pride of King Philip, and of the Spanish as a whole; the grand scheme to unite with Parma, a plan more ambitious than any in the history of man; the dismissal of the English, confidently damned as feeble heretics who would succumb to the righteous might of Holy Church and its crusaders upon the sea: for those fantasies, thousands of men had died. Sabi had died.

Yet even as he wept, mourned and blamed, Juan felt quite another emotion, too. He stopped when he was a little way around the cliff and looked eastward along the coast, past the strange-looking causeway of black pillars that lay on the other side of the point where the *Girona* had perished.

He was standing upon the soil of Ireland, part of Queen Elizabeth's dominion. The *Girona* was gone, and with it the power of Spain over him.

He was a free man. Once again, he was truly Jack Stannard of Dunwich.

God willing, he would come across some friendly Irishmen who might give him sustenance and shelter from the English patrols that were bound to come looking for the wreck; after all, they were hardly likely to assume that one of their own countrymen might be among the survivors. Perhaps any Irishmen he encountered could direct him to a small harbour where he might find a ship or boat to take him to England. Then, if it came to it, he would beg his way across the whole breadth of the country, all the way to Dunwich.

He thought of Venison, the old blind beggar who had frequented Dunwich when he was a young man. Well then, he would emulate Venison if he had to; but somehow or other, he would get home.

Yet all that was for the future. For now, Juan was still in the sodden, stinking rags he had worn for so long. The gashes made by the shattered timbers of the *Girona* looked angry and were increasingly painful, and he was shivering uncontrollably. He felt himself the very old man he undoubtedly was.

He staggered onward, but his head was throbbing. He lost his balance and fell several times, always picking himself up, but with more and more difficulty each time.

Now his eyes and ears played tricks on him. He could swear that he saw Dunwich before him, welcoming smoke rising from its chimneys. But then he blinked and saw it was no more than a few pitiful huts in the distance. He thought, too, that he heard church bells ringing, as the bells of all the sunken churches of Dunwich were said to ring – as he had heard himself, many times. His mind cleared a little, and he realised he truly could hear a single faint bell tolling in the distance, somewhere behind him. It could only be the *Girona*'s bell. Either it had somehow come ashore and one of the other survivors was ringing it to attract attention, or it was being rung simply by the motion of the waves, tolling the death knell of all those who had perished in the wreck of the galleass.

He took a few more paces forward, but his legs seemed heavier with every step. Without knowing how, he found himself upon the ground. He tried to get to his feet again, but could not. He began to crawl towards the distant huts, but now his arms, too, failed him. He somehow crawled a few yards more, feebly and painfully, but his head was a confusion of colours and sounds. His limbs did not answer. He was aware of three or four men approaching him, and that one of them was clad in black. He tried to speak, to tell them that he was John Stannard of Dunwich, an

Englishman, late slave aboard the lost galleass *Girona*, but the only sounds that came out of his mouth were low gasps.

'He's alive!' said the man in the black robe, in clear English. 'Look at the age of him – what was such an ancient doing on a Spanish ship? And how in the name of all the saints did he survive that wreck?'

'Look at his wrists and ankles, Father,' said another fellow in a pronounced Irish accent. 'Must have been one of the slaves on the oars, I'd say. Remember how Turlough said he thought the wreck was a galleass?'

'Then his survival until now is even more of a mystery,' said the priest as he knelt down, 'and a minor miracle, even if short-lived. Ho, fellow, can you hear me? Can you tell me your name?'

Juan tried to speak, but failed again.

'You know the English tongue, though?'

He managed a slight nod.

'Well then, I am Father Ronan MacDonnell, kinsman and chaplain to Sorley Boy MacDonnell of Dunluce Castle, the chief in these parts. Do you understand me?'

A priest, thought Juan, although his mind was a sea of confusion. *A priest of the true Holy Mother Church. God be praised. Deo gratias, Deo gratias.*

'You must prepare to meet God our Father, my son,' said Father MacDonnell. 'Do you believe in Holy Church and the Holy Father Pope Sixtus? And will you receive the sacrament?'

Again Juan nodded as best he could.

He saw the priest produce a small bottle from his belt, saw him dip his finger into it, felt him make the sign of the cross upon his forehead, and heard the familiar words of the sacrament of Extreme Unction, delivered in a tone and a manner so very different to that of Fra Gordillo.

'*Per istam sanctan unctionem et suam piissimam misericordiam, indulgeat tibi Dominus...*'

Jack Stannard of Dunwich, a free Englishman upon the soil of one of the Queen of England's realms, attended and absolved by a priest of the old and true faith, saw and heard no more.

Thirty

The *Margaret of Dunwich* lay at single anchor in the Horse Reach, set fair to sail on the late-morning tide. To any casual observer, no scene would have seemed more natural. Ships had been coming in and out of Dunwich harbour for centuries, and although it was badly silted now, sealed from its direct access to the sea by the vast shingle barrier called the Kingsholme, it was still possible for a skilled navigator to come up to the town's quays, even though most of them were now ruinous, and for ships to get out into the open sea.

In fact, the scene being played out in the master's cabin of the *Margaret* was anything but natural. Tom Stannard and his sister Meg stood by a chair that contained the bound, gagged and utterly furious form of their half-sister Mary, who was kicking at thin air. The brothers Peter and Jack Stannard stood a little way away, Peter leaning casually against a bulkhead while Jack studied the scene before him intently.

'Your word you will not scream or cry out?' said Tom.

Mary, whose cheeks were stained with tears, nodded, and Tom stepped forward to remove the gag. She spat at him.

'You… you *bastard*!' she cried, her words little more than strangled hisses. 'Kidnapping! Abduction! By my own brother, by Christ! How dare you? *How dare you do this to me?* Oh, Sir Nevill will hear of this.'

Meg stepped forward, smiling. 'Sir Nevill, is it? Your great protector?' She circled Mary. 'Think on this, dear sister. How d'you think we were able to smuggle you out of his very house – out of his very bed?' Mary Stannard's jaw fell open. 'He's delighted to be rid of you, to the degree that he's paid half the cost of the voyage you're about to embark upon.'

'Not true!' sobbed Mary. 'Sir Nevill would never do that to me! He loves me.'

'No longer, sister,' said Meg, 'if he ever did. Lust, yes. But love? I think not.'

'Lies! You lie! Let me see him, let me talk to him!'

'No prospect of that, sister,' said Tom. 'Even if he was inclined to see you, which he is not, this ship sails upon the tide.'

Mary seemed utterly bewildered. 'The tide? A voyage? What is this? In God's name, *what is this*?'

'You should be grateful, aunt,' said Peter, chuckling to himself. 'You have a new life ahead of you. A new land, no less.'

'*What?*'

'Amsterdam, dear sister,' said Meg. 'A growing city, I'm told. People from all over the world, and riches beyond imagination. Plenty of sailors. You'll like it there.'

'Amsterdam? Amsterdam in Holland?' Mary shook her head. 'This is madness! You're bedlam-men, all of you! I shan't go to Amsterdam – my brothers George and Harry will hear of this, you'll all pay, you'll all hang, I swear upon my mother's grave—'

'And what a wide grave it is,' said Meg, to Peter's considerable amusement.

'D'you really think George and Harry, or any of their progeny, will care?' said Tom. 'You tried them sorely enough, sister. Besides, they'll receive letters from the eminently respectable Sir Nevill Bourchier, justice of the peace for the shire of Suffolk, telling them the sad news of their sister's sudden death of an apoplexy. And if you do manage to write to them in the fullness of time – why, all of us over the years have been plagued by impostors trying to claim a share of the Stannard monies. Even if they believe you, do you really think either of them will exert themselves to get you back?'

In desperation, Mary's damp, pleading eyes settled upon Jack, the youngest of Tom's sons, the one she knew least well and the only one of her captors who had said nothing thus far. But he returned her gaze with interest.

'You aren't fit to bear the name of Stannard,' he said coldly.

'But I can't live in Amsterdam!' protested Mary. 'I'll have no money! I won't be able to make myself understood! How will I live? Where will I live? What will I do?'

Tom went over to the small table at the stern, lifted a large, heavy bag from it and dangled it before his half-sister.

'More than enough coin to set yourself up with decent rooms,' he said. 'And you'll find plenty of folk who understand English well enough. Jack and I have traded there many times. You'll hear every tongue in the world, and they all find ways of understanding each other. At bottom they all speak the same language, and you'll find that this bag contains a great many words of that language.'

'Aye, more than you deserve,' said Jack.

Mary's eyes were fixed upon the bag, and now had a more calculating look to them.

'As for what you'll do and how you'll live,' said Meg, 'I'm sure you'll find ways and means, sister. They say Amsterdam is full of rich men. It's also full of Englishmen – officers from the army fighting with the Dutch. So I reckon you'll find another man fool enough to make you his whore, and even if you don't, they say there's a fine income to be had there for a woman upon her back.'

Mary's eyes were furious. 'Damn you!' she screamed. 'Damn you all! You can't do this, I say! I'll come back on the first ship I can find! I'll see you all upon the gibbet yet!'

'Of course you can come back,' said Peter, moving a little closer to her. 'But think on this, dear aunt. Who, precisely, will believe you? There'll be sworn testimony from the unimpeachably respectable Sir Nevill Bourchier and from all of us here present that you are dead. As my father says, George and Harry won't lift a finger for you. It'll be the easiest matter in the world for me – for all of us – to put out the word that this impostor claiming to be Mary Stannard is naught but a Spanish spy. I'm sure your much-vaunted Sir Nevill will be happy to testify to that. Then, dear aunt, we'll see who ends up dangling from a gibbet.'

For once, Mary Stannard was utterly lost for words.

'Oh, don't be too downhearted, sister,' said Meg, chucking her mischievously under her chin. 'Not one person in Dunwich actually likes you. In Amsterdam, though, you can remake yourself and have a better life than you could ever have here. Besides, I'm told the fashions there are greatly superior even to London's, let alone Suffolk's.'

For a brief moment, it seemed as though Mary Stannard's eyes brightened.

-

Peter and Jack Stannard watched from the top of Hen Hill, high above Dunwich river, as the *Margaret* set all sail and began to breast the waves of the German Ocean, its course set eastward for the rebel provinces of the Netherlands. Looking southward, they could see their father and aunt strolling by the ruins of St Francis's chapel. It was as though nothing untoward had happened; the two brothers could have been children again, playing on the high sand hills by the harbour. But there were fewer people about now, more buildings were empty or ruinous, and above all there was no Adam, bullying and upbraiding them.

They talked but little of their dead brother. In truth, there was little either could say; Adam Stannard had been difficult to love, whether as a boy or as a man. They had no happy memories of him to share, and each knew that any signs or words of grief from the other would be a lie. They also both knew that Adam would have disapproved vehemently of what had transpired in the last few days – Peter's elaborate ruse to free their aunt, the family's undoubtedly illegal exiling of Mary Stannard. He would certainly have denounced them all as irredeemable sinners, and he would probably have been right in that.

They both stared out over the marshes for some minutes, neither uttering a word. It was clear that as far as the surviving brothers were concerned, there was no more to say upon the subject of their elder sibling.

'What will you do?' asked Jack, finally.

'Back to London,' said Peter. 'Arabella awaits me, and God willing, Lord Carnforth's Men may be able to mount a few performances before the season ends. And you?'

Jack sighed. 'Father's keen for me to stay here, to learn more of the business with a view to taking it over from him one day soon. But look at it, brother. Look upon Dunwich. Already naught but a village in all but name. It'll be a miracle if there's anything left of it by the end of our lifetimes.'

Peter looked out over the scene of decay before them, then turned to his brother again.

'You could go back to Plymouth.'

'Hardly. Plymouth's Drake's town, and I've had my bellyful of Sir Francis. No, I'll winter here, I think, to keep Father company, then seek a new voyage in the spring. There was talk in the Deptford alehouses that Sir Walter Ralegh intends to fit out a new expedition to his colony in the Americas – that might serve, if he'll have me. But whatever berth I find, it won't be on one of the queen's ships. The Navy Royal has seen the last of Jack Stannard.'

'You've changed your tune since last winter, brother,' said Peter, clapping him on the shoulder. 'Then, you desired nothing more than to serve your queen in one of her great ships. You were the most vocal man I've ever known for the flag of St George.'

'Aye, well, I've seen more than I cared to see in that time.'

'I know you, brother. I know that when the ensigns are unfurled and the drums beat once again, you won't be able to resist the call.'

'I'll resist,' said Jack. 'I've seen too much, I say. Learned too much of our so-called betters.'

The brothers took a last look across the rooftops of Dunwich towards the distant tower of All Saints, high up on the cliff.

'You can tell me of it over a pot of ale at the Crown, brother Jack,' said Peter.

'When have you taken only one pot, brother Peter?'

'Ah, now there you have me. But I have a thought – I'll race you there, as I did when we were young! The loser pays!'

'You, race? You, an actor? Look at you, brother, you've grown fat through easy living in London and all those inns you perform at. You might as well give me your money now.'

Peter grinned. 'Ah, poor Jack,' he said, ''tis true I'm an actor, but there's one thing you should always remember about our kind.'

With that, he kicked his unsuspecting brother hard in the right shin, then turned and set off, running down the hill at a fair tilt.

'We cheat!' cried Peter Stannard over his shoulder.

–

By nightfall, an easterly gale had blown up. Pleading exhaustion and a headache, Meg made her excuses from the carousing at the Crown, which she had known in her younger days as the Pelican in its Piety. She didn't doubt that her brother and nephews and their friends would stay drinking through the night, and part of her wanted nothing more than to talk about past times with Tom and of future times with young Peter and Jack. But she wished to keep a clear head. In truth, she was very tired and craved her bed. Perhaps she would dream once again the strange vision that had come to her the previous night, the first she had spent in her own bed for many months.

She had seen her father clearly, as though he were standing before her, but he was a young man again, the way she remembered him when she was a carefree child in Dunwich. She had not dreamed of her father for many years, but when she'd woken that morning, she'd had the strangest feeling of profound contentment. She took out her rosary from its hiding place and prayed for his soul, that it might already be free of Purgatory and enjoying bliss eternal with her mother and all the saints. Then, as she did every day, she prayed for England's return to the true faith, if necessary by means of King Philip dispatching a second and even greater Armada. Only when that was done had she gone down to the harbour to join her kinsfolk.

Meg longed for the dream of her father to return that night; but there were other things she had to do first.

As the storm howled, and the sea lashed against the base of Dunwich Cliff, she made her way across the heath by her secret path, coming at last to the long-dead hollow tree that she knew so well. She pulled away the plug she had carefully fashioned to seal the hole in the trunk, a plug and a hole undetectable to all but the very closest examination, then reached inside and took out her crystals, her looking glasses, her charms and the other artefacts of her secret, forbidden craft, along with the crucifixes, rosaries, candles and other symbols of her faith. Once back at her cottage, she would pray for the coming of another Armada, for the restoration of the old Church, and for the accession of the rightful monarch, King Philip's daughter, Elizabeth the Second, Queen of England *de jure* and by the grace of God.

Before she turned to return home, she picked up and smiled at her clay model of her sister Mary. Out of sheer devilment, she stuck a pin in it. Perhaps at the very least it would make Mary seasick. She did not bury the pin too deeply, for she did not want the ship to sink; that would have been too good and too fast for her sister, and honest Suffolk men would perish if the *Margaret* went down. No, seasickness and then a dose of pox in whichever stew she ended up inhabiting in Holland; that would serve admirably.

Meg wrapped all her artefacts carefully in the cloth she had brought with her. She had been careless to leave the bones and the other items within her cottage; her folly in doing so had almost brought about her destruction. But she would not make the same mistake again – not that she need have any great concern even if she did so, she thought.

She grinned. She knew, for her occasional lover Bailiff Robert Spatchell had told her often enough, that it was still the same irresistible smile she had possessed as a child, and which had won over the hearts of every man and woman in the town. She had ample cause to be in good humour. No one in Dunwich or anywhere in the Sandlings would dream of accusing her of witchcraft ever again, not when she had been acquitted upon the word of none other than the Lord Chief Justice of England. With such immunity, she knew she could outdo even her aunt Agatha.

She could, and would, become the most powerful witch in Suffolk.

Epilogue

24 November 1588

The queen was coming.

The day was bitterly cold, and there was thick snow on the ground from a heavy fall overnight. Even so, the streets of London could not have been more crowded. People were leaning at near-impossible angles out of the windows of the buildings on either side of Ludgate Hill. Every man and woman lining the street craned their necks for just a fleeting glimpse of their sovereign lady, while children who could not find a berth on a parent's shoulders shuffled and pushed between the legs of their elders, trying desperately to make their way to the front. Those without gloves breathed hard onto their hands to try to keep them warm. It being London, and it being a London crowd, there were villains and beggars galore: cutpurses, rufflers, cranks, whipjacks and all the other dubious fraternities of the street. But there were legitimate hawkers too, and those purveying roasted chestnuts were doing a roaring trade. Not a few men, and even some women, were already blind drunk, it being a day of national jubilation and rejoicing. Today, Queen Elizabeth herself, the all-conquering Virgin Queen, would lead her kingdom in thanksgiving for the God-given victory over the Spanish Armada.

Peter Stannard and Arabella Dowling had excellent places in the crowd, very nearly in the front row and with a clear view of the west front of St Paul's Cathedral. This was not an entire coincidence. The pair were flouting every sumptuary law in England; he wearing a short white cloak over his gown, and she a fine overgown above an elegant kirtle. Thus they resembled some young lord and his sweetheart, or perhaps his sister, and this impression was heightened by the presence around them of Lord Carnforth's Men. The actors were wearing a different livery to that which had fooled Sir Nevill Bourchier, and appeared to the untrained eye as the most intimidating body of retainers to be seen anywhere in the entire city of London. True, they risked arrest by any authority prepared to make even the most cursory demand for their credentials; but Arabella had expressed a wish to see the queen, and every man in the company was more than a little in love with her so readily accommodated her fancy. Moreover, Peter reckoned that the guards lining the route, and the agents who would undoubtedly be mixing among the crowds in plain attire, would be concerned solely with the ever-present threat of an assassination attempt by Spanish spies or English Catholic fanatics. None would care how many laws of England were broken this day as long as the queen remained alive at the end of it.

There were cries of excitement from down towards Lud Gate, and the sounds of distant cheers and applause. The great procession was approaching, bringing the queen to St Paul's from Somerset House.

First came the messengers, then the gentlemen harbingers, all wearing brightly coloured liveries. The servants to the foreign ambassadors followed them, then the queen's own servants, then the first band of royal trumpeters, who sounded a succession of fanfares and stirring marches. And so more and more came through Lud Gate and up the hill towards the west door of the cathedral: gentlemen ushers, the clerks of the likes of Chancery, Star Chamber and the Privy Seal, the queen's chaplains, the aldermen of London in their multitude of liveries, knights of the realm, sergeants at law and the barons of the Exchequer. A brace of pursuivants came next, their vivid tabards in stark contrast to the cold November scene, then the highest judges of the kingdom in their scarlet robes. Sir Christopher Wray walked among them, and Peter Stannard took especial pleasure in looking directly into his eyes as he passed and seeing not even the faintest glimmer of recognition.

More and more of the great officers of state – the Master of the Revels, the Lieutenant of the Ordnance, and so forth. More pursuivants. More trumpeters. Arabella was gasping with delight at every new cohort that passed.

The excitement was growing now. Many were recognising gentlemen of the privy chamber, and knew that the queen herself would not be far behind. First, though, came the younger sons of peers, then two of the heralds in their stunning liveries adorned with the royal arms. They preceded the principal secretary, and Peter nudged Arabella as he pointed out the seemingly innocuous, aged and slightly stooped figure of Sir Francis Walsingham. The man dreaded by those Englishmen who knew of him, feared by not a few of the crowned heads of Europe, and whose name Peter Stannard had taken in vain so brazenly, resembled nothing more fearsome than a mild old country parson, slightly stooped and possessed of a thin grey beard; certainly not the malevolent colossus played by Rob Wasdale.

'Christ's tears, boy,' murmured Wasdale, standing just behind Peter, 'I'll never let you have a say in casting again. I don't look the least like him! Old Hetherington should have played him, no doubt in it.'

Walsingham was followed by the other great men of the realm. There was the Lord Chamberlain, Lord Hunsdon, riding alongside the Lord Admiral, Howard of Effingham, who received especially loud applause for his part in the triumph over the Armada. Then came the peers of the realm in their scarlet robes and coronets, followed by the Lord Treasurer, Burghley himself, looking very old. The two archbishops came past, York ahead of and Canterbury behind the Lord Chancellor, the elegant Sir Christopher Hatton, in a huge gown of black and gold. The French ambassador attracted a few boos, despite the two kingdoms being nominal allies, and the Lord Mayor of London attracted rather more.

The excitement was uncontrollable now. The cheering could surely be heard at the Escorial. Men and women alike were weeping with joy, Arabella among them. Garter King of Arms, his livery a riot of red and blue, was preceded by the white-bearded Marquis of Winchester, the most senior nobleman in the realm, bearing the sword of state.

And there, at last, was the queen.

She was not on horseback as she had been at Tilbury. Instead she rode in a small carriage or chariot-throne borne between two white horses, a number of gentlemen pensioners by their sides to keep them under control.

She wore an all-encompassing white cloak of sable; she was, after all, quite an old woman, thought Peter (although he could have been hanged for the thought), and it was a cold day. Her red hair – although any actor could recognise a wig when he saw it – was set high and crowned by a bejewelled tiara.

She waved right and left, but her face was unsmiling. No wonder, thought Peter; it would be simply impossible to smile while wearing all that face paint. Still, he cheered as long and hard as the rest of them. The moment was brief. The queen had passed in a trice, and none then paid much attention to the tail end of the procession, made up of the ladies of honour (although there were many lewd proposals bawled at the youngest and prettiest of these) and last of all, the halberd-bearing Yeomen of the Guard. Peter was one of few whose head did not turn to follow the queen. Instead, he looked intently at the yeomen, finally recognising his uncle Harry.

He was tempted to wave, but Harry would ignore him even if he saw him; he was too good a soldier for such frippery. Peter also knew that Sergeant Stannard of the royal yeomen had not taken the reported death of his sister too hard. Far from it, in truth, for he had mended his bridges with his half-brother Tom and half-sister Meg to the extent of soliciting one of his old commanders to secure for young Jack a reformado's berth aboard one of the great ships being fitted out for an expedition against Spain and Portugal projected for the following spring. This expedition would be so vast and powerful that the knowing men in London were already calling it the 'Counter-Armada'. Much to Peter's amusement, Jack Stannard's protestations that the Navy Royal had seen the last of him, and his inebriated denunciations of the likes of Drake, Cumberland and the rest in the Crown at Dunwich, had proved no more enduring than the ever-shifting edge of the cliff a few yards east of that tavern. England was safe, and now she would strike back. No Stannard could resist such a challenge; well, no Stannard other than Peter, at any rate.

The procession halted before the west front of the cathedral, where the Bishop of London, the Dean of St Paul's and several dozen more clergymen awaited their queen. As she stepped from her carriage, a choir assembled on the upper steps began to sing, and the crowd cheered once again. As the choir gave their all to the anthem, the queen and her retinue processed through the west door and on into the cathedral.

'Oh Peter,' said Arabella excitedly, gripping his arm tightly, 'that I have seen the queen! The queen herself!'

Peter grinned. 'I reckon I play her better than she plays herself,' he said.

Arabella prodded him in the ribs. 'Don't let anyone hear you say that!' she said in a low and urgent voice. 'Such might be construed as treason, Peter Stannard!'

The crowd was already dispersing. The day was bitterly cold, flakes of snow were falling again, and the taverns and alehouses of London beckoned. As he and Arabella turned away, though, Peter heard his name being shouted above the hubbub. He turned and saw his new-found friend of the last five weeks pushing his way towards him through the crowd. The fellow, about his own age, was new to the city. They had fallen into each other's company one night at the Tabard in Southwark, very much a haunt of the theatrical community. Peter found the newcomer amusing in the way that provincials often were. The fellow was from somewhere in the middle counties, had a ridiculous name and a short pointed beard, and fancied himself as both an actor and a writer. His kind were two-a-farthing in London, but this one had something about him, and Peter Stannard could not quite put his finger on it.

On an impulse, he took Arabella's arm. Mayhap, he thought, after all was said and done, and all things being considered, it might be time to assume what old folk like his father and aunt called the true responsibilities of manhood. He had feelings towards a woman that, on a calm night and with a full moon, could possibly be construed as love, that strange and potent word he had uttered so often upon the stage but never truly comprehended. A word that, unaccountably, he also seemed to feel towards the new life growing within Arabella Dowling's belly. Mayhap then he would marry her, settle down, and thus astonish his entire family. And mayhap too he would take his new friend under his wing, and act the master to his apprentice.

Perhaps the eager fellow would sink without a trace, in which case Peter would lose nothing, or perhaps he would swim, make something of himself and provide a return for the man who first gave him a leg up.

Yes, it was time, he reflected. After all, was there not a tide in the affairs of men, in which case Peter's could only be upon the flood.

Peter Stannard smiled.

A tide in the affairs of men. He liked that. Perhaps he should get his eager new friend to write it down.

Historical Note

The defeat of the Spanish Armada is one of the best-known and most iconic events in British history. Yes, British, although it was a purely English fleet that took on the supposedly invincible maritime juggernaut dispatched by King Philip II: for example, to this day legends of Armada shipwrecks and sunken treasures fire imaginations from Fair Isle and Tobermory in Scotland to the west coast of Ireland, where Irish rocks put paid to far more hulls than did English guns.

In the Shetland detective thrillers by Anne Cleeves and the wildly successful TV series based on them, the central character, Jimmy Perez, supposedly owes his surname to an ancestor who survived the Armada, while the intricate patterns of sweaters from Fair Isle, Perez's fictional birthplace, are allegedly inspired by Armada survivors – one of the most commonly used motifs resembles a griffin, the emblem of the town of Rostock, home port of the ship wrecked on the island, *El Gran Grifón*. In Ireland, survivors were reputedly responsible for introducing, *inter alia*, thoroughbred horses, Gaelic handball, and the surprisingly swarthy strain of Irish folk named by some the 'Black Irish'. (A similar legend exists on the island of Westray in Orkney, where the 'Westray Dons', descendants of Armada survivors, allegedly formed a separate caste for more than two centuries.)

In a nutshell, then, a Spanish Armada shipwreck is vastly sexier than any ordinary common-or-garden shipwreck, while the story itself has always been irresistible to Hollywood and its ilk.

Sir Francis Drake? *Check.* Sir Francis Drake nonchalantly playing bowls as the enemy approaches? *Check.* Underdog apparently battling terrible odds? *Check.* The Virgin Queen, Elizabeth I herself? *Check.* Queen Elizabeth I delivering one of the most famous speeches of all time? *Check.* Unlikely victory against aforesaid terrible odds, thanks to either (a) God or (b) climate change, depending on one's belief system? *Check.*

All of which presents a humble author attempting to write a fictional story set against the backdrop of the Armada with a number of problems.

In the first place, the central elements of the story are so well known that there is simply no leeway. The fights off Plymouth, Portland and the Isle of Wight, the pursuit up the Channel, the fireship attack at Calais, the subsequent battle off Gravelines, Elizabeth's visit to the army at Tilbury, and the fate of the Spanish ships, largely shattered on the cliffs of Scotland and Ireland, have all been described very much as they happened, as far as it has been possible to do so. Of course, I have taken some liberties to serve the purposes of my narrative, particularly in the latter stages of the story. For example, the Tilbury speech was delivered several days after the English fleet turned back at the Firth of Forth, but in terms of my narrative, it was better to reverse the order of these two events. The heavily overloaded galleass *Girona* was wrecked on Lacada Point, immediately adjacent to the Giant's Causeway in Northern Ireland, on 26 October 1588, which would have been well after the conclusion of the summer assizes at Bury St Edmunds, but it served my purpose for the two to happen simultaneously. Only nine men survived the wreck of the *Girona*, and it is highly unlikely that a man of Jack Stannard's age would have been among them, even if his survival was only brief.

The central elements of the Armada story are certainly very well known, but on the other hand, several elements of the story that everyone thinks they know about it are myths, if not downright whoppers. The famous story of Sir Francis Drake saying he had time to finish his game of bowls and still beat the Spaniards is almost certainly apocryphal – it appears in no contemporary accounts and first emerges in print almost exactly 150 years later, quite probably the invention of the author and herald William Oldys, a man who was said to be 'rarely sober in the afternoon, and never after supper', his favourite tipple apparently being porter washed down with gin. Similarly, Queen Elizabeth's Tilbury speech was not published in any form until 1654, based on a letter written in 1623, thirty-five years after the event, as a polemical argument against better relations with Spain at that time. (Having said that, the letter writer, Leonel Sharp, was present at Tilbury as the Earl of Essex's chaplain, and presumably didn't miss the queen's speech for the reason I've invented in this book, namely a mistimed trip to the lavatory.) Moreover, there are three entirely different versions of what she said, the two less renowned versions being far more contemporary than that containing 'the heart and stomach of a king'. Having said that, the famous version is exactly the sort of thing Elizabeth undoubtedly did write and say on many occasions – witness her prayer of thanksgiving for victory over the Armada, provided as an epigraph to Part Three of this book, or her 'Golden

Speech' to Parliament in 1601 – so I hope my treatment of the story will be acceptable to those who still have misty-eyed visions of Flora Robson, Glenda Jackson or Cate Blanchett, depending on one's vintage, in armour and on horseback.

Of course, the prevalence of myth in underpinning what many people think they know about history doesn't just apply to the specifics of the Spanish Armada. For instance, in late-sixteenth-century England, as in other European countries, the majority of witchcraft prosecutions ended in acquittal, and by 1588, increasing numbers of those convicted were merely imprisoned rather than executed. In any case, witches had not been burned in England for many years; nor, as far as we know, were they subjected to the 'swimming' or 'ducking' test that seems to be an article of faith in popular perception, at least not between the fourteenth and seventeenth centuries.

Otherwise, those who think that Meg's trial before Sir Christopher Wray (who was the judge 'riding' the relevant circuit in 1588, despite also being the Lord Chief Justice) is too brief to be credible might wish to consider the fact that sixteenth-century trials at an assize court generally took a maximum – *a maximum!* – of thirty minutes from arraignment to verdict, allowing the court to fit in ten to twenty cases a day. I gleaned this mind-boggling titbit, along with most of the material about witchcraft accusation and trial procedures during this period, from *Marks of an Absolute Witch: Evidentiary Dilemmas in Early Modern England* by Orna Alyagon Darr. It's very rare for an author to find a source that answers exactly the questions s/he wants answered, and in exactly the right order, but Darr's book certainly fitted that bill for me. Goody Purton's confession is based on a conflation of the confessions of two of the 'Pendle witches', Alison Device and Elizabeth Southerns; that passage was written within sight of Pendle Hill, so I hope I've done some justice to their memory.

Several elements of the familiar narrative might actually be myths, but conversely, some incidents related in this book that readers may find fanciful, or indeed uncomfortable, are entirely supported by the historical record. The evidence that Francis Drake – who was an enigmatic combination of ferocious patriotism, avarice, and deeply unpleasant religious fanaticism – deliberately ignored an order to display a lantern that the rest of the fleet was to follow at night so that he could secure the *Rosario* and her riches for himself is overwhelming; his effective desertion scattered the fleet and made it unable to resume battle with the Armada on the following day. A furious Martin Frobisher wrote more or less the exact words (about the 15,000 ducats and having the best blood in Drake's belly) that I have him shouting across the water in Chapter Five.

The fact that many men of the English fleet suffered almost as terribly as their Spanish foes, albeit at the hands of disease and an uncaring government rather than a hostile coast, has often been glossed over or ignored entirely in the more gung-ho accounts of the Armada, both on film and in allegedly serious books by allegedly serious authors who really should know better. Sir Francis Drake's paraphrase in Chapter Eighteen of Lord Burghley's hope that large numbers of men in the fleet would die and thus reduce the wage bill is simply a slightly fictionalised version of something the latter actually said. Fra Gordillo was right, too: the famous Armada of 1588 was actually the first of three during a war that would last until 1604; the other two (in 1596 and 1597) were larger, but they were thwarted by bad weather before ever reaching the English coast. (An even more serious threat eventually came from a Franco-Spanish 'armada' in 1779 that actually entered Plymouth Sound; but that is another story, one of countless such inconvenient narratives that have been erased almost entirely from national memory.)

It is also emphatically not true that the English were the 'underdogs' in 1588. For one thing, and just as in the case of Fighter Command in 1940, the home forces were very near to their own bases, so it was relatively easy for the English fleet to re-ammunition and revictual after each engagement. Not so for the Armada and Luftwaffe alike. The largest ship on either side was English (the *Triumph*); the dozen or so of the largest true men-of-war in the English fleet were considerably larger than their equivalents in the Armada, and many of those ships were 'race-built' galleons, which were much more nimble than their opponents; the English gunnery – certainly their rate of fire – was vastly superior; and when the Narrow Seas fleet joined forces with that from Plymouth, their combined strength outnumbered the Armada, which contained many transport ships that were virtually useless as combatants. I have deliberately played down some of these uncomfortable truths simply because an underdog battling against superior odds makes for a much more dramatic story; after all, nobody would watch the *Rocky* films if Rocky Balboa was a six-foot-ten, supremely fit, all-conquering colossus.

Having said that, the English army as experienced by Peter Stannard was a very different affair, and would probably have been dealt with in very short order by Parma's veterans. Anyone who doubts my depiction of the nature of the recruits in the army in 1588 is referred to that most unimpeachable of sources, Sir John Falstaff, in *Henry IV Part One*, Act Four, Scene Two.

Another truth that some readers might find unpalatable is that a small but significant number of English people actually wanted the Spanish Armada to win. Although the numbers of English Catholics had diminished during Elizabeth's reign, and the even smaller number who denied her right to the throne had shrunk following the draconian papal bull of 1570 (alluded to by Meg de Andrade) and the execution of Mary, Queen of Scots in 1587, the fact remains that some looked upon Medina Sidonia's ships and Parma's troops as potential deliverers from slavery and oppression. One of these was almost certainly William Byrd, Elizabeth's court composer, who set to music her poem used as the epigraph for Part Three, for the great celebratory service at St Paul's, the centrepiece of the Epilogue. Yet only months earlier, Byrd had been setting texts that can be interpreted as coded prayers for the victory of the Armada, including that to which Meg de Andrade alludes in Chapter Six. The omission of English Catholics from the Armada story is surely further proof that history is always written by the winners – even if only as self-serving fiction.

There is no direct evidence of the English fleet obtaining intelligence of Parma's dispositions from fishing boats; this was an invention on my part, although it is not inherently implausible. It was one of the principal ways in which navies obtained intelligence from the seventeenth century onwards, so it's virtually inconceivable that they weren't doing so in earlier ages too. Another piece of dramatic licence on my part is the decision to send part of the Armada through the Pentland Firth on its fateful return voyage. None of its ships actually went that way, as far as we know, instead taking the much broader passage between Orkney and Shetland (where *El Gran Grifón* came to grief on Fair Isle); but having crossed the Firth so often, and having a particular affection for Orkney, I couldn't resist the notion of young Sabi Ibaiguren looking out at the cliffs of Hoy and Rackwick Bay.

I've also deliberately emphasised the role of the Narrow Seas fleet, Lord Henry Seymour's motley collection of merchantmen and auxiliary men-of-war. This has always been something of a footnote in accounts of the Armada campaign, its military worth dismissed and its contribution almost forgotten. Indeed, Seymour himself is far and away the least-well-known major commander on either side; it is not even known where, when or why he died, although it was at some point in 1588 after the Armada campaign was concluded. When the Victorians compiled the original *Dictionary of National Biography*, they threw in obscure naval officers galore from every era of history, but even they did not consider the commander of roughly one third of all the English men-of-war that fought against the Spanish Armada worthy of an entry. As a result, though, I have had a considerable degree of carte blanche in my depiction of Seymour, deriving much of my picture of him from one line in a letter he wrote to Walsingham in June 1588, reporting that he, a scion of one of the greatest noble houses of England, had injured his hand 'with hauling on a rope'.

Other elements of this story have been taken directly from the events of the time. Thomas Kyd's *The Spanish Tragedy*, the first speech of which Peter Stannard declaims in the Prologue, was first published in 1587, while many scholars incline towards the spring or summer of 1588 as the time when William Shakespeare first went to

London. Francis Birks and Robert Spatchell were the bailiffs of Dunwich in 1588, although Sir Nevill Bourchier is an entirely invented character. With two exceptions, the songs that Juan Estandar, Jack Stannard the elder, sings or refers to are either contemporary or else so long established that virtually everyone in England would have known the tunes and words. As for the exceptions, Clément Janequin's '*La Guerre*', or '*The Battle of Marignano*', was wildly popular in both France and Spain, while '*Magnus the Emperor*' is entirely a product of my imagination, based on the legend of Magnus Maximus, or, as the Welsh style him, Macsen Wledig.

My description of Dunwich is based heavily on the map of the town produced by Ralph Agas almost exactly contemporaneously, in 1589. Those who want to know more about 'England's Atlantis' and its centuries-long battle against the sea will find it in the historical notes to the first two books in this trilogy, *Destiny's Tide* and *Battle's Flood*.

Acknowledgements

Thanks once again to my agent, Peter Buckman, and to Michael Bhaskar and Kit Nevile at my publishers, Canelo, for their unfailing enthusiasm and support. Again, too, I reiterate my thanks to those in Dunwich and its environs who helped make these three books a reality, notably Jane Hamilton, Tim Holt-Wilson, and above all, John Cary of Dunwich Museum. Hugh Bicheno, author of *Elizabeth's Sea Dogs* and many other superb works of history, again provided invaluable critical input. Thanks also to the BBC for its impeccably timely broadcasting of a documentary about the Spanish Armada, presented by Lucy Worsley, during the period when this book was being written; a not-too-hideously-dumbed-down successor to the series it broadcast in 1988 to mark the four hundredth anniversary, which I subsequently showed so often to A-level students that I can still remember large swathes of the commentary verbatim. Long may the BBC survive to produce such programmes.

Finally, a big thank you to Michael Berliner and Laura Frascona (and Felix!) for providing me with opportunities to explore modern Bromley, the winner hands-down of my entirely hypothetical prize for a British town's worst treatment of a bishop's palace, and to my partner Wendy for her eleventh outing as my premier beta reader and critic-in-chief. Now that this trilogy is finished, I promise that I'll finally sort my sock drawer.

David Davies
Bedfordshire
During the time of the coronavirus lockdown, 2020